WONDERS OF THE WEST

WONDERS OF THE WEST

A NOVEL BY

Kate Braverman

Fawcett Columbine · New York

A Fawcett Columbine Book
Published by Ballantine Books

Library of Congress Cataloging-in-Publication Data
Braverman, Kate.
  Wonders of the West : a novel / by Kate Braverman. — 1st ed.
    p.   cm.
  ISBN 0-449-90656-6
  I. Title.
PS3552.R3555W6   1993
813'.54——dc20   92-54385
                                                         CIP
                                                          AC

Manufactured in the United States of America

First Edition: February 1993

10 9 8 7 6 5 4 3 2 1

FOR ALAN,
not in a million dreary worlds

"Whither goest thou, America, in thy shiny car in the night."

—ON THE ROAD, Jack Kerouac

WONDERS OF THE WEST

1

My name is Jordan Lerner. I am seventeen years old. And the most beautiful words I know are Sybil Brand and Camarillo.

Sybil Brand is the women's prison downtown. Camarillo is the state mental hospital just across the county line. That's where they send you when you have too much clarity, when your mind refuses the wire fences, when you find yourself walking through the gate and never going back.

I am intrigued by the sound of these names. I have a sense of destiny and recognition. This set of possibilities is sculpted in my genetic code. As Roxanne would say, I feel like I have a reservation.

I say Camarillo and Sybil Brand and the air glows. I am the keeper of embers and arrows that flame. I am a burning mouth. I surround myself with invisible forbidden temptations. They form shapes like a delicate origami in another dimension. They are here, now, but in an unknowable future. They are further along on the continuum.

I am convinced that words contain an impossible to measure power. They form an intersection, a gouged-out place where you realize we are only partly here. Above our shoulders are forests of Spanish moss, architectures of stained clouds that invent their own direction, the storms and harbors and all the reasons. Our ideas are older than seashells or birds or masks. Our thoughts are ancient as the air itself, as water on stone and the impenetrable dusk.

This is the moment when you know it is sadness in your mouth. It just comes out. There is no way to count it or fashion a bridge or a dam. This is when you can sense the drift.

Maybe this is how Roxanne feels when she stands in front of a mirror. Maybe she realizes she is engaged in a kind of mime at the edge of a sheeted portal. She is merely practicing versions of herself. Perhaps there is a certain sequence of postures and it is not random but refined and deliberate. Perhaps it is part of an answer she is trying to find, an indication of a breathless sophistication, a reason to walk across half a continent barefoot.

The trick is to keep the versions in a consistent order. I don't always do that. I think chronology is an overrated concept. When my improvisations become visible they seem like mistakes. That's when they threaten to send me to a mental hospital or juvenile hall, reform school or jail.

I become frightened yet strangely expectant. I want to

know if the pain would stop there. And what if it didn't? What if the pain was constant and I was locked in the cell with it?

I decide to stop saying Camarillo and Sybil Brand. I order these words to vanish but they don't. I repeat them in the darkness as if I were already entangled in a form of possession. It's like a motor has accidentally been switched on and I don't know how to turn it off. Maybe this ghastly machine is fueled by terror and there is no mechanism to shut this down. The only perpetual motion device in the universe is the madness inside.

And I can't stop. Even if I manage to still these repetitions, these institutions would remain in my landscape. I can't banish them. They've already landed in my private regions. They brought their artifacts and put statues in my parks. They are players in my world now, as Louie would say. They are entities.

"You don't want to go to Camarillo," Roxanne says.

I walk into the bedroom we sometimes share. I am intoning Camarillo and Sybil Brand so softly beneath my breath it is almost telepathic. I am consigning these slow syllables to the blue gulfs that run between the past and future, the dream avenues and rivers, the fluid realms where we discard our transitory names and become the essence of hyacinth, undamaged, almost innocent.

I didn't know Roxanne was home. She must have just come in. She will take a bath, change her clothing, and repack. She will anoint her face with creams. She will brush her red hair in front of the hall mirror. The continuum will stall and it will be the same day and night always, the same warm amber.

When Roxanne looks into a mirror, it is always Year of

the Fire Hawk, Year of the Tiger Orchid. Here the seasons are translated into paper birds that burn. There is always a delta, a barge with smuggled fabrics and vials. There is always a sense of danger, of arbitrary destruction, of something worth dying to possess.

I haven't seen Roxanne in weeks. When I am near my mother, my mantra of just-born demons stops. They disappear and the air is clean. This is what happens after conflagration and erasure. Everything is redeemed. Silence comes on spools wide as hills. It would take a lifetime to unwind.

My mother is suntanned. She is wearing a gauzy white dress that shows her golden brown shoulders. It is as if she were presenting them in some imaginary televised contest where the stakes are your life. The material reminds me of tissue paper. It is January and Roxanne has banished winter. Since they invented planes, winter doesn't figure anymore. That's what she would say. Winter was the old world, the one that became tattoos and ash. Now winter is for farmers and peons, hillbillies who don't know how to buy a ticket. The great American legion of zombies, in limbo somewhere between indoor plumbing and credit card debt.

Roxanne is wearing enormous earrings that might be made from the interiors of certain seashells. They may have been fashioned from their ripped-open bellies. With such earrings, a woman could hear the ocean all day. The sea would become a kind of permanent fact perched on her shoulder. It would be as if she had never left Honolulu or Acapulco. A fluid weight would accrue. There would be whispered gossip and sudden bold rumors. There would come a time for decipherings.

Roxanne is smoking a cigarette. A glass rests on top of

her bureau next to her perfumes, her eye shadows and lipsticks. I know it is vodka. I can tell by the way the glass holds in the light, how it entices and captures it, how it becomes soft and paralyzed. Moments are actually a sequence of seductions. We negotiate the hours. We barter for our days. There are seasons when the oceans don't lay still, docile and predictable. There are the seasons when we eat bark. Nothing is guaranteed.

"You listening?" Roxanne says. "You don't want to go to Camarillo."

"I don't?" I sit down at the foot of my bed. I think of boats and hurricanes, how it would be to discover a desert island, to invent the gods and name the mountain ranges.

"No," my mother tells me. "Camarillo would be too definitive. It'd be like tipping your hand."

Where I come from, revealing your cards unnecessarily is a sin. There's no excuse for it. It's the worst kind of stupidity. It's like handing someone a map of your interior and a sharpened stick.

"They'll fingerprint you and the food is bad," Roxanne says. "Think about it."

Roxanne is arranging her bottles of perfume. She places a vial between her fingers and holds it up to the light. She seems to smell it through the glass. I think of a photograph from my twelfth-grade science text of Louis Pasteur holding a test tube. Then I realize these bottles are related to the glass in mirrors. They are a form of language, elegant and grave, intangible and sad. It is how women mark their territory, how they see where they have been. In such ways, they can track themselves. They can measure the perimeter. They can count the yards between their cot and the guard tower.

Roxanne is opening her bureau. She removes an armful of shorty nightgowns, black and red and a color that is not white but rather cream. White is unsophisticated. It is déclassé. It is for shop girls and women in the boonies. Cream, on the other hand, is chic.

Roxanne carries her nightgowns to the bed. She sorts through her underwear and arranges everything according to color. She picks up a lacy strip of black, sprays Arpège on it and places it carefully into the suitcase. She is gentle with her nightgowns. She might be putting flowers or infants into the bag. She might be placing melons and branches of cherry blossoms below the belly of a Buddha. And it occurs to me that we merely drift from one posture of supplication to another.

I almost ask Roxanne where she's going but I don't. She would just say location. Location is a holy word in our apartment. It's a quality distinct from geography. The location Roxanne talks about is something you can't find on a map.

If I asked where she was going, I know what she would say: I'm going to put food on your table, that's where I'm going. Or she might say it was none of my business.

By the depth of her suntan, I decide she's been to Mexico. The Hawaiian suntan is browner but it fades in a week. The Mexican tan is rosier and it lasts. Roxanne is an expert on suntans. She practices the process on beaches with pools surrounded by African palms. The pools are carved into cliffs above lagoons. There are thousands of varieties of palm tree and she can name hundreds of them. The saints nest in such trees. Saint Honolulu, Saint Cannes, Saint Acapulco. You show your devotion to such deities by carrying beach towels and drinking out of coconuts. Roxanne used to bring me the tiny purple and red parasols she had saved from the pineapple slices in her drinks. Then she decided I was too old for this.

I am thinking about Roxanne and her tropical saints. It's the twentieth century and everybody gets their own singular way of praying. It's all a matter of interpretation. The obscure road with its many gray areas. The face of God has been broken. You can't tell anymore what he was. You sweep up shards and lie on the sand. You put oil on your belly and thighs. And who is to determine what he said or what he meant? There are the problems with translation, after all, wind erosion, politics.

"I said it's too definitive," Roxanne is telling me. "Listen, you square. What you want to do is play with the edges."

Roxanne knows all about playing with the edges. She is standing in front of our bedroom mirror putting on lipstick. First she arranges her various implements, brushes and pencils and tubes. It's all in the paraphernalia, adherence to the formulas, whether you are blending your rouge or offering up a human sacrifice. You need what Roxanne calls the accoutrements.

"There's no goddamn magic," my mother is saying, evaluating something in her own green eyes. "It's all done with strings and mirrors."

She makes herself laugh. She begins the ritual of tracing the edges of her lips with a special red pencil. Then she fills the outline in with her brushes. There is the slow layering of the lacquers. I've never seen anyone else do their makeup this way. Someone at Columbia Pictures taught her the secret. This is how Lana Turner and Kim Novak do their mouths.

It is January in Los Angeles. It is early evening and my mother has come home. The air is sharp and clear. It seems as if something has been distilled, some contraband essence of winter perhaps.

Roxanne is blotting her lips. She lets the tissues drift to the floor. A series of her lip prints lines the sides like a string of mouths reciting the same words. This is a sudden litany, a kind of mutation. I think this is how deities are born. And I know what they are saying.

Perhaps I will pick up the tissues when she leaves. I will put them under my pillow. I will have her engraved kisses and they will be permanent. I will be able to find and identify her wherever she goes, even in the regions without winter where the borders were long ago lost.

I forget she is my mother. She could be any beautiful woman on a great boulevard in the center of one of the postcards she has sent me. Roxanne has sat in cafés drinking wine on the Ría de la Reforma. She has carried her purchases of handbags and scarves across long afternoons on the Champs-Elysées. She is the sort of woman who wears seasons across her shoulders. She is organized by color. She knows where the airport is and when the ferry leaves. No one is going to point a machine gun at Roxanne, put her on a cattle train, and make a lampshade from her flesh.

Roxanne carries her drink to the suitcase. She folds one last lace bra into the bag. She sprays perfume over the folded stacks of see-through black that remind me of layers of funeral veils.

"You knock me out. You're such a square," she says. She snaps the suitcase shut. The brass locks.

Roxanne pauses in front of the hall mirror. This is the

final confrontation before she leaves the room, the apartment, or the continent. This is when she enters the avenues of green within her eyes. This is where she rides down her secret boulevards, checks into hotels, masters international datelines, currencies, and the history of palms, how they evolved and dispersed. This is where she appraises herself, when she proves her worth to the air.

"They'll have to retire that color when I die," my mother, who has become a woman named Roxanne, says. She might be talking about her hair or perhaps her shoes or belt or shawl. She is a composition accented in red. "When I'm dead, they're going to bronze it and hang it in a museum."

She finishes her drink. She is picking up her suitcase and walking from the room. She doesn't touch me as she passes. I am too old for dolls or a collection of dwarf paper parasols from tropical drinks with the thin wood sticky from pineapple and coconut and rum. And she is concentrating on where she is going, not where she's been. When you walk through the fluid blue gulfs without anchors, you try not to get swept away. You try not to get sacked. You lose points that way and it's bad for morale.

Roxanne has navigated the living room. Her spiked heels on the hardwood floor tap out a sort of Morse code. It might be connected to the portals of glass. It could have something to do with perfume bottles and mirrors and the cool rubbed sides of statues and certain beads. Then I listen to the front door close and the scrape of the screen with its broken hinges.

I stand in the corner of the room where my mother has recently been and begin my night incantation. I stare into the mirror she used. I am attempting to excavate some vestige of her, some red trace element littering the air.

My words leave my mouth and find their way into the periphery. The periphery is a vast internal zone encased in a permanent winter. It is always raining. Air travel hasn't yet been invented. You can't buy a ticket and alter the seasons. It is some random port I have come to by accident, perhaps a shipwreck. No one knows my real name. I stay inside harvesting my terror. Alongside the boulevards, leaves are changing color. It's a city I don't know. The leaves are mirrors that teach me nothing but the certainty of scorch and loss and I knew this already.

Then my magic words slide into the cool night air where they become a kind of flower or bird, willows and lilies and quail in another dimension, in a time that hasn't yet happened. Eventually someone will gather these objects and place them at the feet of a carved wood statue. People will hold these things and confess their shallow cruelties and aberrant passions. It is possible such rare origami could become something else entirely, with a new morphology, measurable outlines, symmetry, parts that moved. But they couldn't be red. My mother has taken that set of possibilities and they are locked away forever.

2

They say I'm in an imbalanced condition. Then they can dismiss my perceptions and the ways I know that they are wrong, fraudulent and hypocritical. In truth, I know exactly what is going on.

By now everyone is making blouses and skirts. I can't believe it. I haven't even made my first practice gingham apron. I finally have the material, three yards of pale blue with a light yellow motif of rectangles. Roxanne had to drive me to the fabric store in Santa Monica. We had to take the car that can be used only in an emergency. She drove the red Chevrolet convertible with the top down even though it was cold. No one is putting Roxanne in a gas chamber. And no one is going to make her take a bus.

"This is my goddamn Saturday," she kept repeating. "My goddamn Saturday." It was like a mantra in reverse, some form of torture designed to induce violence and insanity.

She was looking at the edge of her cigarette. She was squinting, trying to see something. She might have been searching for a place she hadn't yet been. Her eyes were eager for intimations, even a vague suggestion.

I stood in the fabric store, disoriented. I was so nervous and shaken by my mother's impatience that I fled to the first material I saw. I realized my choice was pathetic and intrinsically dull even before she paid for it. I studied the fabric with its mediocre squares like the blueprint for an insignificant and drained pastel city and hated it. It was some kind of suburb with an aggressive street plan designed by malevolent children. Wherever it touched my fingers, I felt diminished.

Roxanne was studying my face. She tilted her head as if the act of accommodating my image was confusing and painful. I could feel her eyes on my skin. I could see her contempt for me, for the store, for marriage and child-rearing and education, for Santa Monica and for things I didn't even know about and had no words for.

"You got a problem again?" she asked. "Jesus Christ."

I was staring at Roxanne's fingernails. They are so long she has to ask me to button her blouses and pick up her keys and coins. Her nails are always a shade of red. I have memorized the names of her polishes. Chinese Lava. Crimson Noon. Tropical Sunset. Summer Burn. Such reds are part of her trademark.

My family appreciates the necessity of a trademark. You must have something that sets you apart, that catches the eye, that makes them want to ask you back. That's why my

Aunt Doris has a box full of rhinestone brooches. She wears a different one to work each night. She pins a cluster of fake garnet grapes on her breast or something that looks like a model of the solar system in pretend amethyst and brass. She says it makes people remember.

No one could let Doris slip into the periphery. Not after they see the stiff blond arches of hair rising from behind her ears like sudden inappropriate wings. Not after they notice her brooch of grapes or the twin circles of mock emeralds. Or the one with the initials in a synthetic substance resembling onyx. HT. Those are not even her initials.

I am standing in the fabric store thinking about the periphery. It's an irredeemable territory. It's like a swamp that is radioactive. Objects disappear there, cities and people and what they wore and what they said.

I am aware of my mother's red fingernails. I watch her encircle my wrist with her right hand and dig her nails into my skin. "Thanks a bunch," she says.

Her mood improves as we begin driving. She removes her vodka from the paper bag in the dashboard and takes a long slow sip. Her head falls back. Then she turns the car radio up, loud, with her long Chinese Lava fingernails. It's "Remember (Walking in the Sand)" by the Shangri-Las. She immediately switches the station, as if she's been in contact with something obscene. She finds Dean Martin singing "Everybody Loves Somebody Sometime." Her hands touch the radio dial, and for that moment she looks as if she's entirely part of the car.

It was all a red collage. Even the wind was tinged with it. It was a wind of spontaneous combustion, of sudden incineration. It played with her face. Everything was vivid and alert. Then it seemed to kiss her.

I was thinking about that Saturday in Santa Monica as I

sat in my sewing class. I studied my fabric with its predictable rectangular repetitions like a flat and decaying litany in dying hieroglyphics. It was a series of pointless cul-de-sacs in a stilted Los Angeles August. Or something worse, an abandoned language, a set of symbols that had been deserted because they tainted the mouth.

Mrs. Carlsbad, the sewing teacher, was glaring at me. I still hadn't stitched a single seam. I couldn't learn how to thread the sewing machine. There were seven or eight separate maneuvers necessary to place the thread correctly in the machine. I refused to master the procedure. I would have to begin by doing something with the bobbin. When I hear the word bobbin, I feel violated. I want to start screaming. I want to throw heavy objects like chairs through the windows. If I do that, they're going to put me in a mental hospital or juvenile hall.

Mrs. Carlsbad is examining me with progressive distaste. I make her world squalid. She can breathe better when I am gone. We both know this. She writes an office slip and sends me to Mr. Gordon.

I carry my small white piece of paper to the guidance counselor. It gives me something to do with my hands. I hold it in the crisp air and pretend it's a kind of flag. Not a flag of surrender but the white of purity and integrity. Mr. Gordon reads the memo slowly. Then he glances at my face. "You didn't sew again," he realizes.

"I can't learn," I tell him.

"You have an I.Q. of 157," Mr. Gordon says. "Of course you can learn."

"If I learned, it would be a bridge to a place I never want to go. If I go there, I'll die," I say.

Sometimes I tell the complete truth. That's how tired

and indifferent I am, how insubstantial and lost I feel. What I am really thinking is this: You are accountable not only for what you know but more importantly for what you don't know. You must master the art of refusal, of violet resistance. You must master the flagrant mime of the lilac. You must learn the dialect in which the ten million words for *no* are catalogued and kept. This is how you take responsibility for the continuum, the past and the future. You must be careful of the debris. There are bridges you can't just burn behind you. You cannot let these constructions into your world at all. You cannot permit them to become players. There are some bridges you must dynamite before they exist. You must eradicate the structures themselves, their materials and even the concept of what they do. That's how lethal they are.

Mr. Gordon shuffles the pages in my folder. It gives him something to do with his hands. It's part of his ritual. The folder might contain elements from dreams, things the night washed up like the faces of women in emergency rooms and bus stations, the women who stand alone on terraces and balconies, packing their hope chests with their eyes.

"You're doing the same thing you did with typing," Mr. Gordon points out. "You're not going to graduate."

We both know I won't learn to type. I have an *F* in typing, sewing, and home economics, where I will not be induced to mix meat, bread crumbs, and an egg together. I refuse to immerse my hands in it or shape the mess into a tin that will, in forty-five minutes at 325 degrees, become meatloaf. That's not the kind of transformation that interests me.

"You're not trying," Mr. Gordon decides.

There is a faint yellow glaze across the surface of his eyes. His face bears the evidence of a complex stain. It is possible we carry out histories with us. We hold our choices and typographies in our arms. When we decipher this in someone else, we call it revelation.

Perhaps Mr. Gordon committed an indiscretion somewhere along the continuum. It was an act of greed or cowardice. Perhaps he betrayed someone, told them where the train station was, shrugged his shoulders and revealed the names of the children.

"Your uncle says he's washing his hands. He's throwing in the towel. He wants you out of the house," Mr. Gordon says.

He's reading handwriting along the margin of a typed page. Later this will go into my Cum Card, the fat yellow packet that contains the other confidential information. Who has diabetes, depression, or asthma. Who has hearing loss, who attempted suicide and how, with a knife or blades, ropes or poisons. Who was born with a defect like no thumbs, a cleft palate, or a heart condition. Who is expected to die before graduation. Who got raped by their father. Who has been arrested, how many times, and for what.

"Uncle Louie's psychotic," I say.

I practice putting my new vocabulary acquisitions into sentences. I'm beginning to understand this word. You could hang this tag on Louie and still face yourself in the morning. You could put one on his wife, too.

I enjoy how quiet the room becomes when I dare to introduce certain words into it. Of course words can command the invisible particles to sleep or wakefulness. This is how we cast spells and how we free ourselves from them.

It is time to take stock. I am in the twelfth grade at West

Los Angeles High School. It is 1965 and I am failing everything but English and I am not going to graduate.

Mr. Gordon and I are sitting at a long conference table in the guidance counselor's office with a pack of cigarettes, two books of matches, and a Zippo lighter between us. There are tributaries and eddies and remote inland seas between us, coastlines of redwoods and glaciers, reefs of coral. We are sitting in the place where the compasses have nothing to do with the journey. These are the regions where you can drown yourself without trying.

I decide to remember this particular room in exact detail. I am going to regard this room as something I loved and would never see again, like a father or a hometown or a pet. It's a curious idea and I like it immediately. I decide to pretend my eyes are a camera and I can study the room inch by inch and record it. It would produce a magical film. Perhaps I could use this in another area of the continuum. If I could somehow develop it. If I could somehow find a way to preserve it.

I turn my camera eyes to the windows. Below, there is a concrete yard between the administration building and the fence you walk through to get out. The sun looks lacquered. It has the texture of paint. This is the sun of my miserable adolescence. I decide to ask myself how it looks. It looks aggressive but defeated. There might have been some promise once but it was false. As Uncle Louie would say, it didn't pan out.

This is a land where they gutted the gold a long time ago. Only the suckers and marks are still sticking around, waiting to trip on a nugget. That's why the hillbillies look dazed. Their minds are on the ores that aren't here anymore.

Beyond the school fence are the San Gabriel Mountains

with snow tinted a slow rose at the peaks. Between the fence and the mountains are thousands of dull rectangular intersections, pastel and flat like the fabric I will continue to refuse to sew. Along these streets are lemon and orange trees. They are strange miles with their gaudy exteriors and how exhausted they are within. Then I realize there is no distance that really matters. It is all a perpetual series of renegade miles we navigate blind with longing.

"You're not performing at a level consistent with your I.Q.," Mr. Gordon tells me.

I am imprinting the guidance counselor's conference room in absolute detail. The walls are wood paneled. Then there is the oak of the conference table and the beaten sunlight that falls in a kind of spasm upon it.

This is the sort of juncture, stalled between nothing, when I like to imagine I have been taken aboard an alien spacecraft. I've been abducted and I must describe Earth rooms with utmost accuracy. The destiny of our planet depends on this. I am the sole representative from Earth. I am taken to an intergalactic court where I must plead the case of the planet. I will describe the death camps with their fields of limed bones and the lampshades made from human skin and the children who became soap. Then I will say these bipeds also produced Monet's gardens at Giverny, Sputnik and the theory of relativity, the Salk vaccine, the Sphinx, cave painting, Greek mythology and poetry.

Then I am shown an image of this West Los Angeles High School room. On the basis of this, I must explain and defend human architecture and all it implies. If I fail, life on Earth will cease. I take a deep breath. I think I can do it.

I will tell them the rooms are constructed of wood. They are contrived from skinned trees, from their ripped openness. They are severed at their roots. They are extracted from their continuum and the dreams that fed them. These subtractions linger in the air and redden it. That's what makes the afternoon charged and singed. It is the hour of wood and the forest is screaming.

Then I remember my Baudelaire. I rummage in my canvas shoulder bag, feeling between my can of extra-strength hair spray and my tube of white lipstick for my paperback copy of *Les Fleurs du Mal.* I gather strength merely by brushing against it. I like to read these poems out loud. I don't comprehend them because I am failing French, but I sense it's not necessary to understand in the ordinary way. Some tactile resolution can come up through the fibers of the fingers. Isn't this the real nature of hieroglyphics and why they fascinate? And it's enough just to carry it near me. This is how history is imparted in the forest, the way bark is a text you don't need a mouth or a high school diploma for. The ocean is that way, too, with her rocks and shells and limbs of wood that drift and whiten, that collude on beaches, sudden and transient, imparting stories, perhaps.

It occurs to me that *Les Fleurs du Mal* is part of the bridge I must invent to save myself. Baudelaire's words swell, fierce red illuminations, and I know their obscure networks will eventually find one another. In time a bridge will form across the immensity of sharp rocks in the tumbled-upon gorge and one day I will walk across it.

"Are you still reading dirty poems?" Mr. Gordon walks to his desk and returns with the book he confiscated last week. It is *Howl* by Allen Ginsberg.

"This is pornography. You know that," Mr. Gordon tells me.

I didn't know. But it would be an act of betrayal to admit

this. Some clutter might be introduced to the river. I always imagine the continuum is a river. I like rivers. Roxanne liked rivers. That's why she named me Jordan.

At the moment of impact at Hiroshima, during the actual flash, people had the pattern of their kimonos tattooed to their flesh. Everything stalled. It was a conflagration of startled crane and heron, singed plum branches, lilies, and chrysanthemums. Then the indelible white. The burned went down to the rivers where many drowned. When I think of this I feel tears in my eyes so I close them.

I can sense the sky, vaguely restless, as if remembering a dream of release and definition. I can smell the sea, tangy like citrus that's gone bad from a wide-open sun that doesn't play by the rules. There was a series of complicated procedures. Time and measurement were factors. It was an intricacy that proved worthless. It didn't help anyone survive.

I realize it's possible to be ambushed by revelation. It would be a brutal night of too many stars. Heaven would be filled with tiny metal pins. You would recognize the constellations and where they were going. Their faces would be familiar as photographs on the table next to your bed. You would remember everything. You would know what they were saying. Nothing would require translation.

3

Because I refused to sew again, because I put my head on the table alongside my machine and pretended the room was laden with nuclear fallout, I've been sent to the counselor's office. That's three times this week. Mr. Gordon has a meeting somewhere. He's walking out of the room and he looks impatient. He manages to point a finger at me. "You better shape up," he says. "You know where you're headed."

I am beginning to decipher the code in this region. You must appear to be coping. And you must say you want to shape up.

Outside the window are half-built apartments with gaps in the wood that will one day be terraces with black metal slats and too much sun and nothing on them. Women will stand on these balconies and remember everything. Now sea gulls circle an alley.

Farther down the street is something that might be a birch. Its bark reminds me of fresh canvas. Perhaps someone unrolled it last night. Or raw silk, smuggled from across oceans. Some fabric that could cost you your arm or your tongue. When I consider rocks or tree trunks, I want to celebrate their intricacy, their subtle deviations.

The world is between purples. We are past the blossoming of the wisteria and before the unraveling jacaranda. And I don't care about shaping up.

I close my eyes and what I see is sky. One day the sky got bigger. It revealed itself. It was the end of blindness. It was a sudden portal. We went through. Then the world began.

It is before we came to California. The sky appeared as if it was a movie prop someone had ordered nailed up. It was the great blue gulfs of sky when my mother started driving.

My mother and I watch "Hollywood Playhouse" on TV every day at four o'clock. I've already come home from school. I am much younger. My mother lies on her side on the green wool sofa with a soft blanket across her legs. She has a glass of brown liquid that burns when you taste it. She says I can have some but I don't want it. The offensive glass is on the table by the couch. My mother's fingers caress it.

I sit near her feet. She isn't Roxanne yet. I am intrigued by the way her legs curve, how a kind of triangle appears to accommodate me. I am sitting on an island of sofa and my mother's legs are like the sea. This is an unexpected port. It could be a noon plaza encircled by honeysuckle and roses. Sun would take up all the sky. Later a person could hear bells and fall asleep.

I don't care about the movies. I sit quietly and watch her face, her mouth that is slightly open, the way she sometimes cries, how her eyes are unusually illuminated, almost yellow near the pupil. A mother knows the properties of candles and flames. She knows how to order and arrange them.

During commercials, she is practicing new names and discarding them. They are like dresses that no longer fit. Ruth isn't right anymore. It's the name she was given at birth but she's changed since then. The people who gave her that name were accidents. They didn't really know her, not the insistent red streak at her center that isn't meanness but something hotter and darker and less identifiable. They knew nothing about autumn bridges above rivers of charcoal and russet where the winds are.

Ruth Ann has the wrong connotations and it's juvenile. It's for someone with braids and knee socks. Rita proved too contrived. Rhea and Rachel and Rebecca stick in her mouth. They are part of the old litany that gags her. They are about rooms divided into sections for women and areas for men and the repetition of tedious postures and no answers. It's about the collapsing universe we are no longer bound to.

In between, she found Ruby. Ruby lasted half a year before my mother decided it was tinny and déclassé. My mother's world is divided into the acceptable and the déclassé. Now Ruby sounds like the name for a hooker, my mother realizes. A hooker from the South. Or somebody cleaning your house, even a black woman.

I imagine this region of déclassé where the shed names

have been sent. It is a kind of lilac closet. Or perhaps it is darker, more like violet, more like the African violets my mother says she loves. In this closet are the stacks of exiled words. Perhaps they are on shelves next to the out-of-fashion hats in their round boxes and the fur collars from my mother's coats that have begun to fall apart and have been folded into bags and tucked away. In this manner, there are no losses. Even the intangible elements are recorded and can be redeemed.

The failed names are in this lavender alcove and also things I glimpse from the sides of my eyes, shapes like sails and butterflies. The air is old and smells of oranges and vanilla and veils worn to marriages and funerals. There is a sound that might be a kind of thick rain. Day has stopped. It is on the border between light and dark, some extended twilight when everything aches.

The names my mother doesn't want anymore are here, on the invisible shelves. This is where they put the residues from spells. When the sorcerer waves his wand and the object disappears, this is where it goes, on this edge between enchanted and cursed. Here you know things while you sleep. I believe my mother dreams of trains and she is always on the platform leaving me.

"What are you thinking?" I ask her.

"I'm thinking I wish Ernie was dead." My mother is staring at the television. She is drinking sherry and smoking a cigarette in a green enamel cigarette holder. The sherry tastes like a fire that is bitter. My mother has decided Ruby sounds like a bar girl from Tennessee. It has all the wrong inflections. Its intimations are flagrant and misshapen. It makes you think of drunken uncles and afternoons that leave coal stains on your panties. Ruby is a wrong turn and the shadow it casts could kill you.

Ernie is my father. My mother never says the word *father*. Her lips will not permit this. Now she has condemned Ruby to the poisoned room of shabby coats and hats without their feathers, the failed place. Now she is vacant and nameless. Does she feel like a ghost? Will her bones start to show? Am I to blame for this?

"What's your favorite color?" I ask. If I keep talking, nothing will come through the cracks at the edges of the room. If I keep staring at her, I can somehow collect the air where she's been and I can keep breathing.

"Red," my mother who is between names says. She lights a cigarette with the stub of the one she just finished and puts it into her green enamel cigarette holder, which matches her eyes. "I wish you'd outgrow that game already," she says. She turns back to the television screen.

"If you could be anyone, who would you be?" I ask. Once I begin the question game, it is impossible for me to stop. It's like a spell. I keep asking questions until I get banished, until my mother sends me away.

"Would I have the same sensibility? Would I just inhabit their body but retain my identity?" my mother asks, squinting at me through the smoke. She looks like she's trying to find something at the corner of the room. She seems mildly interested.

"No. You'd become them completely," I tell her. I think that's the right answer.

"Then it wouldn't really be a change. Then it's just boring," my mother decides. She turns from me to her sherry. The glass contains a golden brown that makes me think of sunlight on walnut trees. It makes me think of bookshelves and pianos. It's the color of what you enter the forest hoping to find. My mother has walked over to the television. She turns up the volume. I know I am finished with questions for this day.

My questions have been exiled to the flawed domain where the hats with torn veils and ripped-in-half feathers are. The place where you must hold your breath. The place of the uncertain seasons with the two mothers with their many names. If I am not careful, I may be sent there, too.

I have decided there are two of her. The way she is when Ernie is home and the way she is when he is gone.

She is always sick when Ernie is home. It's incredible how pale her face becomes. It's the face of the first snow before anyone has stepped on it, before anyone even knows it is there. The face of secret winter. It's so cold and white, you don't know how to navigate, how to read the signs. It's a winter of disguised basements and unbroken solitude filled with sad and incomprehensible tones. It is so far beyond seasons as they are ordinarily known, it is almost elegant.

My mother wears her bathrobe, the pink quilted one with the big white shiny border of ribbon on the cuffs. She buttons it up to her neck. She wears socks under her fluffy slippers. She carries a box of tissues wherever she goes. She leaves pink rollers in her hair all day. She even sleeps with them. She wears her eyeglasses. She stays in bed reading books. She cannot even come out to watch television on the sofa. She can barely sit up. She says she has cramps. She isn't hungry. She says she's coming down with something. She says she has a headache and the flu. Don't go near her.

As soon as Ernie leaves she becomes someone else. It's as if she is awakening from a spell. Maybe somebody kissed her. Now she is Rita or Ruby. She rubs blue eye shadow on her lids and I think of a lake in summer. Her eyes look like August and I immediately imagine water. Then she takes the rollers out of her hair. I unwind the big round ones from the back of her head, the ones she can't reach. I hold my breath.

"Do you think a man would find me attractive?" my mother asks. She takes off her bathrobe. We are staring at her naked body in the mirror. She is the color of peaches and the individual bones in her spine show. You could count them and I say yes.

"I don't mean Ernie. Not Ernie. I mean a real man," my mother says.

I say yes. I can still see the white places left by the back of her bathing suit. She's putting on powder and perfume. She smiles at her reflection. "There's no goddamn mystery," my mother says. "It's all done with strings and mirrors."

She takes down her jewelry box. She opens the lid and lets me choose for her. I consider the permutations of these earrings. There are flat bronze discs and slivers that dangle. There are things that look like bitten moons. I wouldn't want this near her cheek. I hold out round white pearls in my hand. My mother calls them her Mamie Eisenhower earrings. She says I want her to look like somebody's grandmother. But she wears them anyway.

"What are you thinking?" I ask.

"I'm thinking about my brother Louie. That's a man," my mother tells me. "He's a bookmaker on the coast. Last time I saw him, he had forty phones."

"You mean he's an author?" I ask.

My mother laughs. We are walking to the bus stop. I can tell as soon as she turns in the direction of the store with the newspapers and magazines, as soon as we cross the street in front of the house with the three elms. We've been doing this for months, even when it rains. Whenever my father is gone, we ride the bus to the car lot downtown.

I never mention this to my father. My mother who is Rhea and Rachel and Rita and Ruby warned me. "If you tell Ernie, I'll leave you behind when I go." My mother was using her serious voice. She was staring directly into the center of my eyes and I felt wide awake. Then she placed her hands on my shoulders and shook me. I could feel her fingers through my navy blue alpaca winter coat. "Understand? I'll leave you with him."

I envision the chamber of the discarded crescents, the wounded violets, the toy piano with its two stuck front keys, the stuffed bears and bunnies with their legs torn off and the cotton coming out of their necks, and the clothes that don't fit anymore, the shoes with the scuffs and broken buckles. Soon my father will be there with the round hatboxes with their white carrying strings and the thrown-away names that start with *R.*

We are riding the bus and my mother is someone you could not have predicted. She is wearing her red dress with the long sleeves and the red velvet hat with its one tall red feather. Not red, but a burnt auburn. That's what she calls it. And she's put on her high heels even though there are still thin patches of snow on the ground near the curb where a person could slip.

"I'm beyond slipping," my mother says.

I don't have to ask what her favorite color is. We are riding downtown and I watch the buildings become taller and crowd together. There are people everywhere, on the sidewalks and steps. They seem to be staring at us. The buildings are somehow sewed at the seams. They might be falling into one another. They are a brick that appears brown. They were ordinary bricks once but somehow they got dirty. If they get soiled enough and their inner workings become visible, they could be sent to the alcove of lost hats and toys and fathers. Maybe they can also banish cities. There are gestures to decipher on these boulevards in this granite winter.

These are not streets, I know that. She says they are called boulevards. And there are cars and taxis, the buildings spill shadows across the cement and it looks permanently dark, netted, caged. My mother has her handbag on her lap. I know what is inside, the handkerchief with the red *R* stitched in the corner. And inside of the handkerchief is the pile of money. That's why my mother keeps opening and closing the purse, opening it and touching the money with her fingers. She traces it lightly like she does the sides of her glass with the sherry in it. Something is coming up through the tips of her fingers.

"How did you get so much?" I lean toward her and whisper.

"I've been saving a long time." She smiles.

I think she's been saving since we went to the museum and saw the exhibit from China. It was my field trip from school but somehow she went along. We stood in front of the glass display case where the foot-binding procedure was explained. There were reproductions of the way the feet looked in something called plaster of Paris. There were photographs and diagrams. My mother read every word twice. She began crying. That was the year she first considered taking driving lessons. That's when she started trying to find the right new name.

Then we are getting off the bus. Her hand on the back of my coat tells me where to go. She steers me. It is a world of water, after all. She knows the currents, the reefs. We are turning off the boulevard onto a smaller street. Men wear suits and women carry round boxes. They know us at the car lot. They watch us approach, raise their arms, and wave.

Sometimes these men let my mother drive a car. Monty and JoJo and Craig. They are giving her driving lessons even though they're not supposed to. I sit in the office on a folding chair next to a desk with an ashtray and a telephone I've been told to never touch. Above the desk is a photograph of a naked woman standing up. Her left leg rests on a chair. She wears black high heels and a sailor cap. She is smiling with her lips slightly apart. There are paper clips and pencils and business cards and old calendars in the desk drawer. There are matchbooks and dust. Sometimes I wait in the office for hours. Sometimes I remember to bring a book.

Today we sit in my mother's favorite car. It's the red convertible. JoJo takes the top down for us. He shows us how easy it is to do. He turns the radio on. Then he leaves us alone. We sit in the car and my mother changes the stations. She moves the dial back and forth until she finds a song she knows and can sing the words to. It is "Mack the Knife" by Bobby Darin. This is the mother you could not have dared to imagine, singing with the wind against her lips. I stare at her. It could mean anything.

It's the end of a cold season. It's a world of suggestion. I know we won't go until it's warmer. My mother is between names. She is opening and closing her handbag, touching the money with the tips of her fingers. Then she starts talking about China.

She's been talking about foot-binding all year. She recounts the entire process, how the feet were bound in special sheets, how the bones caved in and the toes fell off. This was considered beautiful. This was proper. Then the woman was crippled. She couldn't walk at all. She had to be carried on a litter. They did this for a thousand years.

"She couldn't run away," I say. I realize I'm supposed to say this. It's like a play and we each have a part. I have memorized my dialogue.

"But she could drive," my mother concludes.

She gets out of the car. She is gone for two hours and forty minutes. I time her by the clock on the dashboard. When she returns, she is carrying the car keys.

We are driving with the top down. It is late afternoon. A light snow is falling. My mother stops at a store. She returns with a bottle in a paper bag. She takes a sip and puts the bottle back in the bag under her seat. She's wearing her new red hat and snow sticks in the feather. She lights a cigarette and doesn't bother flicking the ash. She simply lets the wind take it away.

I am looking up and I realize I am seeing the sky for the first time. I have never before understood the complexity of the gray veils, how the whole belly of cloud seems to be shredding, how it is giving birth to the snow. The sky is a kind of basket of white eggs that are falling, shattering, flakes are spilling from their sides. They are more delicate than the memory of feathers.

"They must have figured a way," my mother is saying. "Hobbled on sticks, maybe. The forest must have been filled with them. Hiding in caves. Eating insects and mice."

She is talking about the women in China, the women who may have managed to escape, to stumble crippled from their enclosures, to risk the night. Soon my mother is going to become Roxanne. When it gets warmer, we are going to pack the car and drive to California. We will wait for the snow to melt and the mountains to become passable. We are waiting for the roads to be safe. We are waiting for my mother to find the right name. We are at the edge of winter and waiting for some form of inspiration, a sudden juxtaposition we might recognize.

Then we are going to find my Uncle Louie who makes books but isn't an author. We are going to surprise Louie and I plan to count his telephones. I am going to ask him why he has so many. And now I am staring at the sky as if I have never seen it before. I am putting my head into the air and looking at the shredding and I am thinking that it is possible to drown in up.

Up is a place, it's a kind of banished kingdom. It's like the alcove of exile. It's a region of the déclassé. Up is what hasn't happened yet. It's a white gray struggling for definition. It's where chronology might not help you. This is the area that contains everything you haven't learned yet.

Then we are walking into the house. It's dark, it's night now but Ernie isn't there. Ernie never comes back. I don't see him leave. Perhaps I was asleep or at school. Maybe my bedroom door was closed. He is simply not there and the place of his absence elongates.

"Ernie's gone," my mother finally says. It is weeks later. Just Ernie. He might be one of the guys at the car lot. He might be the mailman or the old man with one arm who sells tickets at the train station. "Permanently," she adds.

How big can gone become? What can it open into? Perhaps there is a trick door you stumble on and chance to unlock. You didn't mean to. By accident you turn a key and then you are there, removed from the world as it used to be.

That other region is veiled in light purples and it inexorably recedes. You recognize you are an inhabitant of another terrain. It is like a secret garden but larger.

Then you realize you are beyond the city walls and night is falling. A rain begins and it is heavy and unusual. The rain is percussive. It contains elements like metal or tin. You think you might be imagining this and all the small pins. You are riding in a car. You put your arm out and where the rain falls you begin to bleed. The rain is filled with thousands of tiny saws. Or perhaps they are fish mouths with rows of teeth that glitter. This is the face of the night. You decide to run away, to go back. But when you turn around you lose direction and the place where you were has been erased.

4

There are shadows against my closed eyelids. The air in the guidance counselor's office is synthetic, the color of nothing that existed in this world before.

I glance at Mr. Gordon. I used to have what he called promise. Now he's probably sorry he gave me the special pass that allows me to walk out of any class and go directly to the conference room. If he isn't there, the nurse calls him. This is because I'm being counseled.

Only three kids at West Los Angeles High School are being counseled on a regular basis. Before he left for college, my best friend Jimmy Nakamura was one of them. Jimmy is a math genius but he has recurrent nightmares about the atomic bomb.

I think he has a right to his reactions. After all, five members of his family were killed at Hiroshima. His father's aunts and uncles died from radiation poisoning. Now his cousin Tamiko has leukemia.

Jimmy has assembled a chronology of horror. It began one summer in West Los Angeles. His father was helping his grandfather paint the porch of their house. There were red roses pushing through a lattice. There were iris and lilies. Then he was saying his prayers outside in a garden of stones and gravel. Everything was black-and-white like a documentary movie. You felt you were part of history. It was already defining your rhythm and possibilities.

By then they knew the soldiers would be coming. Jimmy's father recognized the moment as definitive. He put on his Boy Scout uniform. He had just earned a badge for archery. He combed his hair. Then they were taken on buses to a detention camp on the other side of the mountains. They called it a detention camp, not a concentration camp.

There were unexpected textures in the stark inland place. It was a sky of martyrs and kidnaping. It was always a stasis of birds over water and the repeating sun, one rising and one fallen. One thought of slaughter and the way it lingers above the dried reeds. There were unforeseen couplings. It was afternoon in the camp when Jimmy's father heard a bomb had been dropped on Hiroshima. And they never got their confiscated property back. As Roxanne would say, that's the kicker.

Jimmy Nakamura and I take World War II seriously. The planet is divided into people who think World War II is just something that happened in a textbook and the others who were personally affected.

Jimmy Nakamura can talk about the bomb for hours. He begins with the actual impact. People within half a mile of the blast were completely vaporized. They married the air and lost their destiny. They were singed out of time. They were the moths that found the flame and they can't come back. There is no ritual of return passage for them.

Jimmy believes certain types of incineration last forever. There is no possibility of reincarnation for people who die from atomic bombs. They cannot be reassembled in any other realm. Even their atoms are contaminated. Their generations have been removed. There have been forms of lethal internal sculpture. They can have no afterlife and even if they could, they would occupy an untouchable caste.

Most of Jimmy's family didn't die in the blast. They were killed by radiation poisoning. I have an enormous appreciation for the effects of radiation. I can watch my Uncle Louie dying from it in slow motion. Around here, they call it cancer treatment.

Jimmy's aunts and uncles were outside of the city. They were not instantaneously extinguished. Instead, their hair fell out. They bled from their noses, ears, and eyes. They weakened. They vomited. Often they lost their minds. Then they died. Sometimes they had a baby first. That's what happened with Tamiko. She was born after the bomb fell.

Later Tamiko was sent to live with Jimmy's family while they gave her treatments at Palms Memorial Hospital. Jimmy says his apartment is some kind of depot. It's a death port. After the welcome teas come the treatment schedules, medicines, and clinic appointments. It makes him crazy.

The only other person with a permanent counseling pass is Pamela Bruno. She has a mental illness and a defective leg. She's what we call a double.

Mr. Gordon is putting out a cigarette and feeling for something in his pocket. I remember my eyes are cameras and I have a responsibility to memorize and record this. Before Mr. Gordon began counseling me, I would sit in the room where everyone else was typing or sewing and I would lay my head on my desk and attempt to still my breathing and disappear. There must be cracks in the mural of the world, a passage to the slow blue river with the banks of reeds and red drums. There must be a way to fall through.

"Sleeping is for the nurse's office," the typing teacher, Mrs. Trevino, would say. She exaggerated each syllable, as if she was typing with her mouth, making the words bitter and metallic. She was forcing them to jump and bite.

My teachers despise me because I live in the Courts. I have a 157-point I.Q. and I repudiate them absolutely. I respond to them as if they were trying to poison me and they know it. They are trying to give me radiation sickness of the soul. And they are going to have to put me into restraints to do it.

My teachers think it's a waste of an I.Q. to give it to someone from the Courts. The kids in Palm Courts end up leaving the district. We get sent to relatives in Kansas City or Stockton when our parents die. We go to Youth Authority, mental hospitals, and foster homes. We go to reform school and Trade Tech. We go to buy a loaf of bread and never come back. We erase ourselves. We vanish. We are something you might have seen above a mesa, over a gorge or an arroyo. You can't be sure.

It begins when the kid's mother breaks down. That takes

a year, sometimes a year-and-a-half. Every morning the mother wakes up at six, puts on her secretary clothes, the tight pink skirt her boss says he likes and the white high heels. She polishes her shoes while she boils the water for instant coffee if it's early in the month, if there's still money for coffee. Then she walks to the bus stop. She walks because the car has been sold. The car went after the house and before the amethyst ring her grandmother gave her. It went after the garage sale and the lamps from France. Now she walks to the bus that will take her to her job. She files and types and answers telephones. She has to be careful to keep her voice cheerful. If the boss thinks she's crying during her coffee break, he'll fire her.

Outside the bus are anemic eucalyptus with starved crescent leaves that fill her with despair. They have a strange chalk within them, some property of lingering incarceration perhaps, and how it is stirred by the too-yellow air. Her ear has turned red from the press of the telephone against it. Then she walks from the bus, past the stray magnolias with their plastic-like white flowers. She passes the kiosk in front of the Courts. Then she cooks dinner and washes the dishes, the clothes, the bandages. She irons the short black dress her boss said he wants her to wear more often. Then she visits her husband or daughter in Palms Memorial Hospital. Visiting hours are seven to eight.

The seasons become interchangeable. Who could decipher their subtleties and why would they bother? There are California Monterey pines that seem too green and indifferent. Then her husband loses another limb. Or her son gets a tube because his throat won't work. There are the unexpected problems with breathing, swallowing. You can't take anything for granted.

Then she comes home and puts polish on her fingernails. She smokes too much and her hands shake. She doesn't know where her other son or daughter is. She makes the bag lunches for the next day. She sets her hair. She gets thinner. She thinks maybe she should take a pill for pain. Her eyeglasses break and she doesn't buy new ones. Why should she?

Then she begins to collapse. It doesn't happen all at once. Maybe her boss told her to wear the straight pink skirt to work without panties. He likes her to sit on the edge of his desk, stir his coffee, keep her legs spread. If she doesn't comply, she will be dismissed. He has her lean against the side of his desk while he tells her this. He touches her thigh underneath her skirt with his pen, without looking directly at her, as if it wasn't really happening. How can she be sure?

That's when she develops the migraines. She starts throwing up. She needs a new notch on her belt. Her son makes it with a hammer and a nail. It becomes difficult to tell who's got the cancer. Then she breaks down. That's when the fathers and brothers start drinking. That's when the daughters begin to drift away. They are leaves in a bad season. They know this. Then they are gone.

"Even with your family problems, college is not entirely outside the realm of possibility," Mr. Gordon says.

Not entirely outside the realm of possibility, I repeat to myself. I consider the split atom and the black holes of space. Somewhere, a woman stands ankle-deep in a river, turns in a circle seeking resolution amidst the shadow of legs across parched grass. I close my eyes.

"Do you think about college?" Mr. Gordon wants to know.

I shake my head no.

"What about cooking and sewing? Aren't those skills you'll need? As a wife and a mother?" Mr. Gordon asks me.

I decide to look at his eyes. I am going to risk this. I have a mission. Human evolution in the next millennium depends upon my observations. His eyes are a weak blue. A polluted blue. Algae by an insignificant lake in a decadent tropical city where the language proved inadequate and has been thrown away. I would refuse to have his children.

"Won't you have a family to take care of?" Mr. Gordon is interested.

I say no.

"What are you going to do?" He looks at his folder. I suppose he's attempting what we in twelfth-grade English call a dramatic punctuation. "Obviously French isn't part of your plans."

"I wanted to take Spanish," I reveal.

"Spanish?" Mr. Gordon is suddenly energized. He repeats the word with distaste. He makes a sour expression with his lips. "College-possibles take French. What would you do with Spanish?"

I consider the desert wind that blows from the south and east, the charged wind they call a Santa Ana. I like to feel it rub against my flesh. It's a wind from another dimension. It knows about bobcats and owls and the glare of deserts and how after seventeen hours between plateaus the dawn can seem red, Egyptian, how you might want to kneel down and marry it. This wind can tell you stories about bridges and acts of insolence and supplication. But you must know how to listen.

The Mexican girls at West Los Angeles High School have their eyes outlined in black like organic amulets. This is how Indian princesses must look, draped in turquoise and silver. I like the charms they wear around their necks, thin emblems designating a saint with specific attributes. Saint of lovers and women who travel by horseback and barge. Saint of sick children with withered legs. Saint of hunger and paralysis. I consider the names of these displaced royal women: Rosalia. Marta. Esmeralda.

"What would you do with Spanish?" Mr. Gordon repeats.

"It's so close," I realize. "I could go there and talk to the people."

There is silence. I have said something that induces the end of words. The air has doors and grids and bars, thick mesh, nets that lock. Or perhaps I have accidentally invented a spell.

"Talk to the people? You mean taxi drivers and maids?" Mr. Gordon stares at me. He is angry. "There's been nothing written in Spanish since Cervantes. It's almost a dead language. It's a language of people who work in hotels. Are you going to be a maid?"

I consider this possibility. I envision a hotel I have never seen. There would be a balcony facing the sea and a wide stretch of sand between the terrace and the waves. It would be the dusk after the end of prayer. There would be seashells along the shore, slivers of sand dollars and the separated halves of heavy clam shells, bleached and white like so many severed hands. They would glitter when the moon rose. The sand would seem inhabited. You could get dizzy from picking up so many of them. You could fill entire bags. You could cross borders. Then you could start your own currency. When you became tired, you could lay by the pool and drink from a coconut. You wouldn't have to save the parasol in the middle.

There would be palm trees and above, like a scraped

belly, the sky with its perfumed gas. I would breathe it in, a sequence of mouths, all of them speaking. It would be the blue of grace and absolution.

Mr. Gordon is staring at me. I am about to say something. Then the bell is ringing and I am moving through the door, into the broken sun.

5

I am navigating the horizontal two-story orange sprawl of West Los Angeles High School. Doors open from one corridor to another like a train somehow ambushed and stalled, derailed. Perhaps the tracks have been washed away.

There are only cold plaster walls and yellow lockers. There are only brass plaques engraved with the names of boys killed in Korea and a locked trophy case with marching-band awards.

In the main office the desks are behind a barricade of wood counter. The ceiling has acoustic squares drilled with rows of exactly twenty-five by twenty-five holes. I know because I've counted. This is where they crucify sound.

Then the square of linoleum tile on the floor. The way the light is sliced and hangs on metal bars, suspended, cubed. What is it like, precisely? It is servile and repugnant.

It's a relentless linear realm that finally empties into the wide flat ache of the boulevard. I move south in a kind of stupor feeling betrayed. I search the bleached foliage along the sidewalk for Jimmy Nakamura even though I know he graduated and took a scholarship and went to Berkeley. He shares a wooden house with three other freshmen who study physics. There are sunflowers in his front yard and purple morning glories interspersed like so many fallen stars, not degraded orbs but rather bodies at rest. Jimmy says the city drifts towards the mud flats. He likes the bridges with their impersonal architecture exposed. It's like the end of secrets. And he says the whole world is about to change.

I glance at the entrance to the Courts. I haven't seen Pamela Bruno in weeks. Maybe she's had a relapse and they had to put her into restraints and take her by ambulance to Palms Memorial. Then I am passing the deserted kiosk and the flag pole with nothing on it. This is a kingdom past flying even the skull and bones, past barbarism and piracy. This is the last broken wharf. There are no border disputes here. This is a region no one wants.

I don't see anyone I know. Then I realize it's Monday, follow-up day at the clinic for satisfactory progresses and remissions. Everybody but the air balls and buzzer shots go. That's what we call the terminal cases. Air balls and buzzer shots. They're like the last-second wild throw a ball player makes as he runs out of time, just tossing it up blindly hoping for a miracle.

I begin to think about being abducted by aliens and given

the task of describing human culture at the end of the millennium. I will admit it's been a sequence of concentration camps, genocide, and the atomic bomb. But perhaps this is simply a chaotic transition where the borders are not solid. Maybe that's why poisons are leaking into the water and air. That's why there is strontium 90 in the milk. Someone eats a contaminated peach and their unborn generations are deformed.

But what about van Gogh and his version of night? What about the stars he enticed and hung near his face in a reinvented universe? What about ballet and democracy and the American dream? What about universal education, the equality of women, and the possibility of love?

Then I see the red Chevrolet by the curb. Uncle Louie and Aunt Doris must have gotten a last-minute ride to follow-up. Uncle Louie and Aunt Doris hate to drive.

My family believes Southern California is a treacherous desert outpost where everyone is an informer and thief. Here the Nazis and cossacks come from the Dust Bowl. They are waiting for an opportunity to make you into a lampshade, to yank out your gold and silver fillings and melt your flesh into bars of soap. That's the theme of the twentieth century. Ask Roxanne and Louie and Doris. They know.

You can't trust it outside. Not the pale drained sky with squalid clouds in the rubbed-away mockery of blue. Not the fat sea birds with their malignant strangled sounds. Not the ripped-away shreds of the palms.

Outside is what happens when you walk through the front door. Savage drunken garage mechanics deliberately tear things up so they'll break and cost twice. There are hillbillies and blonds with imperfect grammar. These are the children of the migrants from the degenerate interior. This is what a legacy of incest and wet brain can do for you. Outside is a place where it is always the time of night only, a few broken lamps, maybe, and everything rhymes and twangs.

Southern California is a feudal kingdom, a vast hostile plain. Who knows the rules of these strangers with their inferior dialects and malice, their bad skin and teeth and terrible banjo music?

You must remain within walking distance of Les Downer's Flying A Service Station. In Uncle Louie's hierarchy, just below the doctors at Palms Memorial, the most important man in West Los Angeles is his mechanic. Louie says you have to treat them nice. They're all big and stupid like Les.

Once, before Uncle Louie got in the chair, when he was still able to walk with a cane, he took me to the garage with him. Louie said he had a responsibility to educate me, to show me how to do business with these people.

Uncle Louie stopped and bought a bottle of Southern Comfort. He knows what these people drink. It says Southern on it. It's like a code. That's how these subliterates talk to each other, with codes.

I am walking with Louie and he's approaching the gas station like he was in Africa with wild animals. He's on a safari. He is proceeding with great caution. He's taking slow steps and he keeps smiling. His mouth must ache with the effort. And he's holding out the bottle of Southern Comfort raised at his side like a flag of surrender. His hand is making gestures of supplication. His face looks like he's mentally saying, come here doggie, nice doggie.

Of course Louie can't do that anymore. The cancer is in

his leg bones. He rarely leaves the apartment. He tells me what he needs. I am dispatched to thread my way through the paths of the Courts, beyond the dull lawns littered with the particles that are drifting from between the gauze and stitches and bandages, and you must run as fast as you can. There are strangers waiting to ambush you. They're behind the palm trees with their thousands of varieties. They're crouched beneath the hedges of catatonic poisonous oleander. Maybe they want to skin you and fashion a lamp. Or tattoo numbers to your wrist.

It's a planet of terror and infection. Ask Louie. He'll tell you about his treatments, those insidious beams they bombard him with. It's like he's a city and there is a war. They want to make Uncle Louie into thick ash. They want his highways. They want to eradicate the inscriptions on his statues. They want to rewrite his history. They would demand the words he speaks to his God but he has no prayers.

The treatments make his hair fall out in clumps in his fingers, in a nest in his comb. And his teeth fall out. His legs have stopped working. The bones are curving in. He can't chew food. Everything tastes like dirty cardboard and straw. He's a barn animal now, some stray. And if the hospital staff hears him say that, they'll make a notation about his attitude. Then they might begin talking about tubes.

You can't trust it inside, either. You must be alert. You must check your body for spots that are suspicious, darkening or enlarging. You must feel for lumps or abrupt clusters. We are a kind of ocean where islands sometimes rise. We must search for telltale signs, a leak, an indication, even a symbolic wound. Where do you draw the line? And you must catch it before it spreads. If you wait for the pain you are dead.

Sometimes I stare at a light bulb. I close my eyes and open them as quickly as I can. When I do this I can see half-realized shapes in the periphery. They are some visual representation of the half-lives. And I wonder how many half-lives Uncle Louie has left, after all the cobalt treatments. He is swollen with blue poisons. They spill out of him, enter the air and float to the horizon, which they defile. He's what's lowering real estate values. It is sunset and I can feel the soft pulsing, this ruined underside of blue where small-craft warnings won't be nearly enough.

I walk into the living room and force my feet to touch the floor softly. I consider acres of invisibility and how remote and cool they would be. And I wonder why they call them cancer victims instead of cancer carriers.

When I first heard the words nuclear family, I thought they meant an apartment with a cancer victim in it. A family who dropped their mother or father off at the end of the driveway with a nuclear medicine sign. A family who spent evenings in rooms with metal barriers and machines that hang from ceilings where you need special vests and glasses and even then it's dangerous.

Uncle Louie gets the same particles that annihilated Jimmy Nakamura's family. Now Louie's skin is like tissue paper. If you touch him, he shreds, he bleeds. He could wear the indent of your fingertip forever. Louie waves his cane and yells with his hoarse voice, "Don't come near me."

Louie and Doris have been playing Hollywood gin. I can tell it's gin and not two-handed bridge because they have their score book out. They've been keeping track of their points for years. They're halfway to a million.

I remember the first time I saw the card table. It was the night we came to California, when my mother became Roxanne and had to move around. Somehow I had the notion that the card table came and went. I didn't understand it was always in the center of the living room, that it was a permanent fixture. I didn't realize dinner was what you found on the side across from the fresh decks still in cellophane and the tiny just-sharpened pencils. Dinner was Ritz crackers, cheese cubes, and quartered carrots with onion dip. I was shocked when we studied nutrition in Health Ed. I thought the five food groups were three kinds of crackers and cheddar and Swiss cheese on a paper plate. The only green thing on the table was the money.

When Doris was promoted from waitress to hostess at Canter's Delicatessen, dinner began to improve. With her elevated status, she was able to bring home entire bags of cheesecake that had crumbled, cookies devoid of the cherry in the center, rolls someone had put their thumb through. And the ragged edges of turkey and pastrami that reminded me of the tailings left by nuclear fission, the by-products of the transformation of uranium.

There are transformations on Fairfax Avenue in Canter's Delicatessen, too. Journeys are begun and ended. We are solitary depots in an area of fluid borders and no illumination. Distance becomes abstract, something that can't be crossed in a stalled deficient wind. Character is revealed. It is ineluctable like mountain ranges. Under the glare of the waxy hot light in the thick yellow flecked ceiling there are revelations. I know this for a fact.

The record player is on. It's Ethel Merman singing "Everything's Coming Up Roses." Aunt Doris has the phonograph jammed on perpetual repeat. Everything is coming up roses all day long, week upon week, whether they are in the apartment or not. It's like a monstrous act of voodoo, a concurrent desecration of sound and plaster and light.

The telephone is on the edge of the card table, on the south side where Doris sits. She says she gets better cards in that position. She would have evaluated her hand while talking into the phone instrument. "You know low? You know the lowest? Look under that. Dig a ditch. Then you'll see her," Aunt Doris might have said. She would have been talking about Roxanne.

The TV is in its usual place, unplugged in the closet with a tablecloth covering it. Its dead glass face is invisible beneath a rectangle of frayed yellow linen. According to Louie and Doris, TV is permissible only for the nightly news, which must originate in New York City to be credible. Or else for some catastrophe, something monumental enough to disrupt ordinary programming. That's when they wheel it out and lift the tablecloth from the screen and plug it in.

Louie and Doris believe TV is just American propaganda. It's another pathetic hoax for the hillbillies. It's the new opium for the new masses, as Aunt Doris says. But they are way ahead on this one. They are what Uncle Louie calls too hip.

For instance, Aunt Doris is not just the midweek night hostess at Canter's Delicatessen on Fairfax Avenue. She is not merely the woman who directs you to a booth, the lady with blond hair sprayed like fins near her ears and the remember-me brooch glittering on her breast, that fist-sized fake emerald that draws your attention and indelibly fixes her in your memory.

In her version of events, she has had a few minor setbacks due to her husband's cancer. But at any time she might be returned to her former life as the stay-at-home wife with two furs, the white mink coat and the brown mink stole. She will have back the weekends in Las Vegas at the Tropicana or the Flamingo Hotel. The days when she lifted a finger only to call room service.

Sometimes I think the continuum is a river filled with ports and pawn shops. And my family has mastered disguise. We appear in these transitory roles that cannot define or contain us. We are actually victims of a garish accident. We need to talk to the supervisor.

Since we have been arbitrarily demoted, we can be magically restored. It's a fairy-tale land, after all, this coast of poisoned oranges and no seasons, only heat and its inevitabilities. There is haze on the vaguely Mediterranean hills that seem like a cursed Greece, perhaps, asleep in their own soiled pastels.

And there is no way to determine if you're lighting the candles on the right nights or if you are lighting them at all. Perhaps night has become a procession of slow yellow intervals like sails with lanterns on their masts. No one knows what you are doing or who you are doing it with. Everyone just got here. In a year, they'll be gone.

Anything is possible. Maybe Uncle Louie is not really in a wheelchair with his skin bleeding if you breathe on him. Uncle Louie is going to have the black Cadillac again. He's going to be the bookmaker you used to see in a private box at Hollywood Park. He was the one in the white linen suit in the first row at the boxing matches at the Olympic Auditorium. He would take Doris to Chinatown for dinner first. They arrived late and everyone stared at Aunt Doris in her tight black skirt. Louie, the man with forty telephones, would smile to himself, listening to the crowd whistle.

Now Ethel Merman is singing "Everything's Coming Up Roses." It is late afternoon on a day on the border between the first two months of the year. Soon the palms will stand on the cliffs above Santa Monica Bay, motionless in the sullen evening, in the glare proceeding the contaminated lavenders. Soon there will be no centers. The sun will set in a pink exhaustion like a pale bruise received in a stupor, a drunken collision. Then a morning will come when absolutely nothing will be certain.

6

It is easier to maneuver through the Courts now that I know I am simply gathering information. These are acts of discrete sabotage. This is a form of ethnography. I am purposeful and hidden.

Palm Courts West is subsidized housing for the patients at Palms Memorial Hospital. You can stay here as long as you are receiving treatment. You have to move out within ninety days of the funeral. I am living in the Courts because Uncle Louie is in remission. On a deeper level, as we say in twelfth-grade English, on a metaphorical plane, I am here because Roxanne took some losing flyers and made some staggering mistakes.

Palm Courts West was designed to be a sort of miniature

city. Once you had to drive through a gate past a booth for a guard who isn't there anymore. The kiosk remains as a kind of symbolic statement. This is a land of the bandaged and insomniac, the slow bruises that can't quite heal. These bruises are a permanent light blue. You know you have been touched by something extraordinary and unexpected. You know how big the arbitrary night is. When you live in the Courts, you know there is no way to gather such blues, arrange or redeem them.

Now it is early February. I follow paths past lawns struggling to retain their tawdry suggestion of green. I imagine I am a stranger chancing to glance down the neat rows of two-story stucco bungalows. I might drive down the alley behind the apartments with their laundry rooms and fenced slabs of concrete yard and think nothing of it. A stranger wouldn't know there are never enough linens. It's the fluids that stain them. There is always so much yellow. It is a manifestation of fever and infection and being a bad baby again. You cannot wash or mend these things fast enough.

A stranger might drive past the aluminum-covered garages bordering the alley and not realize we spend our afternoons there in rooms that have been padlocked. We have found a way to get in.

The Courts are a series of deceptive repetitions. As Aunt Doris would say, it doesn't draw attention. There is a vocabulary of lawn, paths like scars, the artery of cement alley. The world becomes a body. You cannot avoid it. Or the blocks that end with a small store where you don't need money, just your hospital card. They will sell you soap and instant coffee, milk, cereal, bread, gauze, baby formula, adhesive tape, cigarettes, and beer. They have decided we don't need more than this. These are the rudiments with which to build worlds. These are the bones of the coping.

On the north side of the three identical stores is a volleyball court and a square of grass with swings where no children ever play. There is a sign near the volleyball court that says NO NOISE. They don't just mean on Sunday mornings or after 9:00 P.M. They mean no noise ever.

If you make noise they could ask you to move. In the Courts, the conventional measurements have failed, the borders, the way we took vitamins and paid our mortgages, the way we voted and made do. Now we are dwellers within the terminal. We must be silent because we never know who is going in for an operation or a treatment, or when. You don't know who is recovering or who is having a setback. After you go bankrupt, after your insurance runs out, after they have passed the hat for you in your old hometown for the last time, you get cut when the surgeon can fit you into his regular schedule.

We are learning better living through chemistry and it makes us puke and shiver, stagger and gasp between the gauze opening up and needing to be changed, between stumbling to the sink to retch in the basin and examine ourselves for infection. The mirror is a portal. We look inside and see that we have become blue. We are the underbelly now, the place where the flame forgets itself. We live in the time of the sand and the rock. We won't be around for the Bronze Age or three dimensions in painting. We just want to make it back to the sofa.

There is the matter of the medications, the pain pills and injections. Sleep is magical and rare and we must protect it. We need our strength for the next procedure, the one they'll try if this one fails.

I walk on my toes and control my breathing. Someone nearby might be on the verge of sleep after an all-night setback, after the unexpected, after asking God to bless and forgive him thirty-five thousand separate times. I consider saints who cared for lepers, who ran out of rags and cleaned the wounds with their tongues. I consider being shot by ten thousand feathered arrows. Such are our night litanies.

In Palm Courts West light is sliced by strips of gray metal. Even with the blinds shut, there is the sense that the boulevard is near. You can feel its agitated fluttering, impersonal and demanding.

I walk down Sepulveda Boulevard and I am struck by how inordinately straight, wide, flat and without deviation it is. It implies a world where buildings are permanent and there is a reason to cross the city, to leave and return. It asserts linear definitions and boundaries you can count on. Such assumptions have nothing to do with us.

On the other side of the boulevard are the residential streets where the intacts live in yellow and blue ranch houses set behind wooden fences. There are trees on these streets where the mothers stay home. They don't go to Acapulco with men they are vague about. They don't stick their faces into coconuts and watch their flesh mimic copper. They don't vanish for months without telephone numbers. In the pastel ranch houses the fathers aren't stitched with a deliberate absence of symmetry. They aren't held together by incisions and pins.

At West Los Angeles High School we are deemed unwholesome. There is a sense that we have succumbed to temptation, that our condition is volitional. We have broken a taboo and brought this upon ourselves. Perhaps we did something with our father or uncle. Maybe it had to do with matches or metal or something about a locked door.

Our mothers take early morning buses to their jobs. They wear makeup. No one supervises our clothing, irons collars, braids hair, puts in ribbons. No one cooks us breakfast. We are allotted change and buy doughnuts and coffee. We are allowed to cross streets and talk to strangers. We can compute sweet rolls to quarters. When we are young we wear our keys around our necks. We don't have to do homework. We don't have braces or Little League, piano or ballet lessons. We are nothing like the children in the pastel ranch houses.

Our clothing doesn't fit right, shows our scraped knees. Fatigue seems to be coming off our skin, rising like elements that have been tarnished. You don't want to ask us about our dreams or hobbies. You don't want to know. We look like we haven't been eating right. We look like we're not college-bound.

They can see us slumping off the green horizon, unstarched and nervous. Something with a cough and a low-grade fever that should have stayed home, but there's no home, really, to stay in.

At West Los Angeles High School whenever someone gets crabs or lice, everyone from the Courts gets called into the nurse's office. The health inspector from downtown comes. Sometimes they look for bruises and burns on our skin, welts from ropes or belts, the lingering petal of a fist. They expect to find evidence of our deformities and abuse. They seem disappointed when they don't.

I can feel the Courts at my back. The buildings are a dirty tan and the wood along the roofs is an undifferentiated green like insubstantial foliage beaten by pollution, by heartbreak, by some mean streak intrinsic to the afternoon.

I observe the kids from the houses on the residential streets arriving with their friends. Their clothing changes with the seasons. They have extra bags containing items they will need for their after-school activities. Soccer balls, flutes, and music books. Even their mothers have cars. They don't have to take buses to work. They don't have bosses who threaten to fire them if they don't remove their blouses.

The intacts don't bother with us. If you live in the Courts, you are only passing through. That's one reason the district doesn't want to spend money on us. The average stay for a family in the Courts is fifteen months. Jimmy told me that.

I trust Jimmy Nakamura's statistics. After all, he knows more about radiation fallout than anyone I've ever met. It's his specialty. He's reconstructed exactly where his relatives were when they were vaporized. They had just woken up. They never even knew they had died. That's why Jimmy thinks they're condemned to perpetual stasis. He says if you die and don't know it, your incarnations are arrested and caged. You look up and see thousands of versions of yourself in identical cells. It's a punishment of absolute duplication. There is no communication. How could there be? You always know precisely the same things. You cannot even argue.

Behind me, the Courts pulse with their insistent sense of the soiled and hazardous. You can't see that we are living our half-lives between the Monday follow-ups. We are living in seven-day increments. Machines tell us how we are doing. We remember to smile. It's the beginning of February and there are no explanations. We have worn them out along with all the paths and cul-de-sacs in greasy lamplight.

There is night and night again and the rancid sheen of the boulevard and the illuminated carcasses of the city. We are living our squalid half-lives, having the procedures, the cuttings, the grafts, and our half-lives are quietly running out.

7

I can remember my second summer in the Courts.
Heat settled in the alley. It smelled of roses and peonies and
a dust the color of lilacs. I thought about New Jersey and
sidewalks with a crocheted oasis of shade from the maples.
There were shadow stars where I walked. The ground was
a kind of mirror. Everything was scented vaguely like laundry, like the sheets my mother washed on Sundays. My
mother was making lemonade. She had pink rollers in her
hair and she smiled.

There is nothing like that here. It is afternoon. The
palms are an implication of a thin linear thing, not a branch
but more primitive. Perhaps it meant something fifty feet
in the air, but by the time it hits the sidewalk, it's not even

the memory of a shadow. Maybe it's a kind of suicide. Now it can't be buried properly and you won't name your children after it. It never happened.

It is August and there is no school. It is before Jimmy Nakamura and Pamela Bruno. The sun is full and makes me squint. I feel it in my mouth. I sit in the alley as long as I can. I feel I've been there for weeks. This is how people turn into stone, how they become part of mountains. I count three hundred yellow cars. Then I count three hundred orange ones. They are rarer. That takes longer than the white or blue or black. Then I give up and go home.

Louie is there, Doris, and even Roxanne. I see them as I adjust to the dark apartment. The blinds are drawn. The room is a sequence of cool indentures that makes me think of steps to dungeons, aquariums and tattoos. I think of lost children fallen to the bottom of wells. Uncle Louie has a blanket wrapped around his shoulders. He must have just returned from a treatment. I am surprised by what they are doing. They are watching television.

It's the summer my family discovers TV. It isn't kept in the closet anymore with the tablecloth across its alien green face, the green of a lake at a fantastic altitude where you consider drowning, where you recognize the fundamental nature of solitude and find you can't stop screaming. The television is gradually becoming part of the room. They are watching more than the New York nightly news and an occasional cataclysm. It isn't just a thing for hillbillies. Now it's on all the time.

They are watching "Queen for a Day." A customer at Canter's told Doris about this program. Doris initiated Roxanne and now they're both addicted. The program features three women who compete with one another as to who has had the worst life. It's a series of desertions and car crashes, heart attacks, bankruptcy and bizarre accidents, things with tractors and cranes. Someone is always in prison.

"Has that got my name on it or what?" Roxanne says. She lights one cigarette after another. She sits on the floor near the TV set, concentrating.

The difference between normal life and "Queen for a Day" is that on TV you get prizes. It's actually about resurrection. The winner is crowned. She wears a tiara. She is enveloped by a robe that falls down past her ankles. It has fur along the collar and the sides of the train. It's like getting the mink stole back with interest. Then she is given a bouquet of wrapped-with-ribbon, long-stemmed roses. Then a washing machine, a dryer, a boat with an outboard motor, blenders and toasters, suitcases and pillowcases with her initials. Then a wheelchair for her son, perhaps, and a dining room table, a portable barbecue and a chandelier.

"Look at that," Doris is saying. "Pinch me. Is that a dishwasher or what?"

I wonder why Aunt Doris would want a dishwasher. We don't even have dishes. We have only paper plates, napkins, and toothpicks.

Doris is sitting on the sofa with her bridge scoring pad adding up the amount of the prizes. She asks Louie and Roxanne what they think each item costs. But she doesn't want exact figures. They take too long. An approximation will do.

"Just ball-park me," she says, holding a pen, glancing from Louie to Roxanne. She's so excited her hands are shaking.

Roxanne decides she wants to be a contestant. She's

going to write for an application. She wants to register. She is going to construct a life no judge can resist. She is going to invent a husband with cancer. She is going to have a bankruptcy and a sick daughter.

"What kind of sick?" Doris wants to know.

Roxanne thinks about it. "Retarded," she decides.

Aunt Doris smiles. Everyone agrees that Roxanne would have the best chance to win. She wouldn't be afraid of the camera. She wouldn't clam up.

"She doesn't know from fear," Uncle Louie says. He is staring at the tip of his cigar. It seems to be a compliment.

Aunt Doris gives Roxanne a diet pill. She says it will help her memorize her new life story. Roxanne has decided to incorporate parts of other people's lives into her narrative. Besides cancer and bankruptcy and a retarded daughter, Roxanne and Doris are going to have a four-year-old son who gets hit by a truck. They may have an infant burned in a fire.

"Make it a girl," Doris says. "A girl pulls your heart strings. What about Shelly? You like that? Shelly? Or Suzette? You like Suzette?"

Roxanne decides to buy a typewriter. She has to trim her nails but it's worth it. She types out her story. It's like a script. She walks around the apartment wearing her short aqua blue kimono and her gold sandals with stiletto heels. She holds her script and a cigarette. She walks back and forth in circles. For weeks, the afternoons are filled with the sound of her voice and her shoes on the shadowed wood. It's almost as if she is building something.

Now the television and the record player are both on simultaneously. In the background Ethel Merman is belting out "Everything's Coming Up Roses." Ethel Merman is the

Los Angeles version of the Chinese water torture. I begin singing it, thinking it will make it less painful. I am singing and smoking a cigarette and walking in circles in my bedroom. That's what we do in my family. Smoke and walk in circles. Suddenly Aunt Doris appears.

"Do that again," Doris says with inappropriate excitement. It's the diet pills. Her eyes are wide and she breathes in husky spasms. Often she has two cigarettes lit at the same time.

"Me?" I look around the bedroom. It's empty. So I sing it again.

"You could be something," Doris decides. Later she repeats this to Roxanne and Louie. "Queen for a Day" is over. She has ushered me into the living room. When Doris gives me the signal, I launch into my Ethel Merman imitation. At the end, Roxanne and Louie look at each other. Then they applaud.

We are energized. We are going to conquer television. There is even an idea that Louie could do something with his hands. Maybe he could learn a trick with magic or juggling. There must be something a man with a cane could do with his fingers and elbows in exchange for a toaster oven. Somebody could probably book a sophisticated novelty act. But classy, nothing that uses the word cripple on stage.

It's celluloid fever. It's in the August afternoon air. It's laying over the cheddar cheese cubes and their pale toothpicks. It's being dragged along the hot cement by the fronds falling from sun-corroded palms. After all, fate has somehow deposited us in this city where they film these things.

"Not film. What are you? Farmers?" Roxanne says, annoyed. She's talking to Louie. She has her hand on her hip. "Tape, Louie. They tape the shit."

We are awaiting a catalyst. We are looking at the sky for portents, some intimation of a direction. Then Milton Silverstein appears. On cue, an agent has been manifested. And not just an anonymous agent but a man Louie knew from the old neighborhood.

"I'm coming out of Les Downer's Flying A. I'm thinking maybe I need a tune-up. Something doesn't sound right. And I'm looking at a guy in a white Caddy. I'm thinking, maybe I know him. He reminds me of a guy from way back and I see he's looking at me," Louie begins.

Uncle Louie is apparently viewing this chance encounter as a saga requiring extravagant detail. We should memorize it, maybe, and pass it down the generations. It occurs to me that this is one of the problems with history, the old sick men who tell it all wrong.

"So I say, 'Milt?' And he gets out of his car to greet me. He makes the first move. He's not pretending he doesn't see me. He gets out of a Caddy with the white on the tires. The deluxe model. You can feel the air-conditioning when he opens the door. It's like they sent Alaska into your face. He comes over and right away shakes hands. He gives me his business card. He's an agent."

Roxanne is alert. "Then what?"

"I invite him over," Louie says. "I explain we've got real talent here. Major-league talent."

Milton Silverstein has been invited for dinner in precisely four days. Everything revolves around this. Aunt Doris takes three diet pills and washes the living room floor. The card table is put in the closet. So it can be disassembled, after all.

Roxanne buys a brisket, carrots, and potatoes. She has to buy the pot to make it in, too. That's how long it's been since anyone cooked a meal.

Sensing a rare confluence, a moment like a channel between possibilities, Roxanne borrows an outfit from her friend in the costuming department at Columbia Studios. She comes back with a navy blue suit and a white blouse trimmed with lace. Roxanne knows what they wear on "Queen for a Day." A real lady is expected to look like she was going to a funeral or divorce court.

We are in our bedroom. It is late afternoon. It is still summer. It will always be precisely this summer, this arrested August. A certain silence has fallen across the paralyzed boulevards. The city is filled with balconies and terraces where women stand stricken and betrayed. They are there, in the windows behind the sad fake white lace curtains where it has all come to pass and yet nothing has happened, all in the same moment that never existed or stopped. And something brittle and deceptive is rising from the singed grass.

In Palm Courts West, through the windows you can hear men and women shouting. It's almost the end of the month. There's no more beer money. The children are drinking tap water with sugar in it. They've probably already gone to Family Services. They've been issued their emergency three-pound bag of macaroni and two boxes of cherry Jell-O. Last year they gave out strawberry. Someone said next year is orange.

But we are having brisket in our house because Milton Silverstein, the Hollywood agent, is coming to evaluate our talent. Roxanne is going to recite the story of her invented life in the hope that she can register for "Queen for a Day" and win lawn chairs and kitchen appliances. I am going to sing "Everything's Coming Up Roses," because Doris thinks I can go on stage. In between, Doris and Roxanne argue about where the portable bar on rolling wheels that she is going to win will go.

It is Friday night and I'm queasy. We've never had a dinner guest before. Milton Silverstein is a tall man who moves slowly, as if the air hurts his skin and he isn't in a hurry. Milton Silverstein has come with a woman named Madge. She is Milton's date. Date is a word fashioned on an extremely remote planet. It is not spoken out loud. He's getting a divorce. Louie whispers that to Doris. Divorce is another word you cannot speak. It must be written on the side of a bridge scoring pad or imparted directly into the ear.

Doris and Roxanne huddle in the kitchen. The meat boils for hours, turns black underneath and sticks to the pot. Dinner is so awful, everyone simply pantomimes eating. Milton and Madge move slabs of brisket from one side of their plate to another. There would be no way to chew such meat. When Milton Silverstein asks Louie what he's been up to, Louie recounts his recent procedures and setbacks and how long he was in ICU each time. When no one says anything, Louie names all his bridge partners who have died in the last eighteen months.

Roxanne and Doris are staring at Madge. All week, they have been referring to her as the woman. They don't give her a name. Her name is whore. Her name is mistress, even if she doesn't quite look the part. Now they are studying her as if they are adding up what her clothing and accessories cost, rounding off and approximating. They look like they're ball-parking her.

Madge is wearing a pink cotton dress with a thin white leather belt. She isn't wearing makeup. She had lipstick on earlier but it's worn off. Her hair is a medium brown. She wears it behind her ears, tied in a ponytail.

Then it is talent night in Palm Courts West. Milton and Madge sit on the sofa. Louie sits in a bridge chair. He isn't in the wheelchair yet. Doris and I sit on the floor. There is nervous silence. Then Roxanne enters from the hallway. She begins her soliloquy about the fire and the run-over son, the retardation and how she is saving money for an artificial limb and skin grafts.

When she has finished, Roxanne bows. Doris and Louie applaud. They glance at Milton Silverstein but he doesn't say a word. Doris and Louie stop applauding. Milton Silverstein is professionally inscrutable. We understand that. So we concentrate on trying to decipher Madge's face. We cannot decode her expression, either. Her face is too pure and immobile. It seems to be cast in a foreign language. Then it's my turn.

I sing "Everything's Coming Up Roses" and Milton and Madge do not respond. Louie acts as if they have somehow failed to perceive that the song is over. So he instructs me to sing it again.

"You don't have to do that, Jordan," Milton Silverstein tells me.

I am stunned that he has said my name. Then I am relieved. I want to leave the room. I want to depart the Earth. There are regions of space where the planets are an intricacy of green, chartreuse, lime, jade. There would be the incredible white starkness of the bone white moon, the clouds that would seem like white fire on the hills. You could sleep with the wind in your face beneath an archive of stars. There would be the faces of the women staring at their acres of fenced barley. There would be their eyes behind the curtains, which are an indication of crystals or snowflakes or heartbreak but you would not be responsible.

I have walked into the hallway and Roxanne grabs my wrist. "You don't walk out of an audition," she tells me. She smiles at Milton Silverstein. "She doesn't know the rules yet," Roxanne says. Her voice is apologetic.

"She can leave," Milton Silverstein says.

"She doesn't want to leave," Roxanne answers. She lights a cigarette. She glances at Louie.

"She wants to stay," Louie says. "Let her stay."

"She can't sing," Milton Silverstein says. "Can't you hear that? What's the matter with you?" He has stood up. He looks from Louie to Roxanne.

"She was nervous," Doris says. "Give the kid another shot."

"Jesus Christ. She's got a tin ear," Milton Silverstein says. He offers his arm to Madge. The woman who is not his wife takes it. She walks to the living room door. She touches the knob with her fingers but she doesn't turn it.

"You're leaving?" Louie notices. He sounds surprised. He limps to the door. He hasn't even had a chance to ask Milton Silverstein about the possibilities of a juggling act for a man with a cane. "Wait. What about Ruthie?"

Louie has used her original name. He is willing to evoke the ancient past. That's how important this moment is.

Roxanne also faces the door. "Well?" she says.

Milton Silverstein starts to say something but changes his mind. He is opening the door. He is crossing the lawn with Madge. There is a tinge of jasmine in the air, perfumed and sullen and unpredictable. We are standing in the doorway. We are watching the white Cadillac drive away.

"Did you see that broad?" Roxanne says after a while. She has placed a hand on the hip of her borrowed suit. "What a mouse."

"She looked like maybe the maid," Aunt Doris says. "He should be embarrassed."

"A man wants a broad like that, you know he's got a problem," Louie points out. He sounds philosophical.

"She looks like she wouldn't know how to speak up," Doris says.

"What would she say? Bowwow?" Roxanne smiles.

"Go figure," Louie says to no one in particular.

Milton Silverstein's business card hangs on the refrigerator door for months. It's in the center inside an accidental frame of Scotch tape. Then one day it is gone.

The television is wheeled back into the closet. A tablecloth covers its green face. The absence of the television is a further silence. I remember lilac and an impartial scented lake off the side of a road where my mother rested her arm across my shoulder. We were driving to California. For a moment, I think I can have it back, and the trees, the way the air was a startled dense green like a form of love or a magic bottle I could drink or rub and I was one with the enormities that told me everything without mouths, with wings and leaves and gestures above fluid avenues in afternoons without edges.

But this was a different green, a green that proved to be false. It was a hillbilly green after all. It was just one more thing that didn't pan out.

8

It's Valentine's Day. I've passed the bulletin boards with their impaled red hearts and doily-fringed borders glaring from the corridors of West Los Angeles High School. That's just what I need. Another bleeding organ.

I'm smoking a cigarette in the phone booth across the street from Les Downer's Flying A Service Station. I'm staring at the telephone and willing it to ring. I'm testing my telekinetic powers and I'm crapping out. As Roxanne would say, it's a bad day for Vegas.

It's a cool afternoon. I'm standing in the phone booth that Jimmy and Pamela Bruno and I call our office. I can't have a telephone call in Uncle Louie's apartment. The phone sits on the bridge table. Everyone listens to each word and answers simultaneously. It's a communal experience. The architecture of a social life is light-years beyond my relatives. It is so much further along on the continuum you might not even want to bet on it.

Then I realize the call from Jimmy isn't coming. For some reason I start thinking about my father, Ernie, and New Jersey. Roxanne and I haven't driven away in a red Chevrolet convertible. We haven't lingered beside mesa walls and deciphered Colorado as we passed. We haven't yet learned the gray rock was merely a meaningless afterthought.

It is before the journey we took into the nothing, into the stones in rows on the valley floor like severed heads. It was a ritual the mountains dreamed in their ache of slow time. It is before we discovered there was no silver, no one to ring the bell or answer, no reason for the lightning or the deserted mines. That was when we forgot what we came for, what we took or why. It was on the drive to California that we saw there were no hieroglyphics in the rocks, no antler gods or women with moon bellies. The stars were merely metal without destinies, so many bullets somebody coughed.

We haven't seen the faces of the women in the windows of the farmhouses along the highways yet. The women behind the streaked glass where the wind is blowing from the south, from the east. It has peonies and gravel in its mouth. The women with the vision of a Greyhound bus station, perhaps, and a chenille bedspread to lay across the place where you don't care if he comes back to sleep tonight or ever. The faces of the women in the windows of the farmhouses along the highways, in the apartments, on the terraces, in the taxis, at the corner liquor store. What are these women trying to say?

What could possibly happen? Where will they go? Not with these men in the blue pickup trucks, not out by themselves running for it across the fenced fields even if they knew where the traps were, even if they had wire cutters, even if the wind would erase their footsteps, if the grass like the sea would cover the indentations. Where would they start over? Boise? Seattle? Tucson? And I realize all the faces of the women in the windows are the face of Roxanne before she thought of Los Angeles.

We haven't been initiated into the residue of impossibilities yet, into the ash of August and all the wrong doors, the ones we should have never opened, never crossed the prairies or Donner Pass or left at all. My father is giving me chocolates shaped like hearts and kisses. They are wrapped in metallic greens and reds and silvers. He has given me his version of the universe, planets in orbits you can swallow. He is calling me Jordy. I stand in the phone booth a long time. Then I walk home alone.

"Everything's coming up roses," Ethel Merman is singing. Her voice is brutal and much too large. It is bigger than the wilderness. It sounds like it's somehow pulling up plants and stones and rearranging them. It is making the earth wretched and incoherent.

"Diamonds? Are you nuts?" Louie is saying. He's holding his cigar in the air and staring at it. "I got six spades. That's not enough, Doris? Six?"

They are playing bridge with the Hunters who live two apartments away. No one asks me how my day was or if I'm going to do my homework. No one wants to read my book reports. Salutations are a behavior my family hasn't mastered yet. It's like computers or the space program. They can't fathom it. It's part of some code that doesn't apply to them. It's the way the marks get conned.

No one looks at me as I pass. I'm on the margin moving through their periphery. I walk my camera eyes into the bedroom I periodically share with Roxanne. I sit on my twin bed. Outside the venetian blinds is a listless court with a hedge of bleached pink hibiscus with singed sides. I close my eyes and remember how Jimmy Nakamura became my best friend.

I met Jimmy at a Saturday matinee at Palms Memorial. Every other Saturday at noon they ran a movie in the lobby auditorium for kids from the Courts. Not that we really needed one. In the Courts, it's a horror and science fiction film festival every day.

It is noon in summer and they are playing *The Time Machine* from the book by H. G. Wells. I stay for the second showing. So does Jimmy. Everybody is wearing shorts and white T-shirts advertising tourist attractions and beer except us. It's ninety-seven degrees and we are both dressed entirely in black. We are in mourning for the twentieth century.

We walk home together and we realize we both like the same part of the movie best. It's the moment when the hero returns to his original time, selects three books from his library, and takes them back to the future.

"What books would you take?" I ask Jimmy.

"The *Bible*. The *Koran*. And the *Bhagavad Gita*," Jimmy tells me.

We are standing near rectangular dark green trash bins in the alley. I'm weighing Jimmy's answer. It isn't the first time I've seen *The Time Machine*. They've been showing it on and off all year. I've been thinking that the underground monsters called Morlocks remind me of Uncle Louie. Louie's eyes don't glow in the dark yet, but with all the cobalt and chemo he's getting, it's just a matter of time. If Uncle Louie lives long enough, he could end up biting off the heads of chickens. He could end up eating small children raw. This is how you get to be a geek in modern America.

"I can't believe how stupid you are," I said. I meant it. I'm so disappointed I almost walk away.

I expected more from Jimmy Nakamura. Everyone knows he has the highest math scores in the history of West Los Angeles High School. Even though he lives in the Courts, he takes college-bound classes. I'm staring at him and thinking Jimmy Nakamura is just another fraudulent rumor that didn't pan out.

"Yeah? Is that so?" Jimmy sounds almost aggressive. He takes out a Zippo lighter and sends a flare into the air like he's looking for something on a molecular level, something you can't find with the unaided eye. Maybe he's looking for dented chromosomes. He sends up a second flame, lower, of less intensity and duration, and then he shuts the lighter and sticks it back in his pocket.

"Your selections stink," I tell him. "It's like duplicating your honors."

That's a bridge term for having powerful cards that don't help your game because they cancel each other out. If Jimmy can't comprehend that, I'm saying good-bye. I'll just sit on the curb behind the volleyball court and count orange cars for a while. Or I can look for glass soda bottles in the bushes along the alley. The skill comes in not getting cut. The small ones can be exchanged in the market for two cents. The tall ones are worth three. The bushes are our private hunting grounds. We search with sticks. No one wears gloves. Your fingers get tough and smart. After a while, you hardly ever bleed but when you do, you usually need stitches.

"One religious text says it all," I explain. "You're just wasting two choices."

Jimmy understands the implications immediately. He's integrating the information and synthesizing it. His head is almost humming. He removes his lighter, releases a sudden streak of fire, and stares at it. "What would you take?" he asks.

As it happens, I've been auditioning books from the recesses of my memory, evaluating them and culling my selections. This is like Noah's Ark for ideas. The weight of human civilization is on my shoulders. But I'm used to this.

"The Complete Works of Shakespeare, The Complete Works of Sigmund Freud, and the *Odyssey*." I am confident of my choices. You don't want to waste a selection on a single book. You want to take multi-volume sets. I can see that from the start. I can dig it from the jump, as Roxanne would say.

"You have to pay your respects to the archetypes," I tell Jimmy. I've been fashioning this sentence for years. "Face it. It's all been a pale variation since Homer."

Jimmy lights his cigarette. "You couldn't start civilization over with that," he says. "You need agriculture, science, and medicine."

Nobody needs medicine, I think. But my selections do lack range. What's the point of being well-read if you starve to death? I would have a declining population with breathtaking monologues and no rice or potatoes.

Later that week Jimmy came to my apartment. I'd been expecting him to play another round of *The Time Machine* books game. I've been preparing myself for this inevitability. I've been to the school library and the branch library. That's how ready I am.

"What about *Images of America*? Would you take that?" he wants to know. He's talking about the senior English textbook. I say no.

It's a warm night. The star jasmine is opening on the bushes along the alley. The flowers are white and starched like certain kinds of linen. They make the night seem sweet and bruised. Something happens in the filtered moonlight. Everything seems damp and stepped on, too open, almost dissected. It smells like a certain type of dust. It reminds me of the properties that reside within eucalyptus, vaguely medicinal and chalky and mysterious. It reminds me of a circus.

"You wouldn't take that?" Jimmy seems surprised. It's a massive anthology. I've seen the seniors carrying it. It's like having a weight strapped to your wrist. He is staring at me. "Why not?"

"Because nothing in there has anything to do with me. It's just about men playing polo in Connecticut or boys on hunting trips," I tell him.

I feel like I'm flying. I almost know what I'm talking about. I've spent entire afternoons interrogating librarians. I've come to the conclusion that the West Los Angeles High School English textbooks are merely the fossil record of the patriarchy.

I'm walking in a big slow loping circle through the Courts with Jimmy. It's a night of moist jasmine interacting with moonlight and things are happening. I imagine I'm a pre-human on the primeval savannah. The grass and air are soft chartreuse. I've been stalking. Now I move in for the kill. "What we call art is just notes from the power structure defending and codifying itself."

Jimmy Nakamura doesn't miss a beat. "You think the senior reading list is just another bureaucracy?" he wants to know.

"It's like the post office will be in a thousand years," I say.

That's when we decided to form our club. We called ourselves the Morlocks. We are the last survivors from a race that has been the recipient of massive radiation. We have been driven underground by contamination. But it wasn't beneath the mountains like H. G. Wells thought. It wasn't about tunnels and ores. It was in our apartments.

Jimmy Nakamura is my first friend in California. I am so jolted awake, so vivid from this unexpected experience that I long to tell somebody. I want to share this event with Roxanne but I'm afraid. I start to tell her but I stop. I start again.

"You're darting," Roxanne says. She glances into the mirror to see me.

Darting means she can sense me somewhere behind her. She can perceive me, and like a fast scurrying rodent I am agitating her. She wants me to state my business. She can't stand darting. She says I remind her of a mouse, something hungry registering in her peripheral vision.

I take a deep breath. My entire life is flashing before me. It's a sequence of glittering yellows. "If you could carry a book into the future, what would it be?" I finally ask.

It's night in West Los Angeles. It is a juncture of pastel lies and intricate fictions. Roxanne is painting on pink lipstick with her many pencils, tubes, and brushes. She studies her reflection in the mirror and changes her mind.

She shakes her head at herself. There is a hint of severity and contempt. Frosted Pink. What a baby color. It's another flyer that didn't pan out. She should have seen it coming. Now she removes the lipstick with a tissue and puts on something darker. Burned Sage, Vermilion Serenade, or Desert Fire. I could give her some names she never thought of. What about Blood on Mars or Kiss of the Morlock?

Roxanne has her evening bag out, the one with the tiers of gold beads. It's a world of subdued suns contained and strung together and my mother is solar-powered.

"A book?" she repeats. She is sucking in her cheeks. She is planning to have two of her teeth removed. That's how the stars get that sculpted look on their faces. It's all a matter of surgery. It costs, but everything costs. It's really an investment. You have to spend money to make money.

Soon Roxanne will turn abruptly from the mirror. She will whirl around once and pretend she is seeing herself for the first time. This is called getting an impression. She will want to see how it all works. She may ask me to pretend I am a stranger. She will ask me to describe what I see. "A book?" Roxanne says, puffing out her hair with her hand. "My address book."

"What else?" I ask.

She spins away from the mirror. She closes her eyes and turns once to confront herself. She opens her eyes and regards her image solemnly, as if she was on the verge of some monumental confession.

"What else?" She lights a cigarette. "My checkbook."

Roxanne has moved from the weird gravity of the mirror with its abstract pull and current, its channel into some unredeemed sea. She has managed to release herself. I think of stories about divers strangling in kelp. Now she is load-

ing her evening bag. She places a tiny gold comb in it and
two lipsticks from the spectrum of red. Then she's pushing
a fresh pack of cigarettes and a lighter into her bag. She is
stuffing them down with her fist.

"One more," I say. I feel tired.

"Rockefeller's checkbook," she answers.

It is night in the Courts. The quiet is so dense you can
almost see it. It's a silence that takes not only sound but
things that produce sound, movements and postures, even
the thinking, the inspiration in the nerves, the places
where the intentions are.

It is an hour that summons you without mouth or
breath. It is the hour of boats with mute horns and bells.
The sky might be raked, welted in ridges above fog. It
might be a sunset the color of lips bruised from kisses. And
when I look up, Roxanne is gone.

9

I walk into the living room because I'm hungry. Mike and Gloria have gone home. Mike Hunter is an open heart from San Francisco. Louie prefers hearts. He says the cancers have too many side effects. Half the time they can't even keep the bridge date. Louie says the cancers lose their concentration. He says they smell rancid and afraid. They get vague, as if their personal histories, the specific facts of their origins, their geography and dreams were so many rats jumping ship.

I glance at the card table. Tonight we have broken butter cookies and a pyramid of pickles, a mound of turkey salad and shards of what might once have been kaiser rolls. I jab a piece of something hard into the turkey and begin edging away.

Doris is leaning in the doorway of the kitchen. She is not eating deli tonight. She is on a new diet. She only eats cottage cheese and drinks eight glasses of water every twelve hours. She carries a half-filled water glass through the house and glares at it. In between, she positions herself near the refrigerator and stares at it with a vast longing.

"You got this in the mail," Aunt Doris says.

I approach her cautiously. She has long nails and an irrational temper. I imagine Doris in a kind of zoo. It's after the extraterrestrials have landed. I have been appointed ambassador for the sector. I am given the job of writing the species description on the side of her cage. My remarks will be behavioral and also psychological and philosophical. I plan to make a moral statement. I will pull out all the stops.

My eyes slowly adjust. Doris is holding a record album. On it is a man with wild hair that looks like it might have sparks in it. He's wearing a long scarf that is obviously a garment for a magic winter. You can decipher intention when wrapped in such fabrics. The man is staring into the camera like he could read your mind. This is unequivocally a photograph of metamorphosis.

"It's from Jimmy Nakamura," Doris reveals. She's holding an envelope that has been torn open. She's already read the letter. I always wondered what would happen if I got mail. Now I know.

"He says this will change your life," Aunt Doris tells me.

"Put it on," Uncle Louie says. He's staring at his cigar and smiling. "I could use a change."

I've never touched the record player before. I've always conceived of phonographs like toasters or alarm clocks, appliances somehow misplaced in the living room. It was something to avoid. It poisoned the air.

I put the album on. There are words written on the back of the cover. I realize they are the lyrics. The album is called "Bringing It All Back Home," by Bob Dylan.

"What the hell kind of shit is that?" Louie wants to know.

"It's his own personal compositions," I say. I surprise myself. I speak right up.

"That's no excuse," Aunt Doris points out. "He could find a singer."

"It's horrible," Uncle Louie says. His smile is gone. I'm struck by the way he holds his cigar, airy, almost dainty in his hand. He inhabits some demonic landscape of red. I understand that now. Embers form pathways and transitions.

"He's no Ethel Merman," Doris decides.

I stare at Doris. She is looking at the refrigerator. No Ethel Merman, I think. Of course not. He's not a middle-aged woman belting out show tunes with a voice that uproots trees.

"Get that crap out of here," Uncle Louie tells me. "And never bring it back."

I carry the record album into my room and read Jimmy's letter again. He says Bob Dylan could save my life. There are two crushed cigarettes stuck into the record jacket. They look dirty so I throw them away. Then I wonder what Jimmy could possibly be talking about.

I'm still attempting to decipher his code as I walk to school the next morning. It's twenty-two blocks from the Courts to West Los Angeles High School. I used to count each separate step. I felt compelled to assign a number to the movements of my feet. I had to create a sequence and a procedure. I dedicated each step to a deity I would invent and forget. I engraved each number with my lips and offered it to a god, a spirit or demon. I would say, you, manifestation of fate, let me live one more stalled and aching afternoon.

My thoughts were damaged. There were thousands of sirens inside my head. I released them like swarms of demented swans. These were my morning deaths, small pine coffins I pushed myself into, suffocating at dawn.

Then I would try to make a deal with the sadistic force I believe runs the universe. I would say things like, let me live the forty-three steps to the next mailbox and I'll go back to typing class. I'll make meatloaf. I'll sew aprons. Do not let me get spontaneous combustion between here and the corner and I will try to start coping.

When I walked to school with Jimmy, we argued about who had sustained the most personal damage from World War II. That took my mind off my obsession that some impulse was about to transform me into ash.

Jimmy said the atomic bomb that fell on his family at Hiroshima was the most barbarous act of the century. It didn't fall, he would remind me, it was dropped. Then I would say the concentration camps in Nazi Europe were more intense and inhuman. In terms of actual numbers, I was clearly the most bereft. Only 140,000 people died in the blast at Hiroshima.

I also claimed that the concentration camps were a more protracted form of torture since it was possible to spend years there. One could lead new arrivals from the train platforms to the gas chambers, say. Or service officers in makeshift brothels. On the other hand, Jimmy's family was vaporized instantaneously. They had the easier, cleaner death.

When Jimmy and I walked to school together I did not have to count each step. I could stop beseeching the cruel skies for safe passage to high school. I could stop seeking postures of survival and supplication.

Then Pamela Bruno joined our club. She was schizophrenic and she had a congenital defect that made her drag her leg. She pulled her limb behind her and hopped as she walked, like a colossally wounded rabbit. She was the tallest girl in the tenth grade. She was almost six feet and she weighed 195 pounds. I knew that for a fact because we were in special gym together and I stood next to the scale when she got on.

Pamela Bruno had originally come to the Courts because of her leg. Then they decided she was crazy. That often happened in the Courts. Someone arrived as a mental and then they discovered they were actually sick. Or else they came sick and the disease drove them insane.

Pamela Bruno became a charter member of our club. She was mean in precisely the right way. She proved she could keep up.

That was the same year Michelle Cohen moved to the Courts. She had strawberry blond hair and her eyeglass frames were pink. I despised her. She had an eyeglass case with a needlepoint pink rose on it. Someone had stitched that with her in mind. She was someone's little pink apple. Someone wanted her color coordinated. The expenditure of effort required for such an activity filled me with rage. When I looked at Michelle Cohen's eyeglasses, I could barely breathe.

In the Courts we got our eyeglasses on Vision Day in the clinic. You took the eye test on the first Wednesday of the year. The eyeglasses were ready on the last Friday of the month. They were always black and round. The frames never varied. They were thick plastic. They were supposed to last all year. You learned how to see through the scratches.

Michelle Cohen seemed freshly minted. She didn't know someone had blown the whistle and childhood had been called off.

I was staring at Michelle Cohen's pink eyeglasses and I noticed she had a heart-shaped locket on a gold chain around her neck. Jewelry, no less. And she had pink ribbons in her hair. That was another sure giveaway that you were looking at a recent arrival. You could tell by how pressed their clothing was and how intricate their hairstyle. After you've been in the Courts for a while and your mother goes to work, there won't be time to fuss with hair ribbons or to iron cuffs.

Even if there was time, why bother? These are the manifestations of the forms that have failed. This is where you see the bones of the ancient world and they are decayed. You can't reconstruct the essence of these buried things, what they were or what they meant. You live in a new world, stilled, quiet, almost uninhabited. You live where the dark is fierce.

I invite Michelle Cohen to our clubhouse. We have taken over an abandoned laundry room now. The door has been boarded up and padlocked. The washing machines are broken and they've decided not to fix them. We've already pried off the coin slots and removed the dimes. We climb in and out through a back window. Pamela Bruno somehow manages to squeeze through, pulling her useless leg behind her.

We are sitting on the cement floor in a circle. It is always the color of a damp and estranged afternoon, a grid with only gray values. I think of ships and being wrecked and lost. It is the perpetual hour before sunset, abysmal with a lack of punctuation and something harsh.

At least we can talk in this room. There is the freeway behind the alley. It takes sound and disorients it. We are muffled. We might be in a chamber at the bottom of the ocean. We have adapted. We are chameleon, amphibian. We can breathe anywhere.

We are officially California Buddhists. We have an altar with a wood statue of the Buddha sitting on top of a bronze tray. We put pink and yellow hibiscus there, an occasional rose, pale purple iris, bird of paradise. We offer lemons and oranges we steal from trees. We light candles and incense. We pray in our own way.

I point a finger at Michelle Cohen and ask her where she's from, the name of the city. Then I ask her what she's got.

"What I've got?" She looks blank.

"What are you here for?" Pamela Bruno clarifies. She seems annoyed.

"Heart?" Jimmy asks.

The Courts have been besieged by hearts lately. They're refining the procedures and a patient here and there is surviving. Somebody Louie played bridge with went home. Aunt Doris told me about it. The hospital gave out free cake and punch. Everybody stood in the parking lot and waved good-bye.

Michelle is staring at Pamela Bruno. Pamela lights a cigarette and offers her one. Michelle seems shocked.

"You don't know what your father has?" Jimmy wants to get it straight.

"I don't know," Michelle says. She looks like she's about to cry.

We decide not to press it. We usually ask the new kids what they've lost. We want the details while they're still fresh. We want to know what's been left behind, what's been sold, repossessed, traded, and pawned. Did you have a ranch near Sacramento? Did your mom have a diamond bracelet? Did she drive a two-toned Buick? Did your dad have a fishing rod and a truck?

We call this the great American game show in reverse. It's the anti-matter of game shows. It's about what's gone. Little League and Brownies, gymnastic lessons, your rock and coin and seashell and stamp collections. A mahogany dining room table, perhaps, that felt cool under your fingertips, and when your mother polished it, you could bend down and smell lemons and see your face. Maybe there was a vegetable patch behind a hedge of honeysuckle. Perhaps there was a swing on the porch. You could study the street from behind your white picket fence. It had red roses along the spokes. There was wisteria near the sidewalk. There might have been a dog or a cat. Every now and then, there was even a pony.

Then it's later, perhaps winter. Jimmy and I have exhausted the possibilities of the Morlocks. We have decorated our club room. Pamela Bruno said she could get a vase and a tablecloth and she has. Now the Buddha sits on a cloth of yellow roses. We have a bedspread on the floor. It's me and Jimmy Nakamura and Pamela Bruno and Michelle Cohen and we've decided we want a new club name.

Pamela Bruno looks like she's been awake since New Year's. Her eyes are red, as if she had been scratching them with her fingernails. And she's twitching. It's as if the air is giving her a series of abrupt shocks. She's a rock in the shore at the ocean. Waves spill over and dislodge her. They're going to have to inject her with tranquilizers soon. That's what they do. Then they put her in Palms Memorial for a chemical vacation.

"I nominate the Psychos," Pamela says, with a complete absence of imagination. She looks agitated like she does when she has the blue sparks in her hair, the small blue fires she says are rising from her skull like flowers or missiles or insects from another world. It's the things she thinks about. They burn her.

"That's too obvious," Jimmy says. "It has no resonance."

I want to offer my suggestion, the Terminals. I like its subtle evocation of departures and voids, its layers and complexities, how it is about computers, death, the Courts, and illusions. But Pamela won't stop talking.

"Okay. I nominate the Mutants or the Blood Bags," Pamela Bruno, who has clearly been thinking about it non-stop for days, said.

"That's ugly," Michelle Cohen realizes.

Everybody stares at her. By now we know her father has a malignancy in his kidney. He's a terminal case.

I can hear the cars on the San Diego Freeway beyond the alley. It sounds like a tortured ocean. Or perhaps a wind infested with metal. Something that had been natural and then tin seeped into it, invaded it, made it sharp and gray. We ignore her.

Jimmy lit a cigarette. There is a staccato sequence of flames from his Zippo lighter. I think of sun spots, of gases releasing themselves on the edges of galaxies. Maybe he was trying to birth worlds.

"What about the Stink Bombs?" Michelle Cohen blurted. She seemed excited.

"Who let you in?" I stare at her. "Jesus Christ. That's a baby name. Tell her," I say in Jimmy's direction.

I'm angry with Michelle Cohen for more than the pink eyeglasses and the locket on the gold chain and the grandfather who picks her up on Friday nights and takes her to the San Fernando Valley for a family dinner with her cousins. I was once in her apartment and something happened.

I was in Michelle Cohen's living room even though I knew it was dangerous to be in a shared area. These fathers have scars and tubes. They are misshapen, bandaged, unnatural, broken. Their vocal cords have been removed. Their bones are fusing or collapsing. They've been tampered with and they will never be whole or normal again. You won't be able to pass them on the sidewalk and not notice. They've been plucked from the ordinary world and there is no return. They can't walk, can't breathe, can't wash themselves or eat or sleep. And the mothers are gone.

We have learned to stay outdoors. We whisper in the alley near the garages and the padlocked laundry rooms. But today it's too cold. It's raining. That's why I'm in Michelle Cohen's apartment. She's offered me food. She said her mother left two cookies. I am licking chocolate off my fingers. The air in the room is severe and gray. The lamp is on.

The glow of the lamp is extraordinary and too yellow, too insistent. It seems cut out of time. I'm wondering if this is how tumors look when they show up on X rays, three-dimensional, like a brilliant island just risen in a place where there used to be only water.

Suddenly Mr. Cohen wheels himself in. I know his name

is Mel. He has just appeared, small, sharp, birdlike, preda-tory. I tower over him. He is dark and frightening, an offended dwarf with a metal body. He is unbelievably pale. It's a land of trolls and dragons. There has been a spell, and this is its residue. And Mel Cohen is the color of exiled clouds. He is ruined absolutely.

"You think I'm some old man," he accuses, breathless. I don't know where Michelle is. And he's panting. He is trying to tell me something I don't want to know. I under-stand this and accommodate it.

"You think I'm old," Mel Cohen persists, fueling his rage. His teeth are startling yellow. They are pointed and make me think of tropical birds, plumage, something denser than lemons, more impulsive and distorted. There is the matter of neon and light bulbs. I consider the possibility that he has somehow been eating lamps.

"Look at me," he commands, grabbing my wrist. He is squeezing my arm. He is hurting me.

We live in the Courts and our mothers take buses to offices. They are file clerks. They spend the day leaning over metal cabinets. They wear the kiss of tin against their hips. They get calluses on the tips of their fingers. The fathers stay home. They have emergencies that require ambulances. Their tubes come loose. You find them on the floor. Sometimes they turn blue. If they turn blue enough it will be over.

In between, there are the side effects from the treatments and procedures. The medicines make them slur their words. For days they are blind. They forget how to turn on the stove. They can't shave anymore. They can't remem-ber their place of birth. They need to go to the bathroom in a pan or a bag.

"I'm thirty-four," Mr. Cohen tells me. "You think that's old? Look at me."

I think thirty-four is ancient. He's two years older than Roxanne. I could stare at him for centuries and not blink once. He could read nothing from my face. I have learned the art of impenetrable silence. I am twilight glazing a ridge of granite on a night without a moon. I am the infinite dusk in a transitional season that will give you nothing. Mr. Cohen realizes this. That's when he lets go of my wrist. That's when he begins to cry.

I am running out of Michelle's apartment. There is a code in the Courts and he has broken it. The mothers cry when they walk from their buses. We expect that, especially at the end of the month when the money is gone. That's when the mothers send you to visit neighbors at dinner time. Maybe they will give you half a sandwich. Maybe they've got cousins in the San Fernando Valley who sent over a stew or a soup. Maybe they know someone with a fruit tree in their backyard.

Later in the month the mothers try to decide if they will keep the telephone on. If they give up coffee and shampoo, they will be able to pay the bill and keep the phone from being disconnected. They must have the telephone. What if they need to call an ambulance?

But the fathers are not allowed to cry. The fathers are supposed to vomit pieces of their stomachs and lungs into a garbage can, hide it under a crumpled newspaper, and not say a word.

In between, the fathers need special food like babies. You grind it up and spoon it into their mouths, carefully, between the stitches and adhesive tape. You don't want your hands to shake. You might spill it on their lip or chin and they will get angry. Slap your hand. Call you stupid. Call you a whore. This is why it's better to wait in an open garage near the alley until the mothers get back.

"What's wrong with the Stink Bombs?" Michelle asks.

"It's not enough to have it mean on your lips. It's got to be mean in your brain. It's got to have a savage kick to it," Pamela Bruno says.

Pamela Bruno's eyes glitter inflamed. She says she has waterfalls of fire in her hair. The cells within her skin seem to be igniting.

"I don't even know what you're talking about," Michelle Cohen decides. She stands up. She walks to the back window and prepares to climb out of the laundry room.

"That's because you're just passing through," Pamela Bruno yells. "You haven't been here long enough. Besides, you're just an air ball. You're a buzzer shot."

We know a malignancy in the kidney is hopeless. Whatever they're doing for Michelle's father isn't going to help. Michelle Cohen's father has reached the stage where the hospital is using the not-on-the-market-yet medicines. The buzzer-shot medicines are so strange and potent, you can die the first time they administer them.

The hospital is probably talking to Mr. Cohen about prayer and vitamins. When they start talking to you about God and the essences of avocado pits, you know it's almost the end. When this happens, you have reached the stage of lingering.

Now another winter is winding down in Los Angeles. I am standing alone near the sewing room. The bell is ringing and the air is a fantastic blue. I am trying to comprehend this and how the air around the palms beyond the fence turns perfumed and bruised and dark. It is a blue that intimates not grace but some abstraction, vast and gaudy and broken.

I realize everyone is gone, Jimmy and Pamela and even Michelle Cohen. Her father's cancer metastasized into his brain. They gave him morphine and still had to tie him up. Everyone said he was a real screamer.

I read the Bob Dylan lyrics quickly. Jimmy has sent this to me from the north he now inhabits. He is farther along on the continuum, where there are bridges and quiet water and the sky between lightning is the color of chilled larkspur. There are clouds but they are irrelevant. And I don't know how a record album can save me.

I am in the corridor of West Los Angeles High School and everything seems damp. Somewhere, there is a remote horizon with stones above a harbor. A legion of fishermen drag in the nets that catch the past and future. At dusk they illuminate the water with their mouths. In such ports, they keep the clarities and edges. One might be reformed by severities. And it suddenly occurs to me that I am alone because I have reached the stage of lingering.

10

Once a year during Health Week, DeeDee "Talk to Me" Dushay comes to West Los Angeles High School. They have removed the offensive construction-paper Valentine's Day hearts and replaced them with sign-up sheets. The P.E. teachers have been encouraging anyone with a problem to make an appointment.

"You might not even realize how wrong your home life is," Miss Wong, the P.E. teacher for special gym, explains.

Special gym occurs in an alcove near the lockers. The room is completely carpeted with thick blue mats. I am curiously lopsided and off balance because only one of my breasts has developed. I am continually walking hunched, trying to conceal my asymmetry. I stand with my arms crossed over my chest, protecting what isn't there yet. It's hard to play basketball that way.

I'm half-listening to Miss Wong encourage us to confide in DeeDee Dushay. She speaks very slowly because we are a class of physically impaired girls. Miss Wong has concluded that if you can't do fifty sit-ups and push-ups, you can't understand standard English.

I am not one of those girls who thinks she is having an adequate childhood when she is not. I am completely aware of the fact that it's going to take me decades to dig out from the debasement and the debris. I am particularly aware of how brutal my home life is because I am now memorizing events and conversations with the aid of my invisible recording devices. I am also taking notes.

When I hear that DeeDee "Talk to Me" Dushay is coming, I begin gathering fresh data. I am going to be able to calmly cite names, dates, and exact quotations. Now it is the day after we had the nutrition quiz in Health Ed. I ambush Aunt Doris by the refrigerator.

Aunt Doris doesn't quite see me. She is holding a gallon of Rocky Road ice cream and a soup spoon in one hand. She has a burning cigarette in the other. Aunt Doris goes three or four months without eating a single morsel. She only drinks coffee, smokes cigarettes, and takes diet pills. Then something snaps. Her entire chemistry is altered. She is in a sort of trance. Her lips move, her cheeks puff out, and her eyes are glassy. She looks like a bloated carp. She looks like the thing you don't want to encounter at the bottom of the pond. She's the reason they put up the danger sign and enclosed the area with a barbwire fence.

"I thought your cholesterol was too high," I say. I've got my notebook out. I am writing the conversation down verbatim. She doesn't notice. Her eyes are veiled.

"Didn't the doctor say your cholesterol was too high?" I repeat.

"Cholesterol," Doris manages. "What do they know?"

I write that down. "They know smoking is bad," I say. I have my blue folder with charts and statistics. I open it near Aunt Doris.

"Smoking is okay for Jewish people," Aunt Doris says.

"How's that?" I have the pen out. I'm ready.

"It's genetic. You get cancer if you drink. It's mixing them produces the bad effect. Just smoking is okay. Make sure you never booze. That's the secret," Doris explains.

I write that down. This is evidence. I'm watching Aunt Doris pile the ice cream into her mouth, one enormous spoonful after another. Why doesn't she just use a ladle? Why doesn't she use a shovel?

I've got a morning appointment with DeeDee. I'm going to begin by discussing our eating habits, the toothpicks and continual grazing at the card table. Then I'm going to delineate the nature of their abnormalities specifically. It's all in the small actions that accumulate and turn virulent. It's what these behaviors imply.

For instance, I'm going to tell DeeDee about the way Louie and Roxanne drive. Or the way Louie drove before he got stuck in the wheelchair. It's a symptom and it should be noted and analyzed. My family drives up to their destination and if they don't find a parking place directly in front of the building, they simply drive away. There are no detours ever.

I am going to explain to DeeDee Dushay what they did to me last year during Earthquake Preparedness Week. By a complete fluke having to do with a substitute teacher who didn't know that no one from the Courts ever wins anything and who evaluated essays on the basis of merit, I was selected as having the most outstanding composition in the entire school on the effects of a devastating earthquake. I felt I possessed an unearthly lucidity in terms of collapsing ceilings and falling walls. I was fearless with my speculations about gas jets. I was chosen to read my essay at nighttime assembly. And Roxanne, Doris, and Louie didn't show.

"I couldn't find a parking place," Roxanne said.

I stared at her. "You could leave earlier," I pointed out. "You could park a few blocks away and walk."

"No walking," Roxanne says.

I plan to remember that. No walking. I don't have to ask why. Roxanne can't walk more than a few yards because of how high her heels are. After half a block, her legs begin buckling. Besides, only hicks walk. Peasants walk. Peons and coolies pulling the master on their naked backs. People with their bare feet in dust and their shoulders stooped from the strap. That went out with leprosy and the yoke. It's the twentieth century and my family has discovered the wheel in a big way.

But being on time isn't a behavior that's developed yet. Or perhaps it's been deliberately discarded. Maybe time as a conventional standard didn't pan out for them. Being on time is for some jerk in a factory. It's California and there are no more timecards to punch. In Uncle Louie's world being on time is for schlemiels. It went out with the whip and the cotton fields. In my family, if a parking spot doesn't open up at precisely the necessary instant, they drive directly home. They take the absence of a parking place as a kind of omen.

"You could have circled the block," I told her.

"No circling," Louie says. "Circling is dangerous."

That sounds like something he might have learned from Les Downer. Louie repeats this like a piece of ancient wisdom, irrefutable, recognized by all people in all places. It expresses a fundamental human desire. It's the soul of man distilled into two words. No circling.

I'm culling through my memories and I'm trying to be objective. I want to present DeeDee with a cross-section of atrocities. I'm considering writing a short introductory and summary section.

I decide to walk through the living room of my apartment to soak up atmosphere. I want to be accurate. You don't just walk through rooms in Uncle Louie's apartment. They are minefields you chance to survive. In these rooms you feel invisible particles lodging within your flesh, under the skin, and burrowing into the architecture of your cells. You can actually feel these contaminated particles root themselves in. They are some form of psychic leech. They drill their way to the marrow and there is absolutely no method by which such organisms can be removed. There is nothing amorphous about them. They build nests. You feel inhabited.

The diseased psychic microorganisms feel as if they are multiplying in the fabric of my skin and denting my molecular structure. It's a kind of psychological mutation, a personality cancer. It's going to affect me for the rest of my life. My children will be deformed and their children for hundreds of generations. It isn't a living room. It's ground zero.

Yes, it's a kind of weird atomic blast right there by the card table. It's in the air, in the greasy lamplight the color of sick dog teeth, in the cigar smoke and stale cheesecake and in the wheels of Uncle Louie's chair.

I decide to interview my mother. I'm going to collect a representative sample of her thinking. "If you could be anything, what would it be?" I ask her.

"If I could have gone to college, I would have been a doctor," Roxanne responds through the mirror. She likes to look at me through glass where everything is unnatural, distant and restrained with avenues and plazas and seasons between us. This is how I see her face. It's all about reflections. Isn't that what children are, a series of stained holographs bearing the sin of your mouth?

I think of the faces of women in windows, looking past the irrigation ditch leading to a creek named for a tree, a river named for a reptile. Above the fence, a desiccated city of cloud.

And the image of Roxanne as a doctor is bizarre and fantastic. "Yeah?" I say, with my pen ready. "What kind of doctor?"

"A rich kind," she says. She reaches for her evening purse. She isn't smiling.

Now it is finally time for my appointment. DeeDee "Talk to Me" Dushay is a pert blond wearing orange lipstick and a cream-colored blouse with a huge bow at the throat. She watches me walk in. She's using Mr. Gordon's conference room. I sit down in my usual hardback imitation oak chair where I spend afternoons feeling my squandered youth go by, measuring the dilapidated seconds with their surprising metallic depth.

"You said your family is doing things to you?" DeeDee Dushay reads from a page in the file. She glances at my face.

I take a deep breath. "Yes."

"What kind of things?" DeeDee averts her eyes. She surveys the surface of the conference table. "Things without your clothes?"

"Without my clothes?" I repeat. "No."

"Do they drink?" DeeDee asks. She's reading something from a page in the folder.

"Drink?" I feel like I'm underwater.

"Alcohol," DeeDee Dushay says. "Booze."

I think about it. "My mother drinks," I reveal.

It's the first time I've considered the possibility there might be something inappropriate with the vodka bottle Roxanne keeps in the glove compartment of the Chevrolet convertible. The vodka seems to accompany her everywhere, like a friend. There are the small bottles she puts in her suitcase, underneath the perfumed cream-and-black panties. And the wintry glass she always places near her wrist like a crystal, an amulet.

DeeDee Dushay made a quick notation. "Do they feed you?"

"Feed me?"

"Do they give you food?" DeeDee began to tap her pen on the table. She seemed to be thinking it was too nice a day to be stuck inside. It was almost spring. A person could drive to the Santa Monica Pier on a day like this, glance in the pails to see what the fishermen were catching. It was a day to count bonito, halibut, and bass. Then you could ride the carousel and feel the wind on your leg. Or you could wash the car, maybe, and do a little shopping. It was the sort of late morning when you could find a new tangerine blouse.

"There's food. They don't give it to me. I walk over to the card table and get it myself," I say.

"They don't serve you. That's not a crime," DeeDee Dushay said. I could see she was losing interest in me. It occurred to me that when DeeDee Dushay played the H. G. Wells take-it-into-the-future game, she played it with blouses, not with books. "Any strangers in the family?" she asked.

I considered my options. It wasn't a moment for metaphors. I could see that. I said no.

"Does your mom bring her boyfriends home?" DeeDee asked.

I stared at DeeDee Dushay. Roxanne would never bring her boyfriends home. They fly her to Hawaii and Mexico and the French Riviera. She brings home the towels with the names of the hotels written on them with bold red letters. She carries back square glass ashtrays, soaps sculpted to resemble rosebuds, individual shampoos in matching gold bottles and once, from Cannes, a thin glass vial of amber perfume.

"Is your mom still working?" DeeDee asks, listless. It's late morning. On the other side of the street, across from West Los Angeles High School, a thick hedge of white oleander looks starched and immune to the sun. There is the powder blue rectangle of a swimming pool in the distance, a blue that seems to contain color variations as if it somehow had its own coral reef. It's time to consider lunch.

"Yes." I think of something. "Night and day," I add, almost aggressively.

"She's trying to better herself," DeeDee Dushay answers quickly. Her tone suggests she thinks I'm not being cooperative. Not being cooperative could get you sent to juvenile hall or a mental hospital.

"Your mother could probably use some help," DeeDee "Talk to Me" Dushay has decided.

"Listen," I begin. I almost stand up but don't. "They're terrible people and I'm having a monstrous childhood."

DeeDee studies her file. She glances at my face. She looks as if she's decided that I am just fine. "Your childhood is over, Jordan." She studies the papers on the conference table to make certain she's gotten my name right. "You're a young adult now."

I don't say anything. I can see a piece of Los Angeles from the second-story window. The avenues of palms are really in the air. I can see their lime fans. And the balconies of apartments with an occasional red or pink geranium poised on the edge in the sun near a broken bicycle, a bent baby carriage, shells where the metal has gone to rust. Then the sea gulls flying above drying clothing, lemon and orange trees. I can sense the ocean, salty through the citrus and the many dull plants, the sheets and towels in the slow dense breeze. I could take an imaginary picture of this. I could call it noon.

I thought about air and memory and their collaboration, their mute sins. These are the things they could shave your head for.

"Do they hit you?" DeeDee Dushay's voice is soft, conspiratorial. She is giving me one last chance. I recognize that and seize it.

"Yes."

"Your mother, your aunt, or your uncle?" DeeDee is all business now.

"My mother."

"What kinds of objects does she use?" DeeDee is holding her pen. She's taken off the cap. She is ready to write.

"Her hairbrush." There. I've said it. Let the chips fall where they may. Outside, I can see orange and lemon trees. We tried to eat the fruit when we first came to California.

It tasted bitter and chalky like something worms would reject. Outside is a flat plain with circus colors. There are boulevards but they are not serious. They have sea names like Wavecrest, Breeze, Shell, Marine, and Pacific.

"You probably sass her," DeeDee said.

Sass her? I open my mouth. Sass her? I shut my mouth. Camarillo. Sybil Brand. Camarillo. Sybil Brand.

"What other objects?" DeeDee sounds like she's heard it all before.

The day is turning unusually hot, livid and inflamed. There are essences of azure in such thick noons. It has to be this way. There is a kind of logic, a stunted progression. It is there, in the rank texture of the palms.

"Objects?" I repeat.

"Belts, sticks, matches. Anything like that?" DeeDee "Talk to Me" Dushay has put the tip back on her pen.

I say no.

"Nothing with the stove?" She sounds disappointed. Her voice trails off. She is definitely thinking about lunch. We sit in silence. It occurs to me that my days are merely notes for an unraveling. "You live in Palm Courts," DeeDee finally says.

I nod my head. Outside I can see a sea gull and a small plane. Bougainvillea grows across the wall of a house near someone's open garage. A car is moving too fast. The sky seems vaguely fierce, a pale strained nervous blue.

"There's nothing I can do for you," DeeDee Dushay says. She closes the file.

I stand up. I examine her face. I can read her expression. It says, if they scald you, call me.

I stand in the corridor replaying the interior tape of my interview with DeeDee Dushay. I'm trying to see where and how I went wrong. I am still analyzing the secret film of our conversation when I walk into the typing room.

The typewriter keys are a form of deranged rain. I consider the way wind sounds against a flagpole where the flag has come down, the way it flutters the red tin of stop signs. Perhaps this is what happens when the elements sin. This might be the sort of diseased rain that falls after bombs, when the clouds are bloated with glass and tin and the thick smoke from charred flesh, that special heavy ash. The rain is black because the ash comes not only from the skin of the dead but from the images and visions the body contained, from poetry that has been read, from a river rafted in June, mist just above the rapids, everything the color of soft weeds.

The typewriter keys sound like the rain of glass Jimmy Nakamura and I used to talk about. A person could survive an atomic blast and the fallout but still be decapitated. It would be a long season of lethal rains carried by winds charged red and crowded with the scarred remnants of human beings and where they had been and what they had dreamed. And further, as a kind of inner structure, the insistent pulsing debris of what they saw and remembered as they stood looking out windows, their sudden illuminations indelible as the marrow of yellow, and the faces of the people that they loved.

11

It is always a season for rituals. I understand this. I walk back to the Courts, and I can remember when my mother and I left New Jersey.

We are packing boxes. We carry the boxes outside to the curb where the red car is parked. It's stopped snowing. The trees have green buds along their limbs. They look like they have a legion of mouths under their skin and these mouths are breaking out. They are going to speak. They are going to tell me something I don't want to know. This is why I practice closing my eyes as I walk back and forth from the car to the house. If I keep my eyes shut long enough, maybe nothing will happen.

We have packed the car trunk with cardboard boxes and

we are running out of space. Whatever doesn't fit in the car we carry to the trash cans behind the house. I don't understand why. If we aren't taking it, why don't we just leave it inside, where it was?

We've been moving boxes for days. I don't have to go to school anymore. Now I'm tired. I want to lay down on the sofa, in the unexpected clearing between my mother's ankles and knees, in the island she creates for me where I am protected from the water, there is no salt, nothing burns. My mother can curl on her side and drink sherry. I can watch her face. That's where the movie really is, in the many strange fires inside her eyes. But the green sofa is gone now. My mother sold it.

"Always leave it clean," Roxanne is saying. She is Roxanne now. The inspiration clarified itself. It detached itself from the horizon and hummed a red thing that was heat and dream. It spoke one word and this was it. Roxanne. Not floral but more metallic with the hard elements compacted, something you could almost wear strung to your wrist, but elegant. "You don't want anyone coming at you from behind. Leave it clean. Protect your flank. It's an overlay, as Louie would say. It doesn't cost."

She has followed me into my bedroom. She is pointing at something but I don't understand. She's gesturing to the shelf with my dolls. I can see what she has in her hand now. At first I didn't recognize it, the plastic trash bag. Is this possible? Is she pulling my dolls down by their hair?

"I need my dolls," I say. I'm frightened. I stand up. I have dolls with porcelain faces and authentic native costumes, starched-looking skirts, stitched aprons, belts with embroidery that you can tie. Some carry their national flags.

"Jesus Christ," Roxanne says. "Forget it." Her face is near mine. She bends down. She is on the verge of hitting me. She has found the fundamental architecture of *R*. She has decoded it and no one is going to make her bones cave in and her toes fall off. She isn't going to be carried on a litter, crippled. She isn't going to hobble into a cave and eat raw grasshoppers. After all, she can drive now. And I can feel how tense the air is between us. There is a current, insistent and unreliable. The world is a sequence of sudden inexplicable motors. I am learning that. I don't know how they are turned on or where they will take me.

"I can fit them in," I am saying. I am making my voice sound reasonable.

"You're almost eleven goddamn years old," Roxanne says. "Girls your age are having babies. And you're worried about dolls. Shame on you."

"Just a few," I try. I turn my head to the side. I don't want her to see my face. Everything has stalled. I have nothing more to take off, no more layers or veils. There is nothing on my shelves or in my pockets.

"Fill this bag now," Roxanne throws the trash bag at me. "Dump them in. I'm going to count to three."

She has the power of the alcove of violet shadows, the place of the up and the gone. She knows the hieroglyphics of the seasons and how to manipulate them. She makes the rivers flow. She can do this with her fingers. She knows how to cast spells and how to awaken from them. Her many names are the doors where entities are born and vanish. This is a region of force fields. This is a country only she can see. And you can't lie down anymore. The sofa in this realm has been sold.

"But Mom," I begin, evoking the ancient syllable.

"Don't you dare call me that," my mother says. Each

word is sharp and distinct. She charges across the room and shakes me by the shoulders. She looks into my eyes and I am afraid.

It is the time of the spreading gone. It is the era of the vast stain. My father is gone. The sofa is gone. The red car is parked in front of the house. It glares at me. It is just before I throw away my collection of dolls with their braids and mantillas and gingham bonnets.

"I'm not just your mother," my mother says. "I'm also a human being. I have a name. Even garbagemen have names. I'm Roxanne."

Roxanne. It glows like a strange illumination in the time of the up and the gone. It's a flare, a tainted series of flames. It shows me the new direction. There will be an elaborate initiation and it will burn and the scars will be permanent. And this is all deliberate. I have seen pictures of tribes where the backs and arms are gouged with rows of tattoos like ridges of gills on fish. Such rites take weeks. One could never forget. And Roxanne is somehow choosing a version of this for me.

I place my dolls in the plastic trash bag. She is Roxanne and anything is possible. She doesn't have cramps anymore. She doesn't wear eyeglasses and round pink rollers in her hair. She has thrown the quilted bathrobe and fluffy slippers away.

Then we are driving in the red convertible. It is me and the person who used to be my mother, me and the stranger named Roxanne. This woman knows about how feet were bound in China and how to protect your flank. She knows about boulevards and car lots and the men who work on them, the ones you wear your burnt auburn feathered hat for.

Now she knows about maps. I wonder how she learned

this. She must have read about these things in magazines and saw them in movies. Then the street is so suddenly behind us that I forget to turn around, to open my eyes wide so I can remember. Then everything is behind us. My father. My school. My mother who is now a woman named Roxanne. A woman with a new name, a red convertible, a car filled with maps and boxes and no husband.

We are driving into America and I have no dolls with wooden shoes and lace collars and red sleeves that puff out. I have nothing to hold with my hands and there is too much air. It wants to take my breath away. I hold the sides of my blouse. Roxanne will be angry if she sees I'm doing this. She'll tell me I'm acting nervous. I will her not to notice and she doesn't.

I imagine the states will resemble my puzzles of America. The states will be red or blue, pink or yellow or green. Their various products will be displayed, their syrup or cotton or cows or apples. A lady with a starched apron the color of clouds will hold up a tray of round cheeses and smile. A man with faded blue overalls will stand alongside a field of corn. He will lean against his tractor. He will be raising his arm to wave. His eyes will be a seamless blue as if the sky knew his name. He will be wearing a straw hat. There will be a scarecrow at the edge of the field, down near the dog and the fence and the well.

America is rustling my hair and spilling shadows on me. America is trucks with boxes and stacks of wire and wood. In the sky above the road, birds are flying nowhere, not even in circles. The road continues, separating the fields of crops I don't know the name of. Roxanne doesn't know either and she tells me to stop asking. There are black birds on telephone poles. They look slick and greasy. There are coffee shops on the side of a highway where Roxanne says we can't stop. There is brick and there is country. There are stray isolated houses behind fences of trees. There are houses all alone on low hills with large sad-looking windows. I ask Roxanne what they do in these houses.

"They suffer," she says, lighting a cigarette. The edges of her lips curl in a kind of smile. I notice that she is wearing red lipstick.

The highway keeps going as if it can't help itself. There are the wire towers with cables strung to them. I can't imagine what they are for. And I have learned not to ask my mother. Then the wooden stakes of fences that have fallen. Then hay in bales piled near the plowed sides. Then places where sand shows and there is no sky, only strips of gravel along the roadside and pieces of broken tires. Then places where the haze is and one stranded rusty barrel. There are outposts of deserted pipe near fields that look parched or overfed. Then hills with collapsed barns and sheds with no doors.

There is wood in the shape of carcasses, human, animal, something too twisted and insignificant to burn. There are abandoned shells of houses that might have been left a year or a century ago. Once I looked through the eroded slats and saw there had been divisions, platforms, the indications of stairs and lofts and separate rooms.

"Are we there yet?" I ask her.

"Stop asking. You're like a baby," my mother tells me. "Here," she tosses me a map. "You can read. You decide."

I hold the map. I understand the route we are taking. It has been drawn in black pen. It lays across the country like a scar. It is the first prophetic wound but I don't know that. We are following the brutal gouged black. I become confused with where we have been and where we are going. Trenton, Redding, Harrisburg, Chambersburg. And Pittsburgh. Did we see the sign, was it off the road, did we go there or not? And what about Wheeling? Columbus? Springfield and Dayton?

In between, we go to motels with names that lie. Mountain Shadows in a place under a flat sun with nothing on the horizon, not even one lone pine or some rocks. The Sleepy Lagoon Inn where there is no water or indication that there ever could have been. Three Trees and there are none. The Island which is set on the side of the highway. Little Dipper but you can't see any stars, there are too many lights from the city, some city sending a thick yellow film into the night air, some yellow I almost recognize. I tell this to Roxanne and she doesn't care. We sleep together in a big bed. She wraps my body into hers and we wake up that way. We stop eating breakfast. We wait as long as we can into the afternoon and then we buy hamburgers and cokes on the side of the highway.

Along the road there are trees with flowers that look like tissue paper. When I touch them, I am surprised. They are composed of some material so tough I would have to saw them off. I won't be picking a bouquet for Roxanne after all. Then the sky looks like glass or a painting of water. It looks like a blue skin. You could touch it, rub your face against it, listen to lullabies.

There are long roads that go through fields and I wonder why anyone bothered to build such structures or why they would want to travel on them. There are mountains in the distance that never clarify themselves and highways with ragged edges and patrolled-by-aircraft signs. Rows of motels are interspersed with fried-chicken stands and parking lots with pale misshapen ears of corn that have been stepped on. There are boulevards that look empty and are named for men. Douglas Street. James Street. Charles and Michael and Tyrone Road. Harris and William Lane. Montgomery Way. In between are cows and dried bushes and places that seem to be some kind of afterthought. And I don't know what this country is trying to tell me.

We get off the highway, we change direction and go to Cincinnati where Roxanne has a friend she can't find. There is something wrong with the address. I watch her argue with a man who closes the door while she is still talking. She comes back to the car and she seems pale.

We drive up and down the same set of streets. I think of insects trapped in glass jars. I begin to recognize the houses and the wooden porches and slices of overgrown lawn. There are women in the windows behind pieces of curtain and stained shade, women in arcs of yellow lamplight. Roxanne says they are thinking about Greyhound bus stations and the telephone bill. She says the problem isn't their hormones or Christmas or the Centennial.

I have no idea what she is talking about. I didn't even know Roxanne had any secret friends.

"Angela ran with jazz cats," Roxanne says. "She couldn't keep away from reefer."

She glances at the street. There are implications everywhere. Jazz men with yellow instruments and yellow sounds doing things with their mouths. I think of floral curtains fluttering in a midnight without punctuation like a black ocean.

"She's probably dead," Roxanne finally decides. Then she starts driving again.

I can visualize the map in my mind. I think we are near

Indianapolis and Terre Haute but I'm not sure. There have been too many Springfields, Newarks, and Washingtons. We are in Cincinnati and Roxanne starts losing bits of herself. She tells me it's called pawning. The stack of dollars in the handkerchief with the red *R* stitched on the side is gone. And this trip is pulling her apart. She stops at a grated storefront and removes a piece of her body.

She instructs me to wait in the car. I wait. She is pawning. I imagine ponies and animal paws. I remember going to the circus. I think of the way a circus smells and it occurs to me that she might be doing something dirty. We are above the state of Tennessee where Roxanne realized that girls named Ruby work in bars. They have run away from the coal mines and their brothers who did things to them under their skirts. Ruby was the wrong name for her. She recognized that and discarded it. Roxanne says she has another friend in Chicago. A woman she knew from the Catskills. Something about musicians. Roxanne says we'll go there next but we don't. It's late afternoon in Cincinnati and she comes back to the car after pawning. She shows me her hand and after a moment I realize her wedding ring is gone.

I am astounded by this stark nakedness. She might be displaying an amputation. I understand gestures and measurements, how there is a hierarchy of texture and burn and how the borders are defined and circled with gold. I know this. And my mother's hands are merely flesh now.

America is trucks with killer faces, with yellow and red streaks on their cabs like Indian war paint. Or the tattoos certain tribes engrave on the faces of their children. Then the groves of trees that seem abandoned. And the derelict farms that look like people ran from them. There are craters in the fields near the highway. I scare myself. I imagine alien spaceships burned these pockmarks into the earth. If I stare at these mysterious scars in the ground, something will wake up and come after me.

There is the constant assertion of water but I never see it. Little River. Little Stream. Little Creek. Little Falls. Little Rapids. Little Lakes. But we find only small bridges with gravel under them and once, an old iron bridge that appeared delicate, almost carved. Some bridges are made of wood and have railroad tracks on them. Who took the water and where did they put it?

St. Louis and another Springfield. Then the signs for towns with Indian names. Cheyenne and Cherokee and Koiwa. And I know there is no Indian nation. The Indians have all been killed. The Indian tribes are partial like violet X rays, miniature blue pulsings you can't find on a map.

There are the ruins of stockyards and depots with pink and purple peonies near shattered fences. And on the horizon, it always looks like it's raining but it isn't. Then more farms, one with a fence constructed from wagon wheels, white, like a kind of lattice. Then cottonwoods and cedars near a canal where a tractor pulls harrows. Aluminum silos look like they're wearing painted silver caps. We cross train tracks as the sky becomes progressively darker.

The trucks have pictures of the food they are carrying painted on the sides, an ear of corn, cans of peaches and cherries. Have they pasted these representations on because they think the drivers can't remember? The men who drive between the American cities look raw and lonely. They seem to be searching the illusionary horizon for something, perhaps a reason to stay.

Roxanne says these truck drivers listen to sad songs,

hillbilly ballads, while they drive in circles cursing the women who have stopped loving them, who have stopped spreading their legs for them and opening their mouths. The women behind the curtains in the kitchen windows who have stopped waiting for their telephone calls, their offerings of beer and cowboy music. I consider these sun-burned men in their circular internal exile. Perhaps they are under a spell. They are trying to wake up.

Have we passed Dayton or Joplin, Shamrock, Richmond, Bloomington, and Sanders? The cities are always hundreds of miles away, you never get there and then you discover they are behind you. And now, out the window, I have missed another city and there are just clumps of stark bushes and piles of yellowish rock. There are fields of dried grasses like fingers waving across the valley floor. They seem severed. They have lost their wedding rings, their reasons. The wind is a detached voice. You couldn't trust it even if you deciphered it, not after the names of the lying motels in the cities with the water and stars that weren't there. And the Indians and mountains that aren't there. Then the ridges of lost hills and the flat lands that might be tiny swamps. And the sudden lakes where you don't expect them.

I am beginning to understand this vast and broken rhythm. There is always the smear of heat coming off the ground. At dusk there is always a man walking with his face set. He wears somber colors, faded and somehow re-mote. I imagine his heart is broken. Behind him is a place that looks like it will be uninhabitable for generations.

Then there is Sparrow Highway and Crow Highway and Eagle Highway but there are no birds. There is a Stagecoach Road across rock. There are signs for forts but I know they are false. Fort Sherman. Fort Worth. Fort Smith. And I have learned that this country doesn't know how to tell the truth.

We get to Tulsa and Roxanne says we are halfway there. I can see that on the map. It's almost where the crease is, the place where we fold it up. This time I get to go with her. It's early in the morning. It's still cool and gray. We are waiting for the store to open, to raise its mouth of black iron bars from across the doors and plate glass window. I wonder how she knows where to go. Could she have learned this from magazines on the afternoons when she stayed in bed, feeling she was coming down with the flu, and don't touch her? Did she gather this information from Angela, her secret friend, who went with jazz men and couldn't resist reefer and finally died on a street with lawns no one mowed, with walls no one painted?

Then we are walking into the store. Roxanne is pawning her watch, the one Louie gave her. We don't need it, she tells me. He'll buy her a new one, a better one with a gold wristband and diamonds for numbers. Louie will take care of her. In the meantime, we have a clock in the car.

I don't know why I'm crying for her lost watch. Perhaps I sense that time is about to be revised. It won't have the same meaning when we get to the coast and Uncle Louie with his diamond watches and forty telephones. There will be a new set of definitions just as my mother has become Roxanne, someone else. She's a woman without a wedding ring or a watch.

It occurs to me that she was once a woman standing with her face behind fake white lace kitchen curtains. Then she turned away from the street and something magical happened.

I study her. She is enraptured with the grandeur of absolute divestiture. She has discovered a further language. She would take her skin off if she could. She wants to let her bones breathe and somehow I understand this. She is seeking a sudden invisibility, a complexity even she can't articulate. She has surrendered to some confusion so complete and monumental it seems deliberate. And a woman who could sell her wedding ring and her watch could certainly part with her daughter. I realize that's why I'm crying.

"Roxanne Jones. Roxanne King. Roxanne Queen." My mother is trying on names as she drives. She conceives and aborts and makes everything bloody. She takes a sip of sherry from the bag she keeps under her car seat. She's Roxanne without a last name yet and she's going to switch to Scotch sometime after Colorado.

The world is a sequence of spring, slow spring edging into summer. It is green intervals, limes, chartreuse. It is cities named for countries like Brazil and Lebanon and Carthage. It is a countryside where nothing is growing. There are the constant highways with names I can't pronounce, foreign names, and I know I have reached the absolute marrow of silence and afternoon is the color of smoke and things I don't know.

Roxanne is driving with the top down into this road that is beginning to feel permanent. The highway is starting to feel alive. America is Coca-Cola, tires, feed supply, auto parts, gas, antiques, and snacks. Roxanne seems to understand these elements, how they accumulate and what they imply. The air is warm and it seems to leave a kind of sticky green film on everything.

I don't have to brush my hair or teeth anymore. She doesn't remind me and I stop caring. We can't even get a comb through our hair, we've tried. It is matted from the wind. Our lips are chapped. We have sunburn and windburn. We have learned to dress in layers, to peel off or put back on sleeves, long pants. We are always both cold and hot. The wind seems too specific. Days unfold in slow motion.

There is no more money for motels. Now we sleep in the car. She pulls off onto the side of the highway behind a hedge of something fragrant and pink where we can still hear cars passing. We push the seats back into a kind of bed. There are the same stars from last night. I am beginning to recognize constellations. I group them together, decide their configuration, their destination, the intricacies of their circumstances, the accidents, the bad luck. Then I baptize them. I call them Snake and Clown and Whirling Dervish, Howling Woman and Broken Dog. I christen the heavens. Roxanne isn't the only one around who gets to rename the universe.

Night feels raw, stark. It, too, has taken off all the conventional measurements, timepieces, wedding rings, hometowns, names you were born with. There is nothing elegant about it. I am afraid extraterrestrials will find us in the isolated dark. The night feels like it's going to open a brutal purple mouth and reveal something terrible. It could impart the terminal litany. It could say something that would fill me with a monumental regret I would have to try unsuccessfully to forget for the rest of my life. I am terrified.

We eat in the car now. We can't go to restaurants or markets. People stare. They think we are stealing food, eating as we walk in the aisles, stuffing bags of corn chips under our shirts, candy bars, dried fruit, loaves of bread.

We are wearing our road clothes, pants under our skirts.

We have mosquito bites on our eyelids and cheeks. We wear scarves around our necks. We put them over our mouths when we drive through dust. Now we look like robbers. And everything costs too much money and there is nothing left to sell. This is what America has done for us.

We go to fruit stands on the highways. Sometimes when Roxanne makes them lower the price, we buy cherries and peaches from these roadside shacks. Roxanne asks them if they can't find something in the back for us. She leans against the counter. You can see where her blouse isn't buttoned, the freckles, the white lines from where the sun hasn't been. She is wearing red lipstick and she smiles. Sometimes they give us a bag of plums that have gotten soft, have blackened. We spit the bad parts out.

We drink water. We put sugar in it from the packets we saved from restaurants. Cincinnati where Roxanne had a friend she couldn't find is behind us. A woman who got divorced and liked to dance with men who gave her terrible cigarettes. The wedding ring she pawned there is behind us. And Tulsa where she sold her watch.

Now there are towns named for animals. Buffalo. Elk. Bear. Eagle. Snake. We are partway through New Mexico and everything is behind us. The lilacs on the side of the road. The sudden patches of tiny white flowers that looked like an incoherent border of snow. The elms with their curved branches that could embrace you.

Now we put the blankets on the ground. We have sores from sleeping on the car seats. Every night Roxanne says she'll get sleeping bags in the morning but she doesn't. We just keep going. Now we have to stop and walk around every two hours. We have to touch our toes and stretch. We lie down near the car on our blankets. I am too hungry to sleep.

Roxanne opens a packet of catsup from a hamburger stand in Texas. She pours water on it and says it will taste just like tomato soup. It doesn't.

"Don't cry," she says. "Half the world goes to sleep hungry. They have since the start of time."

I don't understand her tone. Is being hungry acceptable or is it déclassé? This is an abrupt new terrain. I don't know how to read this map.

That week, we first see the sign. Wonders of the West, 470 miles. I begin to decode the sequence. There is a sign every fifty miles. Each time we pass a sign, Roxanne reads the words out loud. The diminishing mileage makes her smile. Then she decides we have to see it. It's the one detour we're going to make. After all, we didn't go to Chicago. We didn't try to find her other friend, Miriam, the one who once went to North Beach, California, and met Jack Kerouac. We're going to do this instead, turn north, wind our way up into the state of Colorado. We are going to see the Wonders of the West before we find Uncle Louie on the coast.

"Roxanne Frances. Roxanne France. Roxanne London. Roxanne Dancer. Roxanne White. Roxanne Black. Roxanne Rain. Roxanne Green. Roxanne Gold. Roxanne Black. Roxanne Day. Roxanne Night." My mother tries.

I stare at her lips mating with the dusty air. Her mouth is a cluster of spoiled plans, a place where sadness and wind collide.

It is after Colorado, Wyoming, Idaho, and Utah. It is after the detour we both regret. I know California isn't a real destination. You can't get there from New Jersey, not simply by following a drawn line on a map. The process of arrival is more subtle and complex. It involves acts of contrition. You must appease the gods. You must find novel forms of penance. You must tattoo your children and look at the wonder. It's about conjuring and awakening and intuitions you wish you never had. It's about being chapped by a wind of erasure and losing pieces of yourself. It's the prairies of ghost animals, the hallucinatory towns, the neon on the motels we can see behind the cottonwoods where we have parked our car and spread our blankets on the ground.

Amarillo. Gallup. Santa Fe. Denver. None of it seems possible. Not these mountains that look like painted seashells somebody found and laid down on their glistening sides. Not the siege of rocky cliffs where you know you must have a password to cross. Now the desert.

"Roxanne West. Roxanne East. Roxanne Kansas. Roxanne Kan. Roxanne Jan. Roxanne Lan," my mother tries. Her hair is splayed by wind. It looks like she's pulled clumps of it out with her fingers.

"What are you thinking?" I ask.

"I'm thinking about money." She takes a sip from the bag she keeps on the seat next to her leg. She doesn't put it in the glove compartment anymore. The cops are only in the cities. We know that now. And it's her last pint of Scotch. She is trying to make it last.

"What's your favorite color?" I think she may say yellow, how it reminds her of polished skulls, agate and silk. She might say something about lamplight or moonlight.

Roxanne smiles. "Green."

"What's your favorite food?" I consider cherries and vanilla ice cream. Above, the moon looks like it had something to say, like it had an answer but it didn't really matter. You've probably heard it before.

"That's easy," she says. "Scotch."

"Do you believe in God?" I need to know this.

It is night. We have pulled off the highway. We are on the edge of a town. Sometimes dogs come to us in the night, barking, we can feel their breath near our faces. We have started to sleep in the backyards of churches. We believe there are fewer dogs near churches and somehow we feel safe, even though Roxanne mocks the crosses on the door and above the steeple.

"There are no nailed boards in the outlaw night where I have always lived without regret," she tells me.

We are in an enclosed brick yard. I can smell honeysuckle and roses. Roxanne is thinking about God. Then she says, "No. There is no God."

There is a pause where I would like to reach out and hold her hand. Sometimes she lets me do that.

"Go to sleep," she says. She doesn't want to speculate about God. And my hand stays curled in the cool black air between us.

We have come down from Idaho and Utah, after our detour to the Wonders of the West and there are no more mountains. All the Miamis and Augustas and Jacksonvilles are behind us. We are gathering momentum and there will be no more sudden deviations. We have seen where that leads. Now we are moving toward a kind of revelation. The trees growing between rock and sand seem cursed. Someone important has shaken their fist at these trees and they have doubled up, stooped over, and lost their leaves forever.

We are crossing the final desert. The car has been sick since Colorado and Roxanne drives slowly. We carry water in plastic jugs. Every twenty miles we stop and pour water into the radiator. She has learned how to release the hood, how to make it stay open, how to wrap her hand in a towel and unscrew the cap and pour in the water. She has learned how to leap back if the radiator sizzles and the old water explodes in a shower of rust.

It is the desert with its hexed plants called cactus. She has a pamphlet that names and describes them. She says she found it in the gas station and I know she is lying. She pours water in the radiator. Then she identifies plants. She tells me they are called creosote, agave, indigo, and palo-verde. We are looking at Joshua trees. She tells me these plants have medicinal properties. Roxanne is staring at the vegetation with longing. She wishes she knew how to open them, how to unlock their mysteries. She calls a thin gorge an arroyo, says there are bobcats and owls and snakes there. She looks like she could unravel geography with her eyes. She is almost out of Scotch.

There is nothing in this desert now, not even stones. We sleep in the day under our straw hats and whatever shade we find, a bridge across the road, a piece of a wall someone began and abandoned. We drive at night into the cold. Everything seems abstract and obsolete.

Then even the desert is behind us. We have survived the ritual of purification. In our own way, we have been tattooed. We have searched for visions and found them. I look up. The sky has been savaged. It's the texture of blood and torches and lipstick kisses. I wish I had my crayons.

"What is it?" I ask. I am afraid.

"Sunset," Roxanne answers. She gestures to the sky. She smiles and opens her fingers. She seems confident and possessive. "Sunset over Los Angeles," she says, as if she had just invented it.

Los Angeles doesn't even sound like a natural word. It is

absolutely foreign. It is alien like eating stone. No one could possibly live here. The sky is abnormal. We are driving in the red convertible that needs constant water. We are going to surprise Uncle Louie. The sky is spread above us like a mutilated body. Roxanne is putting on fresh crimson lipstick. When she smiles, it's as if she has rubbed the sunset into her face, as if she is wearing this colossal wound across her lips. And I know she somehow likes this.

12

It has turned into a hot afternoon. The orange trees seem poised and alert, clearly predatory. They might be superimposed, jammed awake, insomniac, up to no good. If they don't watch out, rumors will spread that they are not shaping up or coping.

The lawns are dense with a sequence of pinks that seem broken and drunken. I am alone on the boulevard. I have fallen back through time, regressed to the place where I must count each step I take and offer it up to the arbitrary referees of fate.

Inside the apartment, the stung wounded air has accumulated and forgotten everything it might have once known. It is ancient and amnesic. It might be an era before electricity, before prophecies or language. It's the place of the palms with their alarming dullness, their effortless mediocrity. It is the time of no measurements or postcards, no souvenirs as I have previously understood them.

The sunlight might have been cut with surgical precision by the blinds. Perhaps the room has had a treatment, a procedure. The lamps are on even in the afternoon. In the Courts there is never enough light.

"No trump? No trump, no less," Uncle Louie is saying, angry. "We got eleven spades between us."

Uncle Louie and Aunt Doris are playing with Johnny J and Maureen. Johnny J is an open heart from Fresno. Louie likes the Hunters better. Mike Hunter is a bypass from San Francisco. Louie likes to make his Tony Bennett joke when he plays with the Hunters.

"Hey, call Tony up. Tell him you left your heart in San Francisco, too," Louie says, as he lights his cigar, stares at the ember, and laughs.

They're playing with Johnny J because Mike Hunter had an episode during the night. An episode. It could mean anything. Now he's back in ICU. No one knows when he's getting out or the extent of the damage. At least Louie has a backup set of hearts to play with. His spares. That's what he calls them.

"Cancers? What's the point?" Louie says. "By the time you learn their system, by the time you get the bugs out, they're dead."

"You got the ace of clubs. You got the stopper," Aunt Doris tells him. She sounds calm.

"I got the stopper? You goddamn nut case. We got nothing in diamonds." Louie yells.

Uncle Louie wheels his chair around and puts it close to

his wife. He's going through the stack of cards that used to be her hand. He's reconstructing the game trick by trick. He's like a plastic surgeon rebuilding a face from a photograph.

"Nothing in diamonds? I got the king twice, you jerk." Aunt Doris lights a cigarette. "You call that nothing?"

"You should have bid it. Why don't you bid your stinking cards? What am I? A mind reader, for Christ's sake? What am I? Louie the Clairvoyant?" Uncle Louie wheels himself into the kitchen. "Where's the ice cream?"

Uncle Louie has pulled the refrigerator door open. He has managed to get out of the chair, lean forward, and open the freezer.

"We're out of ice cream? Doris?" Uncle Louie is back in the chair. He wheels himself past me and almost runs over my foot. He is prepared to elbow me out of his way. He's got to get back to the card table.

Louie is talking about the ice cream and he's incensed. There are rules in this family. No circling. Nothing mechanical ever. Nothing from the ground. No plants that might leave dirt on a person's hands. That's for hicks. Hillbillies have vegetable patches. No fruit. That's what farmers eat. Winter doesn't figure. No one can come near the car and touch it but Les Downer and then only after you have prostrated yourself before him and offered up a bottle of Southern Comfort. And most importantly you cannot run out of cigarettes or vanilla ice cream. If you run out of these things, you will be burned from the planet. Somebody will drop an atomic bomb on you. Your alphabets and gods will be ash. It will be as if you had never been.

Behind me I hear Aunt Doris talking to Maureen, the wife of the open heart from Fresno. "You know the lowest?

Look under that. That's the mother. After God made her he broke the mold. Then he had to invent disinfectant." Aunt Doris is talking about Roxanne.

I walk into my bedroom and there she is. I feel I've manifested her presence by remembering our trip to California. Jimmy Nakamura and I believe in the power of thought and its destructive potential. We interpret the history of demonic possession and the persecution of witches as evidence of extrasensory perception.

I stand in the doorway of our bedroom. First she became Roxanne. Then she began passing herself off as my sister. That's what I'm supposed to call her when anyone is around. Sis.

"It's a small thing," Roxanne said. "It doesn't cost. You call me Sis. It's just a word. It's one little syllable. What do you care?"

"I care," I said.

"You're a square," Roxanne told me with contempt.

Now she glances up at me. She almost smiles. She has a towel wrapped around her wet hair. She's wearing her aqua blue kimono and she's got her bottles of nail polishes balanced near her side. Volcanic Eruption. Maui August. Fire Symphony. Burned Molasses. Who has the contract on supplying these names? Roxanne is painting her left thumbnail.

"Do you believe in reincarnation?" she asks me.

I sit down on my bed. It's a vital subject for me. Jimmy Nakamura and I both believe in it, but somewhat differently. I think it's a metaphor with archetypal dimensions. It speaks of a primal human need, the impulse of which can be traced through art and religion. Jimmy, on the other hand, is convinced it's physically possible, only not for people who have been vaporized by atomic bombs, who have had the flesh on their arms and chest melt and hang down from their bones like a series of gray cobwebs.

The complexities of reincarnation spread in front of me like a high desert valley seen from a vista point, airy and light blue and without boundaries. Roxanne and I have been to such valleys. I am evaluating how best to approach the subject when she decides to answer the question herself.

"I don't," she tells me. "You know why?"

"Why?" I ask.

"Because everybody says they were a queen in their other life. Everybody's royalty. Everybody's a goddamn princess. All of them, ladies at court." She looks disgusted.

Roxanne holds her nails up to the lamplight. Then she blows on them. Her hands are impervious. There are no months or years here, no ancient cycles that proved empty and fraudulent. Roxanne never gets older. Maybe red is a kind of frontier for her, a border she has placated, subdued. There was a war and she won. At night, it might be a kind of lullaby.

"It's not statistically possible," she is saying. "Think about it. Jesus, people are morons. Why don't they come out of these reincarnation classes and say, yeah, I went back to the Middle Ages in Europe and I was a servant. I got knocked up. Then I got cholera the next week and I died bad."

Roxanne has her tweezers out. She's got the magnifying mirror balanced on the bed by her side. As soon as her nails dry she can start on her eyebrows. Then she will set her hair. Then she will pack.

"No. Everybody is Eleanor of Aquitaine. Everybody is

Cleopatra and Mary Queen of Scotland. Scotland, no less. Nobody just says they served ale somebody made in a backyard still. They got their ass pinched in some medieval dive where the sound of retching was their version of a jukebox. You know what I think?''

"What?" I want to know.

I can read the names on the bottles that are still in the polish box. Wild Scarlet. Vermilion Promise. Apples in Flame. Primitive Rouge. I wonder how the process of selection works. What is the role of excess? How does one recognize aberration? Is it possible to be too red?

"History is actually made up of spear carriers," she is saying. "For every Cleopatra there are fifty thousand of us. That's the generations of this family. We're always just out of the frame. We're the static behind the major forces. You can't even see us in a crowd pan. We're the ones saying, don't go. You won't find a parking place. You won't like the food. Stay home instead. Have some more ice cream."

She shakes her fingers as if her hand hurt. Then she makes them dance in front of her face. The boundaries are fluid and crimson. We celebrate death. We worship fire. As for beauty, don't kid yourself, Roxanne likes to say. It's a full-time job and half the time it doesn't pay.

There is a piece of lawn outside the bedroom window. A bush with pink hibiscus. A magnolia with a white blossom the size of a bucket that looks welded on. Everything is afflicted with sun. The sky is flat and distant, retracted. The sky is becoming withdrawn. Maybe it isn't coping. It once wanted something but now it can't quite remember what. It's been consigned to the periphery. It got repossessed along with the station wagon. It got pawned with your grandmother's gold and pearl bracelet, the one she hid in the scarf and walked barefoot with from Kiev to Antwerp. You can never get it back.

"I can just hear your Aunt Doris. You know what she'd say to Joan of Arc? She's say, Joanie, take off those ridiculous boy's pants. Joanie, you listening? You don't want to get involved. Politics is a can of worms. It's a jar of ca-ca. Don't get started. They won't appreciate you. Listen, Joanie. In the end, they'll show their gratitude with a match," Roxanne says.

Today Roxanne has nowhere she has to be. She's not decorating a movie set in the valley. She's not helping someone put on their costume, pulling on their boots, adjusting the hat with the veil, the cape with the fur collar. This afternoon she is not lifting a tropical drink to her lips on some island twelve plane hours away where the time zone is different and even the sun isn't the same. A place where it rains constantly and sunset is a violet delirium, and later there are flagrant stars above macadamia groves.

"I'll do your nails," Roxanne suddenly offers.

She motions me closer. I sit at her side. She is holding my hand. I let her select the color. I want to be surprised. I will be anointed and this will last for days. It will be a kind of benediction and I can wear it.

"You have nice hands," she says. "Show them off. Make the most of the pieces."

Later Roxanne plucks her eyebrows. Then she takes a bath. The room smells of oranges and musk, alcohol and almond and vanilla and something that makes me think of lace. I can feel her light powder in the air. All at once it seems as if we are at camp. We could tell ghost stories and try to scare each other. Would she let me have the top bunk? Would she walk to the barn with me? And the lake? We could share a flashlight.

"You don't ask me questions anymore," Roxanne realizes. "I guess you're too old."

This night Roxanne is sleeping in her bed. The air between us is layered with organic things. I hear them breathing. I remember we are only partly here. Above our shoulders are forests of moss where we are encased in our impenetrable dusks. Our solitudes are distinct, a soft and morose silver. It is the hour of orchids and doves and deserted women on derelict balconies. The clouds have hidden fluencies. They are relentless with births and shipwrecks. Always a coral reef breeds and dissolves. And we are the broken shell. Nothing can release us.

It was breakfast time in Hiroshima. Jimmy's family never got their tea. Some of his aunts and uncles in the outskirts of the city survived the blast. The skin on their faces came apart like stained gauze. They might have been wearing masks with curious eye holes and cat's whiskers. Then the death rain came.

"Do you think history can touch us?" I ask.

It's a question I've been saving for Jimmy. Now I want to know what my mother thinks.

"I've been touched by history," Roxanne says. She is lying on her back, smoking. Her legs are crossed at the ankle. She is staring at the ceiling. "The Queen Mother came to Central Park. Not this dumpy Elizabeth but the real queen, her mother. They let us out of school and gave us paper flags. Half were British, half were American. Mine was the Union Jack. That was the only thing the school ever gave me. A paper Union Jack with two staples that fell apart the next day. Everybody was hungry. Right before the queen came, the teachers passed out bread with jam. That woke everybody up.

"They took us in a bus. Then she was there. She came

through the park in a horse-drawn carriage painted gold, no less. It was exactly what you imagined a queen traveled in. She was wearing a blue hat with a feather in it. One gray feather. I've never forgotten.''

I am watching my mother's cigarette smoke rise in the air. It is taken by the breeze through the room, toward the window. It looks like it's trying to say something, to curve itself into symbols.

"I saw history at the World's Fair, 1939. It was the marvel of long distance. They had phones installed in rooms with signs saying Paris and London and Rome. You could go in and call anyone. My name was picked. I was always lucky. My name was selected but I didn't know anyone across an ocean.

"I sat at the phone they gave me, but I couldn't remember names or cities. A few years later, anyone I would have called was gassed in the camps. Sometimes I think I was meant to call them. I could have saved their lives." Roxanne puts out her cigarette and laughs. "Isn't that moronic? They didn't even have phones."

I lay in the sheared and unsolid darkness of the bedroom made strange and heightened by the presence of my mother whom I now call Sis. It doesn't cost. This woman of the shed selves who has put out her last cigarette of the night. She might have telephoned her aunts and uncles and cousins, might have warned them about Hitler but she didn't know their names or the villages they lived in. And they probably wouldn't have believed the little-girl voice from New York.

I can feel her sleeping. I realize the process of metamorphosis is continuous, is constantly unraveling, cocooning and reinventing itself. We turn away from this revelation because it is shocking to watch.

There are images you can't clear just by the act of shaking your head. You can't stamp your feet and make them stop. These are our interior lakes, our ports within where we are washed with a kind of lavender vertigo. We are breathless and afraid. Then the air exposes itself and its violet architectures.

Night is brilliant with insight and punishment. Our words are inadequate lamps in this darkness. There is only mourning in our mouths.

Later, if you survive this, there is dawn across the coast of poisoned oranges. Then there will be the extended brass afternoons beside the ravaged orchards where everyone is dying in this region of funerals.

Perhaps that is what the women in the windows of the kitchens we passed on our journey across America were thinking. Maybe they were deciding that they were solitaries. They might have been abandoned. Or there was a circumstance. Maybe they chose to go.

What do such women see out beyond the pane of window glass? There is the uselessness of the blue spruce. The sense that it has always been this way. The dusty blue pickup truck going fast down the numbered road leading to the interstate, does it matter which way it goes? Such women are born to be solitaries. It is like some chemical in the blood. It can be no other way.

Or perhaps they are considering trees. The cottonwoods, the willows by the river, the rumored eucalyptus. And if you live long enough, you can come to the land of the palms.

13

I feel compelled to compose a complete emotional catalog of my life. Maybe it will have an effect along the continuum, behind or ahead of the awkward me I currently am. Perhaps this record will cause a manifestation somewhere else, an island or a pier when I someday need it, a breakwater or a lighthouse in a drowning season.

My life is a history of divestiture. In the beginning there was the self-created Roxanne, predator of the Rs, a mutation of sorts, a spontaneous generation birthing itself during the commercials of "Hollywood Playhouse." Then she has taken the rollers from her hair and she is driving the red convertible, pawning her ring and her watch.

I can remember Pennsylvania and West Virginia and the

highway turnoff we took to Cincinnati where Roxanne sold the wedding band that could no longer define or contain her. Then St. Louis where she begins to talk about selling her watch but she doesn't until Tulsa. It's daybreak when she finds the shop. We wait for it to open. She takes me with her. A few words to the man and it's done. We know time will be different. The increments we once accepted have dissolved. They are obsolete.

The towns and cities look the same now, with windburn and chapped lips and not enough sleep. It's nothing like I thought it would be, hills yellow with mustard and stretches of sand a cool peach, the color of a suddenly glimpsed face. I had imagined borders of strawberries and fists of orange poppies. Instead everything looks muted and raw. Roxanne sold her watch because it doesn't matter what time it is.

"It's not like we're expected anywhere," she says. When I hear that I become afraid. We have already taken our disastrous side trip into Colorado, Wyoming, Idaho, and Utah. We have seen the Wonders of the West. We are still two states away from California and maybe nobody knows we are coming. Maybe there is no Los Angeles or Uncle Louie. And if we get hungry enough, we'll have to sell the car. If Roxanne sells the car, I have an intuition that I am next. The car is our last tangible object. But it is not the last thing we can sell. I sense this distinction and I am terrified.

We have left New Jersey and we have no conventional time or family anymore, no religion and no father. We have escaped the ruins of the old world, God and snow, the foot binders and people you are accountable to. We have escaped, but barely.

We have divested ourselves of the false trappings, the hat

boxes and rule books they make for squares. We have left behind everything that doesn't fit in the car. We have entrusted ourselves to the elements. We have crossed borders so camouflaged and complicated you can't find them on a map and no one can track us.

My mother is in a new incarnation. She has named herself Roxanne. She is both the ship and the people who christen it. She can stay and go simultaneously. In a few years she will become my sister. Sis. Now the sky perches on top of the car like something that has had its intestines ripped out. It looks like it's suffering. It looks like somebody should put a bullet in it.

"What is that?" I ask, pointing.

"Sunset in Los Angeles," Roxanne says, pronouncing the made-up word that doesn't even sound like a city.

I know cities. I've had a map across my lap for most of the summer. I've been collecting cities for months, cities we drove through or passed or saw the signs for, like Kansas City and Detroit. We could have stopped there if we had wanted. If Roxanne had been in the mood. We could have gone to Chicago or Dallas or Seattle. We could have taken the turn-off.

Now we are driving through the gate of Palm Courts West, past the kiosk with its locked door and no guard. There was some kind of contagion, I realize. A poison cloud, perhaps. Maybe nerve gas. The guard must have died.

"It doesn't look right," Roxanne keeps saying. She's driving slowly. She is staring at the apartments with their comatose lawns and legislated quiet and how even at sunset the air is gray and strained. There was something tropical once but it was filtered out.

This cannot be our destination. We have reached the Pacific, there must be a wharf above a harbor. I had imagined a Saturday market where they stack fish and flowers, fresh maple syrup and apple cider. There would be almonds, melons, and bolts of silk with stenciled leaves and embroidered village scenes, perhaps, and pagodas. There would be masks of gods or dragons.

Roxanne stops the car. She checks her lipstick. There's an empty volleyball court. The shades across all the windows are drawn. She places her arm around my shoulder. It's the first time she's touched me in days. Then she rings the doorbell.

Aunt Doris looks us over. It doesn't take much. We are carrying our history with us. We haven't yet learned how to shake the bad dream off and pretend. We have sores from sleeping in the car. We have windburn and brown lines around our lips, small cuts. We have learned the malice of the air. We have red blotches from insect bites, spiders and fleas and deer flies. Our hair is matted.

This is what the road has done for us. We are broken and shocked and rearranged. We have been jolted beyond awake. We have left the father and we have barely survived. We've got the clothing on our backs and that is all. We haven't had food money since the Nevada border. We have seen the tables under the tents in the parks of America where the pelts are displayed. We have seen the steel foot traps, the bitten-off legs and the bled-to-death silver fox, river otter, and badger. We know what freedom costs.

"We can pay," Roxanne says through her cut lips. She puts her hand on her hip and smiles.

I want to memorize my mother's face when she's lying. I look at her the way I studied our map of the United States.

I traced rivers and mountain ranges, highways and unpaved roads. I made distance approximations by measuring the air between my fingers.

There were towns that smelled like steak and lilacs. I could identify dead animals in the road as we drove by, the black-and-white pattern of the skunk, the rings on the tail of the raccoon, the big ears of the jack rabbit, how large coyotes and deer are. But you can't stop and eat them, no matter how fresh and intact they seem. Now I am staring at Roxanne. There are features here I must learn.

"Louie," Aunt Doris says to the room behind her, the room we can't see through the screen door where we are standing. "Your kid sister says she can pay."

Uncle Louie appears in the doorway. He can still walk with a cane. The cancer hasn't lodged its nests in the interior of his legs yet. He doesn't recognize he's in a steel trap. He doesn't know the wheelchair is coming. He doesn't realize he is slowly turning to powder.

He looks like somebody's grandfather. His hair is white. I know the kind of rock his eyes resemble. I have seen these rocks on the highway. His eyes are obviously coal.

I am peeking into the living room behind him. I am searching for the forty phones. There is a square in the center of the room. It's a card table. Two other people are sitting there. It's Dolores and Chuck Buckner. Dolores has a shaved head and what appears to be a plastic disc embedded in the top of her skull. And there is a kind of blue tube coming out of her ear.

There is so much cigarette smoke in the room, it's hard to see what they're doing. They're playing cards. I have small cuts around my eyes. The air did this to me, the night. I have recently crossed the Utah deserts, then the

Mojave Desert and Death Valley. I must be imagining the woman with the tube in her ear, the disc in her skull. The woman who seems to be wearing a bathrobe.

Later Uncle Louie will explain that the Buckners are his favorite bridge partners that year. Louie will tell me how much he likes brains.

"Brains are a contained area," Uncle Louie says. "Throats are good, too. They got a good cure rate with brains and throats. Other cancers, forget it."

"Give the kid a sandwich, Dorrie. Go against type. Be a sport," my mother says, edging closer. The sky is in agony above us. It's the middle of summer and apparently these people are going to let it suffer, let it linger and corrupt the air. In this region, the inhabitants have adapted to this extravagance of magenta. They breathe through it. It doesn't seem to hurt their eyes. Then Roxanne pushes me hard with a hand to the small of my back. I take a step and we're in.

I know at once this isn't what I expected from Uncle Louie, the bookmaker. Not the Louie my mother has been talking about all the way across the country, when we pulled off the highway and slept on the ground near the parking lot of a motel we couldn't afford to go to. Roxanne let me do this, sleep near the motel where I could still see a piece of the neon sign, two of the *n*s from the blue glowing inn. I felt safer. There were always too many taunting stars reminding us we were dull and expendable and no one knew where we were. And this can't possibly be the Louie with a Cadillac and his own box seats at the world-famous Hollywood Park Race Track. The Louie who is going to take his sister and his niece out for pastrami sandwiches. They must have them in California.

It is our first night in Los Angeles. Roxanne and I are in the spare bedroom, the one Louie and Doris got by mistake. They whisper when they tell us this. Something about how the hospital made an error so they got a two-bedroom.

I lie down in the bed closest to the wall and Roxanne is near me, smoking one cigarette after another. She's telling me about the kind of sport Uncle Louie used to be. He'd make a special trip into the old neighborhood just to look her up, make sure she had a coat in winter. He stayed in touch. He made an effort. He pushed a guy through a plate glass window once, a guy who made an obscene gesture to her. She got respect after that. She could walk down the block at midnight and everyone knew she was protected. And Louie would come around with chocolates in a box during the Depression when everyone was hungry.

I imagine the Depression was like our trip across the country. Everyone was selling pieces of themselves, only they weren't moving anywhere. Roxanne is talking about Louie's candies, two-pound boxes wrapped with floral paper and big yellow ribbons. Each candy had a fluted wrapper. Not just paper but almost an individual design. You never knew what you were biting into. There were no indications. It might be raspberry or caramel or even something like lemon. Something vaguely citrus. It would startle the mouth and linger, abrupt and yellow and full of mystery. You could find yourself dreaming about the ocean. That's when she first started to think about the coast.

"I didn't know he was sick," she said. "How could I know?"

Even in the darkness I feel that she is pale. Something has leeched the color from her face. Something has brought the desert in, vast and whitened. I think she's going to cry but she doesn't.

Then it is morning in this terminal region where time and climate have been revised. This is the land where they drop poison gas on the guards and the skies writhe.

I realize she is going to leave me with them. It suddenly becomes clear to me. I am standing in the hallway that leads to the living room where the card table is. I still think it's collapsible. No one says anything to me. After a while I sit down on the sofa.

Uncle Louie and Aunt Doris are already occupying their bridge chairs at the card table. I notice they always sit in the same ones. Louie is holding a deck in his hands. They aren't playing. I can see that. It's just part of some nervous ritual. He needs to feel the cards in his fingers, his palm, the cool plastic and inside, the faces of the four royal families. Then I turn to the place where Roxanne was and she isn't there anymore.

She is partway across the lawn with its stilted dry grass, its impossible grass. She is almost at the curb and she is absolutely resurrected. She is wearing a white suit with a white straw hat I didn't know she had. She is wearing her pearl necklace. She looks as if she never slept on a blanket on the side of a highway in her life.

I run after her. She sees me and darts toward the car. I lunge forward and catch her by the calves. I am holding her ankles and I refuse to let go.

"Stop it," she screams. "I'll be back. I'll be back maybe next week. You slow me down and I've got to move."

"Move where?" I ask. I look up but I can't see her, only the sun.

"Around. I have to move around." She prepares to hit my shoulder with the white purse I have never seen before. When did she buy these things and where did she hide them?

I am almost eleven years old. I am lying with my left cheek in the hot grass holding onto my mother's ankles. The grass smells like old pine needles or a drawer that hasn't been opened in years and has filled with inexplicable residues that have nothing to do with dust. I can smell my mother's powder, her trace elements, the vague insistence of citrus and vanilla. The sun is burning the side of my face. Roxanne has pried my fingers from her ankles. Then she is driving away.

First Ernie and my dolls and New Jersey. Then America, which was nothing like my puzzles with the women holding cheeses on trays and smiling. And the farmers standing by enormous stalks of corn, waving. Then she became Roxanne. Then she pawned her ring and her watch. Now she is gone.

"She was always trash," Aunt Doris says. She's been eating a jelly doughnut and watching from the steps in front of the apartment. "You know low? You know the lowest? Look under that. You'll find her. She's the layer under the scum. She's where the maggots breed."

"Shut up," Uncle Louie says to her. He's pushed the screen door open with the handle of his cane. "You got no taste saying that in front of the kid." Louie is limping with his cane onto the lawn. "Come here, kid. Want a piece of cheesecake? We got chocolate cheesecake."

"Have some cheesecake. Two-ninety-nine a pound," Aunt Doris tells me. I can't determine if she's pleased or not. "Come on, Jordan. Stand up. People will think you're sick. They'll call the paramedics and you'll make trouble."

"What kind of name is that? Jordan? What is that? A goddamn river?" Uncle Louie is asking.

I am sitting up now. The short brittle grass is starting to make me itch. The sky is a brutal white. I had imagined this port of Los Angeles as a clean blue with ferries, perhaps, going out to an island. There would be the smell of bread and cinnamon and coffee. Now everything has been rubbed away. I can see inside the screen doors of the apartments. Everyone is wearing a bathrobe and smoking.

"Don't look like that. Don't look sad like that," Uncle Louie says. He is standing on the grass near me. They are afraid I am going to make trouble. They are afraid someone is going to call an ambulance. "Listen to me. Boy two apartments over died last week. Fourteen years old. He had thirty-six separate operations in two years. I knew him the whole time. They did things to him Nazis in the camps didn't think of. Two years of torture. His mother had a nervous breakdown. She weighed eighty-four pounds. You would have thought she had the cancer. They took her away in a straitjacket. Then he died. Now that's sad. You don't know from sad."

Since I cannot remain on the lawn indefinitely, feeling the sharp stubs with my fingers, pulling pieces of grass out like it was my hair and staring at the driveway where the red convertible isn't parked anymore, I walk back to the apartment. Uncle Louie is telling me I need to develop a sense of perspective.

"What are you? Twelve? Thirteen? You need to be more grown-up," Uncle Louie decides. He offers me a cigarette. I lean over and he lights it for me.

"Listen, Jordan. Your mother has to cover a lot of ground now. She has to make up for lost time. She'll be back," Uncle Louie explains.

"They always return to the scene of the crime," Aunt Doris says. "You want some two-handed or what? Louie? You playing?"

"I'm playing, yeah," Uncle Louie says. He settles himself carefully into the bridge chair. He leans his cane against the table near him.

Outside is a pale green lawn where nothing is moving. Outside is a gate without a guard. Outside is the country where the puzzles of the states have nothing to do with the broken highways, the empty trucks, the faces of the women in the farmhouse windows, the barns and towns that look like people ran from them. Outside is a light tentative sun that smells like the memory of dust and doesn't mean anything. I decide that the last year of my life never happened.

"I want my mother," I announce to no one in particular. I put out my cigarette.

"Don't we all, kid," Uncle Louie says, picking up his cards. "Don't we all."

14

My mother is making up for lost time and covering ground. First she gave up her watch and now she is somehow running behind. These are the chances you take when you strike out on your own, when you look the country in the eye, when you see the demonstration of early American skills of the West in parks and along the sides of rivers. This is what happens when you are tired of lying and being afraid. You risk rupture and exile. We have done this.

In this city with its alien name everything is confusing. Roxanne is memorizing the north-south streets and how to pronounce them. She didn't count on this, the goddamn foreign-language problem. God forbid she should say something wrong and they would think she was a farmer. She didn't expect this deceptive city webbed with intersections you don't know how to pronounce and boulevards that stop and start. She didn't expect so many hillbillies. And there are no monuments or landmarks, hills with spires, bridges and statues, no way to navigate by sight.

This is an abstract landscape, cut-and-dried like geometry. You can't talk to it sweet, let it sense your musk, your tangy essence. You can't bat your eyelashes and make it change its mind. And she is learning where the steep hills are so she can avoid them. She can't trust the car. She's gotten stuck twice. Now there's something wrong with the brakes.

Then Roxanne gets the job at the studio. Sometimes she sleeps at home that year in the other twin bed in the guest room Uncle Louie and Aunt Doris have because the hospital made a mistake in assigning them their apartment. In the guest room Louie and Doris rent to us. Roxanne and I have matching pink chenille bedspreads. Roxanne is vague about how she got them.

Then Roxanne makes a friend. Her name is Jeanette and she's divorced. Jeannette helped her get the job at Columbia Studios, the job in the costume department. Jeanette lives in an apartment with a swimming pool. It's a garden apartment. When Roxanne says garden apartment she has a dangerous intake of breath. I repeat this to myself, garden apartment.

Roxanne says we might be invited there soon. Maybe in the summer for swimming. It would be an invitation for the four of us. A family invitation is the way Roxanne phrases it, making it glitter. Jeanette would include the entire family because she's got a classy background. She went to boarding school in Philadelphia.

We have been invited. Hers is a wide street over the hill in the San Fernando Valley. Roxanne calls it a street but I'm convinced it is a boulevard. I suspect that makes it déclassé. We are standing at the wrought-iron gate. We have to ring a buzzer to get in. This is called a security building. Roxanne savors the words when she says them. She watches them hang their invisible origami in the air and she smiles.

We have been talking about the impending swimming afternoon for weeks. I haven't seen a swimming pool since I've been in California. Roxanne took me up on Sunset Boulevard once. She parked the car and walked through people's gates, onto the sides of their lawns, staring at their gardens, trying to find their gazebos and guest houses and swimming pools. I refused to go with her.

"What are they going to do? Call the cops?" She studied me with something that might have been amusement or the beginning of contempt or some border between the two where they meet and spark. "You're such a square."

Jeanette's swimming pool has become enormous and midnight blue in my mind, a lagoon or inland lake. Perhaps there are tiles on the side, a white that startles like porcelain or bleached bone. And blues that seem cobalt or violet or darker. I imagine the sky will be like a blue skin you could touch; rub your face against it and there would be no fever, no sickness, no one to visit in the hospital.

I am not sure what I expected but this isn't it. We are standing inside the gate—she's buzzed it open for us—and I am staring at the pool. It is shaped like a kidney. I know the structure of all the major organs. You learn this when people explain their diseases to you at the Courts. And the kidney-shaped swimming pool takes up nearly the entire courtyard. It has a blue and white rope around it. Not even a railing, just a rope.

Jeanette shakes hands with me and Uncle Louie and Aunt Doris. Roxanne has explained this unique behavior to me. It is called being gracious. It is part of being born right and going to boarding school.

Jeanette has dark brown hair that hangs down past her shoulders. It is cut into bangs. She is wearing a terry cloth robe over her bathing suit and no makeup. She looks like my sixth-grade teacher.

We are sitting by the pool. There are downstairs apartments and a second floor built around a balcony that circles the courtyard. Everything overlooks the pool. You can see it from all the living rooms and kitchens. There is no sign of flowers. There is no garden.

Jeanette has brought out a pitcher of something called margaritas and a box of salt. She shows Louie how to make the salt stick to the glass. She pours him one drink after another. Doris tells him to stop drinking so much. She whispers this in his ear. He tells her to shut up.

Roxanne and Jeanette are swimming. Other women are in the pool now. They are all thin and blond. Roxanne says they are stews. She explains that means they are stewardesses. I can't tell if this is good or bad. Stews. Doris isn't swimming because she doesn't have a bathing suit. She has one but it doesn't fit. There's no reason to buy another. She just has to start another diet. Then she could fit into the clothing she already has. Louie is sitting in the sun with his hand wrapped around his cane.

"Get Grandpa in," one of the stews says. She is pointing at Uncle Louie.

Uncle Louie stares at the pool. "I can't swim," he replies. "I can't even feel my goddamn legs anymore."

"Come on, Grandpa," the stew repeats. "Don't be a baby."

"Divorcées. They're all whores. All of them. Whores," Uncle Louie says. He lights another cigar. He finishes the pitcher of margaritas.

Everybody keeps swimming. It's almost too crowded to swim. It's more like a form of marine play. The thin blond women do a few handstands, a lap of backstrokes.

We are sitting in the sun on chairs made of wound-together plastic strips like stained bandages that might have been braided. It's incredibly hot. My thighs keep sticking to the chair. I have red welts. I begin to think of the flash at Hiroshima, of being a kind of silk scroll, of having plum branches and swallows engraved into my skin.

I can see TV antennas reflected in the upstairs windows. I look into each apartment. It's like enclosures where humans are displayed in their natural habitats. I watch a woman talk on the telephone. Someone is writing a note. A woman comes out of a shower with a towel in her hand.

I know what the women in the windows are thinking. History can be collected like rows of bottles. It is always the hour of prophecy. You imagine unborn daughters while standing on a veranda in the twilight of stunted orchids. There is the constant sound of a piano.

The sky looks Cloroxed, white at the center, seething. It isn't hot or cold but something else entirely. The water is the same color as the sky, a blue so light it has been rubbed away of intentions, it has been erased. There is only some faint laughter left on the surface and somebody calling Louie Grandpa. There is absolutely no way I am going into that water.

Jeanette and Roxanne come out of the pool. Jeanette makes another pitcher of drinks. I've noticed that every half hour, a child walks up the steps to the second floor apartment in the back. One little girl goes up the stairs and another one comes down. There is a blond with two braids, shorts, and red thongs. Then a girl with curly black hair. Then one with eyeglasses and a green sundress. They are eight or nine or ten. They are much younger than me.

"What's going on?" Roxanne asks, watching the child in the green sundress climb the stairs to the second floor. "Some photo session?" She seems interested.

"Piano lessons. Some old bag gives lessons," Jeanette says.

Roxanne seems startled and confused. If she was a wild animal, she'd be paralyzed in your headlights. You could run her over. "Piano lessons?" she repeats. She looks directly into my eyes. "They still do that? In this day and age?"

Later there was a kind of barbecue. The blond stewardess kept calling Louie Grandpa. He would call her a whore and she would laugh. Even Doris started drinking. When the food came, when the various blond women brought out the chicken legs and salad and rolls, Doris stared at it and shook her head no.

"What was it?" Doris asked in the car on the way home. "Chicken with a sauce? Was that it? Southern?"

I kept thinking about Roxanne's face when she realized the little girls weren't going to auditions. They were taking piano lessons in this day and age. Louie threw up in the car and no one said anything. Roxanne never mentioned Jeanette again. She joined the probable dead, like the woman in Cincinnati who smoked reefers with men who played saxophones.

Years passed before Roxanne made another friend. It was our third or fourth summer in California. I didn't have to go to the clinic for my clothes that year because Roxanne found someone willing to give me her daughter's used clothing. I didn't have to go to the clinic where twice a year they give you a cardboard box with your age written in red marker on the side. If you're too tall or fat you learn to accommodate.

Roxanne is walking into our bedroom at dusk with clothing in plastic bags, the kind of containers you put leaves in after you rake them. You can't find leaves like that in Los Angeles, the ones that turn color and fall. You probably can't even find rakes here.

Roxanne's friend is named Samantha. Her daughter attends a private school. Samantha is the head makeup artist at MGM or Paramount. She used to give her daughter's old clothing to her Mexican maid, but she doesn't think her maid really appreciates the gesture, the quality of the fabric and the styling. So now she gives them to me.

These are not just used garments but magical vestiges of life in another region. They are clues and beacons. That's how Roxanne sees it, how she says the words private school. It is more serious than saying security building or garden apartment. These words are intoned. If you say private school often enough, something might rub off and we could be elevated. This is the moment you unlock the stone and decipher what coils at the core. This is where you must be alert. This is when someone could get lucky.

"Private school," Roxanne repeats. She is simultaneously stunned and grateful, almost breathless.

To me they are just blouses that don't fit, skirts that are too long, and once, a maroon sweater with a black tennis racket stitched on the collar. It clashed with the rest of the mismatched items that came out of the trash bag. Roxanne was studying my face.

"You're never satisfied," she said. "No matter what I do, it's never enough for you."

Roxanne is sitting on the floor beside the two plastic trash bags. She has them near her, as if they were already intimate. She leans into them. She is examining each skirt, blouse, and dress as if the fabric might be imparting history into the fibers of her fingers. Maybe the cloth was a kind of text.

"You know how clean private-school girls are," she says to me.

I don't respond. I don't know how clean they are, so Roxanne explains it to me. Private-school girls have regular shampoos. They take a bath every night. They can do that because they don't have to wait to use the tub. They don't live with somebody like Louie who needs the bathroom for hours at a time, you never know when. There are the medicines, the spillage and cleanup, the ointments, the bandages and the secret procedures, the things Doris has to help him with.

Private-school girls have their sheets changed at least once a week. They live in a region where the shortage of linens is not a problem. Their sheets are ironed for them. They are perfumed. When some article of clothing becomes flawed in even a minor way, they discard it. Sometimes they give clothing away just because they're tired of it or because their concept of fashion has changed. Or perhaps it no longer pleases them. It's that simple.

I glance at the used clothing Roxanne has managed to assemble and stuff into plastic trash bags and I am thinking that this particular private-school girl gives her stuff away because it is just plain worn out. I'm looking at a powder blue angora sweater with a thick brown band along the collar and cuffs. Roxanne is holding the sweater tenderly in her arms, as if she might press it into her chest and attempt to nurse it at any minute.

I have developed a monumental hatred for the sweater. All of the buttons but one are missing and there is what appears to be a bullet hole in the right front pocket. I would never choose such a sweater for myself, with or without the buttons. In fact, I've never selected an item of clothing for myself in my life. I wouldn't even know how to do it.

Roxanne is still enumerating the superior hygiene habits of private-school girls. It's like the plus side of the patriarchy. You can see why it's been in business for millions of years.

Private-school girls have their own bedrooms. Someone's new boyfriend isn't coming into their room in the darkness, isn't leaping from hallway shadows with his bathrobe undone. Private-school girls have locks on their doors. Strange men aren't going to pull down their panties in laundry rooms on the sides of alleys bordering freeways. Their mothers are married. There is a father in the house.

Private-school girls have their own individual backyards. They don't play on the sides of boulevards behind apartment complexes. If a stranger entered these yards behind white picket fences and rose bushes, the father would shoot him.

I'm thinking they should post a sign in front of the pastel ranch houses on the other side of Sepulveda Boulevard where the intacts live. It should say BEWARE, FATHER INSIDE. People should be warned like they are about dogs and burglar alarms.

Roxanne is gazing at the powder blue sweater with an expression of immeasurable tenderness. "You're not sophisticated enough," she concludes. She seems almost resigned. "You don't appreciate."

She motions me to stand up. I stand. There is an article of clothing she wants me to try on. I put it on. It is a green-and-red-checked skirt that looks like a tablecloth from Christmas. It might have covered a banquet table in Bavaria.

The skirt flares and puffs and billows. It's like it has its own climate and it is a cloudy season. It makes you think of wind and feasts and winter. The skirt touches below my ankles and I am already one of the tallest girls in my class. Roxanne is fastening the waist of the skirt with a safety pin.

I am standing in the Black Forest Christmas tablecloth that is down to my ankles and pinned at my waist. I know I'm going to have to climb steps like I was royalty from the Middle Ages. I'm going to have to hold my skirt in my hands and pretend it's dinner time at Versailles. I'm going to have to pin and unpin the skirt for gym class. That fact alone fills me with a kind of grief. Something metallic is turning inside my flesh and in another region, somewhere along the continuum, I am beginning to bleed.

I have put on one of the private-school girls' immaculate white blouses. It has yellow stains under the armpits. Roxanne refuses to see this. The blouse is so tight the button won't stay shut across my curiously developed chest. I am wearing my old maroon sweater with the tennis racket on the collar and the initials WIM embroidered on the breast pocket.

"Imagine," Roxanne is musing. "Private-school girls'

clothes." She examines the place where I am standing but she doesn't see me.

"It looks like Christmas," I say. This is a dangerous moment. I keep my voice tentative and neutral.

"So?" Roxanne comes out of her reverie. She lights a cigarette.

"So we're Jewish," I try. I wonder what will happen.

"That's nobody's business," Roxanne tells me. There is something tight at the corners of her mouth. I think of puppets with strings that get pulled. Maybe Roxanne will start to dance soon.

"But I have to say it. You have to write your religion on the forms." The air between us is becoming charged and chaotic. Soon there will be luminous debris. It's a renegade night and water is falling.

Roxanne stares at me. "What forms?"

"At school," I tell her.

I am draped in a sort of banquet tablecloth that should be in a room with arched windows, torches, carved wood, and banners hanging from the ceiling. I am wearing a ruined maroon sweater with someone else's initials. I am squinting through my thick black plastic clinic eyeglasses with the nest of scratches on the thick lenses and I can't get new ones until Vision Day in January. I am fourteen years old and I need a cigarette.

"At school?" Roxanne repeats. "They've got some nerve. It's none of their goddamn business. We have separation of powers."

I am confused about religion. Once I told Aunt Doris that I wanted to go to a temple. It was a night when Roxanne was gone. A night when Roxanne was on location, perhaps. That's what she said. And if I had a definite religion, I could beseech the god of film sites to make my mother telephone.

"What is she talking? What? Like a Buddhist temple? A Moslem temple?" Uncle Louie asked. He was holding a deck in his palm, caressing the surface with his fingers. "They have that here?"

"She means a synagogue," Aunt Doris said.

Aunt Doris was sifting through the cigar box she kept her jewelry in. She was examining her collection of pins. She is going to be picked up for her job as hostess at Canter's Delicatessen. Tonight she wears a quartz triangle. It might be a stained arrowhead. It is some configuration that makes you think of barbarians, betrayal, a spoiled and stagnant wind. It makes me think of the women in the windows by the highways, staring out past the irrigation ditches, trying to remember where they put the steel traps and the chemicals.

Doris is getting a ride to work because Les Downer says there's nothing more he can do. The car is on its last legs. It can be used for emergencies only. It's as if Roxanne's red convertible got us to California and now it has cancer. It is spreading through its bones. I think it should chew off its leg and make a run for it.

"A synagogue?" Uncle Louie repeats. "No. We can't do that."

I want to know why. Doris is standing in front of the screen door. She has put on the tarnished quartz pin. It makes you think of sin and some hopeless regret, something you did that you're not sure of, so there's no way to make amends. Aunt Doris has orange lipstick on. Her hair is completely yellow. She calls it platinum. It must be summer. She isn't wearing a sweater.

"Synagogues are not for people like us. You got to know the rules to get in. They got a whole special code. They got passwords. They got sentries at the doors. They don't let people like us in. You have to know the right answers. Besides, that's a place for squares." Uncle Louie stares at the tip of his cigar.

No temples. No circling. No plants. No unnecessary driving. Always ask for the supervisor. Demand your money back. There is no God. Winter doesn't figure. Everything's coming up roses. Do not run out of ice cream. Make them remember you. It doesn't cost.

Now Roxanne walks over to the mirror. This is a moment you need a password for and even that might not save you. Roxanne recently became a blond. It would be an experiment that didn't pan out. After a few months she would become a redhead again.

"Only hillbillies fill out forms," she says. "People on welfare fill out forms. Look at me. It's America. I could be anything. Look how blond I am." She nods her head at her reflection. The two Roxannes sway.

"You dye your hair," I point out, remembering the vile-smelling bottles, the special plastic gloves. Roxanne had me time the procedure exactly. I had to watch the clock for eighteen minutes or her hair would fall out. And I would be responsible. Then there were ugly stains on the towel. Doris said she would have to replace it. She was going to have to charge Roxanne for it. And the border of her forehead turned red and looked burned. I began to think about atomic bombs.

"How dare you say that? How dare you lie like that?" Roxanne turns around. The mirror is behind her and she's crossing the room. She is what happens when the spell is lifted. You wake up hungry and mad. You want the lost time back. You want it with interest. "You stinking little square. Look at you," she says.

My shoulders tense. She is going to hit me. She has the hairbrush in her hand. I protect my face with my arms. I make the little shell around my head. I close my eyes so nothing can get in. This is my metal armature. She can hit me on the shoulder now. I am used to that.

"You wear private-school girls' clothes and it doesn't change you. What you are. A liar. I should have left you in Jersey with that other drag-ass." Roxanne hits my shoulder with her hairbrush. "I'm going to tell them at school you're lying again. They want my reports, you can be sure. They know I'm a keen observer. They're astonished by my vocabulary. I can tell. Get out of my sight," Roxanne says.

I am pushing open the front door. I am standing on the lawn and I keep going. I hold my skirt in my hands. I am Marie Antoinette and I am running for my life.

15

There are winds in our skulls I am certain. There are currents and oceans. Images become buried and sunken, remote and lavender, in the periphery, below the surface, behind our foreheads.

I wake up thinking about this, how I will have to recover these lost artifacts, these vessels and who was on them and where and why they sailed. I'll have to go diving and retrieve them.

That's when I suddenly remember the flood control, the artificial concrete river on the other side of the boulevard just south of the Courts. It was empty and aching from sun. When it rained, an abrupt urban river formed, gray always and reckless.

The flood control was behind a locked fence but there were gaps in the wires. Aunt Doris has forbidden me to go there. I go anyway. I am attracted to the bushes with their thorns and rancid black berries with bitter yellow juice, the way there isn't really a path and how stiff the grasses are, the strident weeds. I am intrigued by the possibility of danger, of getting cut or stained.

I walk alone along the edge and the Courts disappear. I pretend I have traveled back through time. I am exploring a primeval wilderness.

I once read a science fiction story about a man who went back in time and accidentally stepped on a butterfly and the entire course of human history was changed. Something hadn't been able to eat that particular butterfly, a bigger creature that starved and all along the line everything was different. Eventually, some primitive man came back empty-handed from hunting mammoths and died. And the universe was completely altered because of this.

I walk beside the flood control wishing I could find the comparable things to step on, to crush utterly, some beetles perhaps, a row of black ants or a stray lizard. Then there will be no Courts, no Aunt Doris and Uncle Louie. It will not be a form of erasure but rather a correction, the extinction of aberration. There will be no mourning. Instead there will be a celebration.

It is the summer I am almost twelve. I am learning that in the Courts it may be more painful to survive than to die. I am considering the permutations of this and the two fears everyone in the Courts share. There is the fear of the iron lung and the fear of having to move.

When someone says the word *move,* it opens in slow motion like a disturbed flower or a death kiss. Moving is a neon orange that pulses. Moving is in the category with biopsy, exploratory surgery, malignancy, and recurrence. It is a kind of radioactive sin.

It is August and I am alone. I push the bushes apart, searching for tossed-away soda bottles. I throw rocks into the flood control, chips of asphalt, pieces of white gravel. I consider the concept of bone-dry and how this concrete channel is exactly that and how the sun seems to hurt it. I wonder if this is deliberate.

I am thinking about the unwritten law in the Courts that says you must never do anything that will allow them to make you move. You can't draw attention, as Doris would say. You can't jeopardize.

If they make you move, you could lose your cleaning deposit. That's rigged from the jump, as Roxanne would say. It's like a tax on breathing. They know you're going to spill something or nick the side of a wall. Somebody is going to vomit. You know they're keeping the deposit no matter what.

Then you would need a first and last month's rent for a new apartment. It wouldn't be subsidized housing either. It would be four or five times more than what we are now paying. And you would have to rent a truck or find somebody with access to a hick with a pickup and make a deal.

And what makes you think they even want to rent to you, at any price? A man with a cane who might end up in a wheelchair and a brooding kid with her nose in a book? Nobody wants to rent to kids and cripples.

What if you are living a few miles from the hospital and something with the fluids and bandaging suddenly opens or closes? What about infection or a problem with breathing? What if they change the treatment schedule and your bus is late? What if you can't walk from the bus stop? What if they begin to think you're trouble and decide not to give you any more pills or chemicals, surgeries or screenings, tests or follow-ups? What if you make somebody angry?

It is a suspended summer when nothing has coalesced. There are no directions and the compass points are all an identical bleached blue. They are born used up. There are no decisions that can make a difference. There are no destinations worth mentioning.

Roxanne is somewhere moving around and making up for lost time. The afternoons when she curled on her side on the sofa watching TV. The twilights when she wore her floppy slippers and said she had a headache, don't come near her. Then the days in the car lot and saving the money. Now she is somewhere without a telephone number.

I am wandering along the cement gash they call flood control. In this region rain is rare and the inhabitants cannot endure it. Louie says they are hillbillies who don't know how to drive. He says it's the in-breeding. So they have created a network of concrete gullies to dispose of the feared water when it comes. In this Southern California, rain is perceived as a danger. It's a form of poison.

It is before I become friends with Jimmy and Pamela. It is before the clubhouse with our shrine and candles in the laundry room. I am all alone in California. I will always be all alone. I can feel it. I have crossed the boulevard and squeezed through a warp in the wire fence and walked through stiff weeds that scratch, wrap around my ankle, and make me fall. I like getting cut.

I pretend it's a real river with magical properties. It's a channel into the past and future, into the portals. When you look at such waters, you can see blue flames and ridges of magnificent bruise. You could never divest yourself of such waters. They would become a part of you.

It's late afternoon. The air is a startling white, the color of ruins. I imagine it's the end of the world. It's a war and the nuclear bomb has fallen. Fortunately, I am not in the city when this occurs.

In my fantasies, when the bomb falls, I am always camped along an impossibly blue river in the country beyond the desert. It is the blue of glaciers, mourning, and amulets. Nights are Joshua trees and shooting stars. The air is inordinately thin. You need to be rooted here, above the valley floor, beyond the date palms in rows, above the tumbleweed and lemon trees. There are stones along the river shore. They are not just pebbles but an augury, a prophecy the mountains birthed.

The bomb falls and I am protected. I had an intuition. Something spoke to me in a dream. I hid behind rocks and buried my head in the shell I made with my arms.

Survivors from the surrounding countryside find their way to my camp. There are rumors about my extraordinary knowledge. They bring their sick children. I know the intricacies of the plants and how to decipher them, how to make medicines, foods, cloth. I organize agricultural and educational units. I assemble plants that make ink and leaves that can become paper. With these I rewrite the history of the world.

I alone can determine what should be preserved and what should be cast into the radioactive wasteland of perpetual forgetting. The place where the words are singed off. It is my responsibility, these acts of salvage and erasure. I am fluent in sorcery. I know the avenues of solace and grace.

Now it is just before sunset behind the gauze of the

clouds. It suddenly feels like the place of the gone, the alcove of the severing. The time when my father vanished, when Roxanne drove him away with her pink plastic rollers and her cramps.

I'm trying to remember what my father looked like. I don't have any photographs. Roxanne left them in New Jersey. We carried the photo albums out to the trash cans and dumped them in. We had to keep our flanks clean. We threw the pictures away with my collection of dolls in native costumes, with the sofa pillows we couldn't sell and the frying pans too heavy to carry. My mother said they didn't figure anymore. She was looking at me as if trying to determine whether or not I figured anymore. Was I too big for the trash can? If she took me, would they still come at her from behind? What if she left me by the side of some road? She could say I wandered away when she wasn't looking. She could say it wasn't her fault. Figure. What a strange word, conjuring simultaneously bodies and mathematics. Then I look up and see him.

He might be one of the fathers from Palm Courts. He has the right kind of shirt and pants, faded and shabby, some shade of green like a stain or hospital walls. He is motioning me over to him. He is in a hedge of wild coral oleander. Maybe he is stuck there. Maybe he has a trap around his ankle, some metal thing like the ones they use on fox and bears, raccoons and coyotes. Maybe there is a tiny swamp, quicksand.

The man is bending over and I realize that he's hurt. It's something with stitches or a tube. Perhaps a sudden pain or a spasm. Maybe I should make a tourniquet.

In the Courts, we are taught life-saving procedures. They show us films before we get our clothes in the cardboard boxes with our ages written in red marker on the side. They sign the clothing distribution forms after the film. If you don't see it, you can't get the clothing box. The films teach us how to give mouth-to-mouth resuscitation and how to stop the flow of blood with direct pressure and where the points are.

"Over here," the man says. He's calling me with his hands. "I want to show you something."

I go because I think he's sick and for that curious moment I'm half-convinced it's Ernie. It is the verge of sunset. It feels like sunset is a direction. I have the sense that the world is holding its breath. Maybe it is wishing for something it doesn't dare to name. And this must be Ernie returned from the place of the wounded gone. He wants me to sit on his lap. He must be my father or why would he want me to do that?

I don't think there is anything wrong yet. The sun is setting in trenches of fuchsia and maroon and plum above the flood control, which isn't really a river. It won't go to the sea. You can't raft it, can't take the survivors down to the ocean and teach them to fish with nets and lines and sharpened sticks. I've been considering the many ways there are to fish. If you're going to rewrite the history of the world, you must know these things. It must be seasonal, the implements. After a time, you would learn the currents and what they bring. The bass and halibut would return. You could use the teeth from sharks to make weapons. When whales chance to wash ashore you could have oil. When you got bored you could invent lamps.

"Put it in your mouth," he says. "It'll fit. Go on."

I see he is right. I can accommodate this. It's when I taste the fluid I become afraid. It tastes like the sea water Aunt

Doris says is polluted. There are signs at the pier at Santa Monica Bay not to eat the fish or the mussels. They are contaminated. There are accumulations and reckonings. Uncle Louie says white people don't eat such fish. Now I have the clammy stuff in my hair.

It tastes like something that should be in a tube. You should have the doctor look at it, maybe run a few tests. That's when I start to go and suddenly I know I'm supposed to run. Then I am in the living room and Aunt Doris is bending over me. She's shaking me by the shoulders. She must be getting ready for work. She's wearing the garnet-like *T* on her breast, the one with the big blue stone at the top. The initials have nothing to do with her name. Uncle Louie keeps staring out the screen door. He is searching for something on the other side of the lawn. Then the street lamps go on. There are arcs of orange everywhere.

"You're going to make trouble," Aunt Doris is saying.

I slowly realize she isn't talking about me. She is aiming her words at Uncle Louie. He is trying to open the screen door with his cane but Aunt Doris won't let him. She's grabbed his sleeve. She's pulling his sweater. She may tear it.

"Let go," Uncle Louie says. "I'm going to kill him."

"What are you talking about? What? A kid says something? A kid says something and right away you believe?" Aunt Doris is still pulling the sleeve of his sweater. It's a pale green like certain pebbles you find at the edge of rivers and oceans. It's cashmere. It's the last sweater Louie has from the old days. He had a pair of white leather shoes from Italy but he wore them to follow-up one Monday and they were stolen.

Uncle Louie is staring at her. "Don't you believe her?"

Aunt Doris thinks it over. She lights a cigarette. "That's not the point," she says. She has let go of Louie's cashmere sweater.

"What's the point?" Uncle Louie asks.

"Moving," Aunt Doris says. "You want to move? You want to jeopardize?"

Uncle Louie is considering his options. It is early evening. If the bomb fell when I wasn't in the city, I might survive the initial blast. There would be the fallout, the black rain of invisible death particles, the hurricane winds carrying torn glass in enormous sheets the size of walls and buildings. There would be a morning of decapitation and severed arms. You would get used to this.

Then there would be the barbarians in the streets, killing one another for cans of peaches, cigarettes and beer. They could have a party by the side of the river that isn't a river. They could mutilate one another with pieces of automobiles and Zippo lighters. They could have little girls sit on their laps and open their mouths. They could think that the disintegration of the world was just like going to heaven.

Aunt Doris walks over to the couch where I'm sitting. I have pulled my legs up near my chest. I have wrapped myself in my arms. I can see the white fluid in my hair. It's dried and it flakes off. I can close my eyes and it smells like night and old flowers. It smells like night in the last harbor at the end of the world. Aunt Doris is studying my face.

"Did he get inside?" Aunt Doris asks. "Did he get under your panties?"

I say no.

I can hear the sirens of an ambulance driving into Palm Courts West. Somebody's sister or mother is bleeding and they can't stop it, not even with direct pressure. Somebody probably tried to make a tourniquet and it isn't working. They keep a list of how many times you call for an ambulance. If they think you are abusing the staff, if they think you're crying wolf and not coping, they could ask you to move.

"Are you sure?" Doris turns her attention from me to Louie. "Are you hearing, Louie? Tell him. Are you sure?"

"He only," I start to say something and stop. "No. He just—"

"He didn't get inside you, right? So nothing really happened," Aunt Doris says. "You hearing, Louie? Nothing really happened."

"But he—"

"—didn't get inside so nothing really happened." Aunt Doris finishes my sentences for me. She's already decided what I should say.

"She should go to a doctor," Uncle Louie decides. He isn't looking out the screen door for the man anymore. I told him what the man was wearing, pants green like hospital walls and fluids that have leaked, that spilled, that make you think of aquariums and tubes and some stretch of ruined sea. If the man from the flood control walked by now, Louie wouldn't hit him over the head with his cane after all.

"A doctor?" Aunt Doris repeats. "A doctor, no less. For what?"

"She should get checked," Uncle Louie says. He's just going through the motions. I can tell he doesn't care anymore.

"And jeopardize? And have to move? What are you, crazy? What is this? The two-thousand-dollar insult? You that insulted, Louie?" Aunt Doris flicks the ash of her cigarette.

Doris walks over to the bridge table. She's touching a fresh deck. She opens and closes her fingers around it, slowly. She's trying to hypnotize Louie. This is a variation on a technique employed in the taming of wild animals. I can tell which deck it is from across the room. It's the ballet dancers with their coiled black hair and pink legs.

Maybe Doris and Louie can play a few rubbers of two-handed bridge before she gets picked up for work. In a few minutes they'll sit down at the card table. Louie will lean his cane against his leg, in case he needs it, and light a cigar. Maybe Doris will fill the candy dish with the party almonds. Maybe it's a party night.

"But he made me put it in my—"

"Take a bath," Aunt Doris says. "Then go to bed. It's bedtime."

I take a bath and run the water as hot as I can. I use some of Roxanne's emerald bubble bath. I don't refill the bottle with water so she won't know. I don't care if she finds out. I wash the white paste out of my hair. I shampoo it twice. I use mouthwash when I brush my teeth.

I would tell my people in the desert that they could survive the nuclear holocaust. I would explain to them that there are no unforgivable landscapes. On closer inspection, vacancy reveals itself as a series of paths between creosote, yucca, and agave. You must navigate the sand that burns. You must risk the abrupt night and the valley floor the color of flesh. Then you see it, indigo bushes and paloverde and the violet flower of the ironwood.

Roxanne appears the next afternoon. It occurs to me that she really does have a telephone number. Louie and Doris must have a way of reaching her. She's a woman after all. She isn't a bird that we have to lure with special seeds and wait motionless in the hush before dusk, hoping to get lucky.

I walk in from school and there she is at the round Formica table in the kitchen where no one ever sits. Louie says it's too steep and narrow. He has to sit in the middle of the room so his knees can bend. It's like his legs are made out of metal now. And Doris doesn't like the kitchen table because it's too close to the refrigerator, it's too much a temptation.

Roxanne is doing her nails. She has the cotton balls out, the polish remover with its vivid lemon scent that makes me think of our journey through the West, and the various vials and bottles. She has a new black velvet case that opens to reveal a pouch where brushes with silver handles stick out. They look like forks with bristles. They look like something from the desert.

Roxanne has her reds lined up in order of intensity. They are illuminated with heat and garish promise. Perhaps she has arranged them according to the severity of their burn. There are reds that seem inspired, tinged with purple. That's the night insinuating itself, tarnishing it. I am staring at the polishes and trying to understand them in a broader context when she says, "I heard."

Louie and Doris are gone. It must be a Monday. The Buckners must have picked them up to go to Palms Memorial for follow-up. Dolores Buckner hasn't had the cancer spread to her liver yet. She still thinks the disc in her skull and the tube in her ear are it. Roxanne is listening to the radio news.

"What is this shit with the moon?" She asks. "The moon, no less."

She is studying her left hand. It looks like a leaf, a tacked-on afterthought. So much of the world is like that, vacant and half-formed and accidental. Places of the vast gray nothing and no one cares anymore.

"You know what man is?" Roxanne asks. She is looking past me, toward the living room table where the radio is. In my family people stare at the radio like they believe that will help them hear and understand better. "Man is a baboon. We're baboons with panties on. We're baboons with car keys and machine guns."

I realize she's talking about the man by the flood control. The man who gestured to me. I went over to him because he seemed somehow broken and I thought he might be my father. Now this other man has also vanished. It's a world where men flicker into invisibility. First the soft lavender pulsing you convince yourself you are imagining and then there are the half-lives and then there is nothing.

"I was afraid you'd be mad," I realize.

"I'm not mad. You know why?" Roxanne is watching the light glance off the polish on her nails of her left hand. The left hand is about intuition and the soul. It's about artistic impulses and solving mysteries. Somebody in the prop department at Warner's told her that. I don't say anything. I know she'll tell me.

"I'm not mad because I don't take it personal. It's like a random act of nature. It's like a tornado. Who are you going to sue? That man, he's some kind of psycho. You were in the wrong place at the wrong time. It's like being hit by lightning. He's an accident and now it's over," Roxanne said.

Tonight there will be a full moon, an aching white that wants promises, wants to tell you tales. It hasn't occurred to me that I should memorize these events, their textures.

I haven't yet thought of personal history in terms of sequences and strata.

"It's like a street tax," Roxanne says. "That's what it costs to grow up in a stinking city."

"Can you spend the night?" I ask. It is later. I am trying to keep the tear that has formed from falling down my cheek. No farm products. Nothing that has roots or comes from the ground. No circling. No touching of the car. If you can't sue, forget it. No God. Protect your flank. Winter doesn't figure. No crying.

"I go to Vegas tonight," Roxanne says. "Sinatra's in town. Everything's jumping."

Roxanne has finished her nails. She's plugging in the new electric rollers for her hair. What a century, Roxanne likes to say, everything from the bomb to the birth control pill. And they keep developing new beauty products.

I am leaning in the doorway of the bedroom we occasionally share. There will be a full moon in Las Vegas tonight. Everything will be jumping. I consider acres of insects on sand, frogs, grasshoppers, locust, and crickets. I try to imagine what she means.

"By the way," Roxanne says, her voice false and light, "if Louie comes into your room some night and tells you to open your mouth, open it wide as you can and scream."

I see it's a one-suitcase situation. Roxanne is packing the medium-sized red one. I can often determine where she is going and how long she'll be gone by which luggage she takes. I also study the bathrobes. The bathrobes give you some indication of climate. You can't tell by the packages of birth control pills. Roxanne always takes at least half a dozen. Just in case. She might have to be gone half a year. Something could happen. One medium red suitcase. It could be anything.

"Please, Roxanne," I say. I almost call her Mother.

"I'll come back later," she tells me. She is near the front door.

Doris and Louie have come home. She is handing something to Doris. Money. I can see the cab turning in past the padlocked kiosk. I didn't see her telephone it. Perhaps someone called it for her.

"When?" I am staring at her. "When will you be back?"

"On the weekend, maybe," Roxanne says. She has the suitcase in her hand now. She sounds vague. Then she is moving out the screen door and across the lawn. She is being careful with her high-heeled shoes and the grass.

It is a full moon in August and I am nearly twelve. I can sense the star jasmine opening itself to the night. Soon Roxanne will be on a plane with the city immobile below like a beast too numb and slow to run, something with a brain of stone. She will be above the hills where dry brush waits for sparks.

I am also dry and white and still. I feel like I have a forest fire in my forehead. I have some fever they will never diagnose and I know there is no treatment. And I don't want to watch her leave. It's better to walk into my room, pretend to do something with my pen and the lamp. That way, when I look up, Roxanne is already gone.

16

It is autumn when I discover that I have one breast. It's after the man who wasn't my father by the river that wasn't a river, the flood control at sunset when the sky fell down like a violet net and I was caught. It's after the man that Louie and Doris say never happened. I made it up because I'm selfish. I tell lies because I don't appreciate. They report that to the teachers at school. It's the year Roxanne has become somebody I'm forced to call Sis.

It is the land of tainted burgundy air and too much strange orange falling from the sky and rising from the pavement. It is always a brass noon. There are the streets that remain after experiment and regret. This is what the ground refuses.

My mother has been juxtaposed. She is living in reverse and we are becoming siblings. My Uncle Louie is becoming a cyborg. He's in a wheelchair now. He has metal legs. He pushes buttons to move. He's had another cobalt vacation. They are trying him on chemo, too. There is the matter of the residues. Anything can happen.

It is morning. I am silently counting my griefs and arranging them in hierarchical order. I am standing in front of the bathroom mirror and I suddenly see it. One of my breasts has emerged fully developed. It's what I later find out is a size 36C. The other side is practically flat.

I wonder how I failed to notice this earlier. One of the fundamental rules in my family is that you must constantly examine your body for indications of cataclysm. Things manifest themselves in the night. There are revisions in the cool darkness where the borders are not resolved and the land masses shift. There can be a crawling out. You must pay complete attention.

Obviously I have not been sensitive enough to subtleties. After all, there really are seasons in Los Angeles. August follows July with a stark coherence. And it is nothing like November. In August you want to leap from a roof. Your flesh craves pavement and a mouth full of gravel. November, on the other hand, is almost plausible. You sense the unexpected could happen. And it has.

I am standing in front of the square mirror above the bathroom medicine cabinet, which is filled with bottles of diet pills, sleeping tablets, tranquilizers, and pain medication. My first thought is that I must immediately ingest a bottle of sedatives and kill myself.

I can't believe how many pills are stuffed in the medicine cabinet. They fall out when you open the door. We may be out of food, even canned goods, but we have our medicines. We need them like we need air and a roof. Doris has dozens of bottles of diet pills. She takes five or six tablets a day now. Roxanne takes a few, too. Sometimes even Louie needs some.

Uncle Louie's got an entire shelf of sleeping pills. He's been hoarding them for years, siphoning off a few a week. In the Courts, everybody secretly stockpiles Seconal. You need them as a hedge against lingering. You need them in case they threaten you with the iron lung. You're supposed to overdose then. That's called going out with class. This is known as doing the right thing.

I decide to move to the bedroom mirror. Perhaps there is a distortion in just that particular glass. I walk into the bedroom and I look precisely the same there. I am holding a bottle of Seconal and I immediately think about *The Metamorphosis* by Franz Kafka. "As Gregor Samsa awoke one morning from uneasy dreams he found himself transformed in his bed into a gigantic insect." That's the first line. I liked it so much I memorized it. Now this.

I have always viewed *The Metamorphosis* as the first great tale of mutation. Gregor Samsa had a terrible family life. Perhaps his physical distortion was a kind of visual cancer that grew from the contempt and indifference his family felt for him. I can relate to that.

I wonder if I let Gregor Samsa become a player in my world, an entity. You have to be careful about what you read, what you allow into your flesh and your molecular structure and memory. It is possible images also have half-lives. Perhaps it takes generations to subdue and erase them. I can appreciate that now, but it seems to be too late.

We are skilled at first aid in Palm Courts. We have

learned not to panic at the first appearance of a dislodged tube, organ, bone. You must remain calm. If you keep calling the ambulance service, you may give the staff the idea that you are not coping.

I move slowly as if underwater. I open Roxanne's drawer and take out one of her cream-colored bras. I fasten it and then stuff a gym sock in the other side, the one without a breast. It's like I've already had a mastectomy. I have always suspected that all things are contagious and now I am convinced. Something from the Courts infiltrated my body, it invaded me, perhaps while I slept and now I am deformed.

I go to school. I am wearing my white blouse with the snaps and my regulation black gym shorts. I walk around the room bent, worried that my sock is going to fall out. No one seems to notice how I move in a weird crouch. I wave one arm in slow arcs for balance. I feel simian, like I'm canoeing and everything is wet.

They've been threatening to banish me to special gym class. I've refused to show the right effort in normal gym. I don't care if I don't do fifty push-ups and fifty sit-ups. I don't care if I can't walk fifty miles. I am incapable of taking such activities seriously. There is some kind of collective hysteria about the number fifty. It has nothing to do with me.

Later that week Roxanne comes home from Mexico. I can tell it was Mexico by her tan, the red in it. The Cannes tan is a tease. You lose it on your way to the plane. But you can count on the Mexican red to last at least ten days. Roxanne says it's like wearing rose petals.

I tell her we need to talk. I close our bedroom door. I remove my blouse.

"I don't see anything," Roxanne tells me. She blows smoke between us. "Jesus, you scared me. I thought you were pregnant."

"Pregnant?" I repeat.

"You got the equipment. You've got the right," Roxanne says. She sounds philosophical. She picks up a skirt and studies her hand through the material. She makes her hand sway. The fabric looks like a veil. Maybe her hand is getting married.

"Don't you see a certain asymmetry here?" I am breathing evenly. My voice is low. I am spacing my words appropriately. I am not suggesting we telephone the paramedics. Anyone can see that I am coping.

"No." Roxanne says. She is staring out the window with its slice of lawn beyond the blinds, its hedge of hibiscus singed pink with a desperate yellow bud in its center. Trees are a greenish black that have no shadow. There may have been a shadow once, but it was lost between the fronds and the sidewalk. It was lost in translation. Then they said it never happened.

"What do you see?" I ask.

"Some selfish kid saying they have a problem. Stop complaining. You don't have a problem. Nothing you won't grow out of," Roxanne tells me. She opens her bureau. She puts a pair of nylon stockings over her hand and evaluates their color. There are nuances to consider. Things can happen to taupe and beige and cinnamon between the air and your skin. There are universes of bronze shades and how they react on your leg.

"So there is something to grow out of?" I persist. I am prepared to be completely objective. I walk back to the bedroom mirror. I am totally disfigured. "So there is a problem," I repeat. My voice feels small and ragged. It's something you could put back in a drawer and forget about.

"Auschwitz is a problem," Roxanne says, annoyed. "They tattoo a number to your wrist, put you on a train, and send you out to the lime pits with a shovel, that's a problem."

My eyes moisten. I blink them dry. I have cast-iron tear ducts. No circling. No walking. Avoid soil. No television. No contact with the ground. Stockpile Seconal. Prepare for suicide every day. That's called having dignity. No sissy-ass God stuff. That's for morons and hayseeds and cowards. And no crying. Crying is a luxury activity. It belongs to a class of people who haven't had to worry about where dinner was coming from for generations. If you're crying, it proves you have time on your hands.

"Dachau is a problem. They pull the gold fillings out of your mouth and make a lampshade out of your infant's skin, then you got a problem," Roxanne tells me.

I stand in front of the mirror and shut my eyes. Maybe something seeped into the glass and infected it. But the necessary correction has occurred. I will open my eyes and the temporary aberration will be removed. I open my eyes and it is still there.

"The camps? What am I talking?" Roxanne says. She shakes her head to indicate a revision of her thought. "You wake up with a lump and it's cancer. One day you're humming on the sidewalk, then they tell you you've got six months left." Roxanne lights a cigarette. She examines some configuration outside the window, some sequence of shadow. I think of willows, bridges, hyacinths, a new moon. "These are the camps," she says. Then she glances at her watch. "I have to make a phone call," she decides.

I study the place on the bed where my mother who is now my sister sat. I hear her voice on the telephone. I smell the separate elements that comprise her, powder, hair spray, perfume, and some essence that comes off her skin, like wild oranges, perhaps. And something that is left by heat and lilacs, a trace you can't actually identify but recall later and only with uncertainty.

I envision a train crowded with one-breasted women being sent to the lime pits. They are carrying shovels. The sun is screened by clouds. It looks like a thin violet crescent.

"You need to develop a sense of perspective," Roxanne is saying. She is brushing her hair. "You got food, a roof and nothing coming at you in the dark. That's better than most. That's a good season, believe me. That's a winning season."

"I don't feel the thrill of victory," I say.

"That's because you're selfish. And you've got to tough up," Roxanne tells me. "You're like sheltered. Jesus, you're like a convent girl."

When Roxanne walks out of the bedroom I follow her. I am at her heels. She is halfway to the curb and I'm still behind her. I'll walk to Vegas if I have to. That's when I look up and see him, a man with a belly and no hair waiting in a gold car.

"It's my sister," Roxanne gestures behind her shoulder. She doesn't turn around. "She got some bad news. She got a bad paper in math."

"You should get her hair fixed. You're so good at stuff like that," he says to Roxanne. His voice is light. He's not criticizing. Nobody criticizes Roxanne. He's just observing the world, no big deal. He's gotten out of the car. He walks around and opens the passenger side for her. "Look. It's hanging all over her face. She needs a haircut. Here," the man removes something from his wallet. He hands it to Roxanne. She glances at it before she gives it to me.

It's a five-dollar bill. I watch them drive away. Roxanne gives me her biggest smile. It's the movie star on the riverboat yellow chrysanthemum float at the Rose Parade wave. It's not just me but all of America she's waving good-bye to. She's wearing her red silk scarf. I can see it blocks away. I let the money fall to the curb. It's still there, in the gutter, when I walk back to the apartment.

A month later, I go to Family Day at the clinic at Palms Memorial Hospital. This is when families of the patient receive their annual Christmas physical examination. You get to select what kind of doctor you want to see.

The girls usually check the box for gynecologist. That's the formality before you get your automatic six-month renewable prescription for birth control pills. In the Courts, the boys go to Youth Authority or disappear. The girls get pregnant. The district doesn't want to spend money educating us. Why should they? It's becoming increasingly difficult to transcend your circumstances. This is what I'm thinking about as I fill out a form requesting an appointment with a plastic surgeon.

Then I go to the Family Aid Special Projects office in the basement. This is where we get our annual Christmas gift and food package. The holiday food package usually consists of a twelve-pound turkey, a can of cranberries, a yam and a white potato for each family member, and a loaf of bread. Sometimes there are extra donations from a factory or a restaurant. Occasionally they have ham and sometimes a pound of butter. Last year Aunt Doris and Uncle Louie picked up the holiday food package late. All the turkeys were gone. They ended up with a can of tomato sauce and six apples.

The Christmas gifts come in two imaginative varieties. There are the masculine blue boxes or the feminine pink ones. That's it. Last year, the gift in my pink box turned out to be the board game Candyland, which would have disappointed a seven-year-old.

I give the receptionist at the Special Projects window my name, age, and sex. I show her my hospital identification card. She studies the photograph and stares at my face. She's trying to determine if that is really me or if I'm some stranger who has heard about the incredible Palms Memorial gift packs and has illegally obtained a card. There must be a colossal black market in Candyland.

She finally decides to give me a package. She doesn't look convinced, but it's Christmas, after all. What the hell. She returns with something called a hygiene kit. I'm thirteen now so I don't get a toy. I'm a young adult so I get the female version of a standard hygiene kit. It's a pink plastic box containing three Kotex pads, a nail file, a tiny bottle of shampoo that has no smell whatsoever, a deodorant stick, and a tiny square tin containing eight aspirin.

As I walk back to the lobby, I pass a group of carolers. They are singing "Deck the Halls" and shaking straps with bells attached to them like rows of huge lesions. They are wearing green and red sweaters with sleighs and reindeer depicted across their chests. Their ski caps have red balls on the top. I am mildly curious about life on their home planet. I can barely contain myself, that's how festive I feel.

I carry my prize to the main lobby. It is crowded with

families from the Courts. I know almost all the people sitting on the orange plastic chairs near me. I have seen the older girls in the alley at night drinking beer with the boys. Their transistor radios are on loud. Their lips glisten, inflamed by street light. Sometimes they let the younger children finish their beer for them.

They are fifteen and sixteen. I have seen them in the summers in the alley when I am searching for empty soda bottles. If I find ten bottles, I would have bus fare to Santa Monica Beach. Now these girls seem subdued, perhaps embarrassed, waiting to be called for their Ortho-Novum. I keep a magazine filled with holiday recipes in front of my face. I memorize the procedures involved in making apple strudel and pretend I don't recognize anybody.

Louie and Doris have a rule about fraternization with the other patients. The rule is simple. Don't. You play bridge but that's it. You don't want to know them and you don't want to get involved. You start saying hello and the next thing is that they're hungry. They want to borrow a few bucks. Then they're back in intensive care and they expect you to show up with a plant with a ribbon on it. Then they're dead and you're supposed to watch the soil fall on the casket and send flowers. In between, they're using your telephone. They've got their inbred double cousins they have to say good-bye to from Tallahassee to Juneau. Then they're buried, you get your phone bill, and you're the one who has a heart attack.

The lobby is standing room only. There is the traditional maniacal rush to see your doctor before he goes away on vacation, before the hospital comes as close to closing down for two weeks as it can. It's amazing how everyone manages to get a recurrence at Christmas. December, let's have a lump. Yes. Let's develop a major new symptom and while we're on a roll, what about a dramatic setback?

Then the mentals go over the edge. They all cut their wrists and turn on the gas and drink their hoarded-up sleeping pills in December. I guess they can't contain how festive they feel either.

The lobby stinks of grief and wounds. You can see it rise and hang in the strange too-cool air, this air of pronged shadows that seems painted and unraveling.

You can almost identify the shapes of what's been lost, little glittering violet pulses at your personal horizon. Christmas was once wreaths and long-distance phone calls. There were people to expect. They said they were coming and they did. Nothing happened on the way, no spasm that doubled them up, took their breath away, and then they got confused and turned back.

Then my number is called. We don't have names in the Courts. That's what you have if you're a private patient. We just have numbers. It's practice for later on, when we wait for our numbers to be called in the welfare office or in prison.

I enter a cubicle. I remove my blouse. It is cold in the room. I realize it's an unnecessary chill. They've designed it this way. They don't want you to get too comfortable. You might return with a suitcase, start rearranging the furniture and expecting favors.

"I'm a plastic surgeon," he speaks slowly, so I have a chance to comprehend this complex information. "You've just got a cosmetic situation." He looks at me like I've let him down. I don't have a harelip or burns. He tells me to put my blouse back on.

"But I have a real problem," I begin.

"Time will take care of some of it," the plastic surgeon says. I don't have a cleft palate or a scar down my cheek so I'm not really there. I'm at the extreme margin. I barely register. He is moving toward the door. He is going to open it and send me on my merry way. "You'll be more mature later," he says.

So this is permanent, I realize. It won't go away just by my promising to never read Kafka again. I'll have to wear expensive and unusual underwear. I'll have to ask Roxanne to drive me to a special underwear store and she'll be so angry she'll punch me. I'll have to cover myself in the showers at school, in gym, at the pool at West Los Angeles Playground in the summer. It occurs to me I won't be able to go swimming. How can I get my sock wet?

I feel as if the skin on my face is coming apart. I swallowed an incendiary device. It's a deliberate act of sabotage. I could have been a Kamikaze. Maybe it's not too late.

"We all have something painful to live with," he says.

Is that so? What's the worst thing you're living with? Your golf handicap? I open my mouth. I almost say it.

"Everybody wants to be a movie star," he is telling me. He sounds disgusted. He doesn't care if I go to the pool at West Los Angeles Playground in August or not. Such a thought would never occur to him. "Come here. I want you to see this."

He's got a box with files on his desk. He's taking a sort of book out of it. It looks like a photograph album. It is covered with a thick brown leather such as I imagine books written in obsolete languages are. Such manuscripts would be kept in locked glass cabinets. You would need a special pass. It would be given only to people who had names, not numbers.

I'm standing near the plastic surgeon's desk. He is flipping through the pages and I realize they contain horribly disfigured women behind cellophane. They must have been in airplane crashes and had metal doors fall through their faces. They have holes for noses and eyes. They are blind now, twisted, melted, partial, without cheeks. These are the faces from dreams, the wax that has found the flame. I feel dizzy.

"See? You're not like that," the plastic surgeon points out.

Of course not. Those are head shots and there is nothing wrong with my face, I think.

I decide to look at his name badge. I am keeping a book of accountability and he is going in it. I have my own images behind cellophane in my own version of leather, in some material infinitely rarer and more difficult to find.

He cannot open the office door fast enough. He's back on target. He's staring at his watch like he just realized he's late for the last plane to Acapulco. He must be a Christmas special, one of the doctors who donate a day of their year to the clinic. They do this so they can sleep better. It has nothing to do with us.

"See what I mean?" He is holding the door open. "I bet you're feeling better already."

I'd like to be your bookie, I think. You could make me rich. Then I'm walking through the lobby past the cluster of people I know and ignore, past the carolers with their oddly patterned sweaters and their dangerous straps filled with bells that must mean something recognizable in some other world.

17

I am introduced to the guy in the gold Impala convertible. His name is Sid Greenbaum and he's bald, he's got a belly. His face seems to be sinking in on itself as if it had seen enough. It's not a case of crevasses and wrinkles. This is more like quicksand. And his eyes are rodent-size. He's got fat cheeks and his chin comes to a point. When he walks he appears to be looking directly at his shoes. He's got flat feet and he chews gum. This is Roxanne's boyfriend?

"Don't judge by the hair," Roxanne says before I meet him. "He's some spender. He comes to Vegas and they send a car. They meet his plane. He signs for everything."

It's Christmas Day and Sid Greenbaum shows up with a

big box. It's the kind of box you could put a coat in. Sid Greenbaum says it's for me and I feel uneasy. This has been the year I graduated from Christmas toy to hygiene kit. It's the year I am elevated and become my mother's sister. It's the year I get one breast. I don't know if I can stand any more.

"Go on, go on," Sid Greenbaum says. "Open it."

Everybody is staring at me. I'm the center of attention and it makes me feel disoriented. I remember the night of my audition for the agent, Milton Silverstein, who never telephoned us again. It's Christmas and I've filled one side of my bra with a white gym sock. Uncle Louie has wheeled his chair next to the box. He's gazing at it like he thought he had X-ray eyes and could see through the paper. Maybe he has begun to think that all the radiation and chemicals he's had could be causing a visual enhancement. Aunt Doris is sitting with her company posture, back straight and chin up. She looks like she's in pain. She can't take her eyes off the Christmas gift. She's trying to figure out what's inside and how much it cost.

I remove the Christmas paper carefully. It is a scene depicting what may be family life in another galaxy. They wear bright outdoor clothing and ride in a horse-drawn sleigh. They wear caps with balls on the top. This must be the natural habitat of the hospital carolers. That's what I'm thinking as I fold the paper. Doris has taught me to open packages without injuring the wrapping paper. Wrapping paper is holy in my family. Doris has a shelf of paper she has rescued. When someone says the word heirloom, I think of this.

Now I pull the thick red ribbon apart. I manage to lift the lid. White tissue paper is folded in a perfect sharp crease. It feels crisp and new under my fingers. I reach to the bottom of the box. I can't believe it. The box is empty.

"Is he funny?" My mother is laughing so hard she's gasping. We recently had a chapter on asthma in health education and I think she may have it. "Did I tell you? He's the funniest man in the world."

I want to remember every nuance of the wrapping. It was an elaborate bow, not one of those simple pull-the-tab-and-paste-it-down jobs. You needed skill to produce this configuration. You needed a lesson. It was obviously professional wrapping with store-quality ribbon. You have to pay somebody to get a package decorated like that. This wasn't a sudden impulse toward bad taste. It was no minor incursion. This was premeditated. I am considering the sheer deliberation required for the wrapping of that package as I walk into my bedroom.

I can hear Uncle Louie behind me. "She's sensitive," Louie is explaining. "She's like a better type. You know what we call her? The Poet. She's always reading and writing. She's one of those quiet types. She's like from the nuns. Tell him, Dorrie."

"She carries a notebook everywhere. A journal she calls it. A journal, no less. She's afraid to speak up. She sees a sales clerk, she puts her arms over her head. She hides," Doris tells him. She sounds apologetic.

"Give Sid a kiss," Roxanne says. She's breathless from laughing and running into the room. She must have taken a diet pill. Her eyes look black and her hands are shaking.

I stare at her. "Are you crazy?"

That word unhinges Roxanne. I've noticed that. Now she's springing into action. She's got the hairbrush in her hand. I've covered my face with my arms. I pretend my arms are driftwood. Or perhaps the horns from the animals we saw in the West, antlers from deer, elk, or moose. The moose grow new antlers every year and shed them in winter. They can weigh eighty-five pounds. I learned that in Wyoming.

"You're always giving me a hard time," Roxanne says. Her voice is loud. She's hitting my arm with her hairbrush. "Did you see that man? Don't you think I'm having it tough enough? Jesus. I could have been in Palm Springs."

I sit in my room all day. The city becomes an eloquent monologue at dusk. I understand this clearly. I can sense the moon above some inverted bay, brutal and vivid. There are avenues somewhere where lamps gather like ships in a port.

I imagine the intacts in their houses on the other side of the boulevard. Their houses are creamy yellow and powder blue set behind wooden fences with rose bushes growing through their slats. There are paths of flagstone through the grass to the front door. Flowers along the path create a border of canna and iris. It is a region where the edges can still dare to be floral. You don't need wire fences with padlocks and electric charges yet. Here people are still known by their names and these names are spoken out loud.

Geography has not failed them. No one has loaded up a car, driven away, and never been heard from again. They haven't lost touch yet, as Roxanne would say. Relatives visit at Christmas. They sit down together at a table covered with a cloth someone's grandmother stitched.

Christine Baker and Susan Towne live in such houses. They're in my homeroom and my sewing class. Their mothers made them cheerleader outfits with blue and white pom-poms. They bring gingerbread cookies with candy eyes to school on holidays. They get different lunches every day. In the summer they go to Yosemite and sleep in a tent by a river. They learn to water ski and identify plants. Their fathers take them fishing. Their fathers put the worms on the hooks for them. I know this because I have to keep listening to their compositions about what they did over the summer.

Christine Baker and Susan Towne live across the street from each other. It is a neighborhood of streets named for women: Iris, Ivy, Patricia, May, Dorothy, Rose. At night they dream of veins of violet water and they know the earth is theirs. It's always been theirs. Christine Baker and Susan Towne probably have relatives who knock on their doors instead of bursting in. That's what I'm thinking as Uncle Louie wheels himself into my room without knocking.

"Shake it off," Uncle Louie is saying. "Shake it off. That's what a pro does. Shake it off and take another swing."

It is dinner time in Los Angeles. Christine Baker's grandmother comes with a pumpkin pie she made herself. Christine Baker's grandmother is also named Christine. There is an order to the naming of such people. They can trace their family trees for hundreds of years. There is a wreath on their door and stacks of wrapped presents under their Christmas tree. None of the boxes are empty.

Such people have Christmas trees and they have family trees. In school, they make us do a family tree each semester. They give us that assignment so they can identify people like me and cast them out.

Last year they gave us special cardboard. I drew the trunk and the branches. I decided to ask Doris for names because

I sensed it would be easier than trying to talk to Roxanne.

"I'm doing my family tree," I began, carefully. I showed her the official-looking thick gray paper. "What was Louie's mother's name?"

"I don't know," Doris said. She was studying her pins in the cigar box where she kept her jewelry. She was considering a glittering pendant with false initials.

"You don't know Louie's mother's name?" I try to sound reasonable. "Your husband's mother's name?"

"Louie's mother was no good," Doris says. "And don't ask him. Don't start. Don't upset him. Something could happen."

In the Courts, something could always happen. If we make noise or turn on the radio, somebody might hemorrhage.

"But I want to know my grandmother's name," I tell her. I am holding my tree and once again I realize I'm not even going to get the first branches filled.

"That's propaganda," Doris says. "You don't have to tell them anything. They give that information to the FBI."

"The FBI doesn't care about my grandmother," I say.

"Just don't start with mothers," Aunt Doris tells me. She glances at the paper in my hand.

"You want a name? How about Fanny? Or Sophie? Or Pearl? That's a good name. Or Sarah. That's another good one. There. Pick a name." Aunt Doris is brushing her hair. She's not actually brushing it. It has too much hair spray to be brushed. She is sort of pulling it up and then sending it out from her ears. I think of solar flares and celestial aberrations.

"But I want the right name," I insist.

"The right name," she repeats. "Christ. That shit is

from the time the Earth was flat. That's from when having a piece of bread and maybe a candle was a good time. Go away. And don't bother Louie."

Susan Towne can trace her family tree back beyond the *Mayflower.* She needs to use both sides of her cardboard. She can do the generations in America and then back across the Atlantic to England and Ireland and Scotland. She has asterisks on her family tree relating to the specific names of farms and the family patterns on kilts. Her family tree becomes three-dimensional. She attaches pieces of fabric. Her mother helps her glue them on. I know this because each semester every teacher has her stand up in front of the class and explain in nauseating detail how she devised her outstanding project.

"You know what happened in the old days? If you couldn't keep up, you got left by the side of the road," Uncle Louie tells me. He's wheeled himself into my room without knocking. "You don't want that. Come on. We're going out to Christmas dinner. This is major league. Roxanne's sport is paying."

Then Roxanne is standing in front of the bedroom mirror. She's putting on her powder and perfume and spraying her hair. She's taking her white mink stole from its sacred resting place in our closet, from its sanctuary inside the plastic and mothballs on the top shelf. I consider the various pelts we saw in Wyoming, silver and red fox and the black bear that changes to shades of brown, yellow, and a reddish cinnamon. I think of beaver and porcupine, buffalo and badger and muskrat.

Now it's Christmas and rodent-breath is taking Roxanne and her daughter who he believes is her sister and her brother and sister-in-law who he believes is her aunt and uncle to a restaurant. Roxanne could have been in Palm Springs but she wanted to share her Christmas with us. She could have been standing on a tile terrace above a backyard with a pool and a tennis court and a crew of gardeners so sophisticated and skilled they are called landscapers. She has even given up the most prestigious of all tans for us, the winter tan.

And we're going. Louie in his chair with Sid Greenbaum helping to load him into the backseat. Then Aunt Doris who has taken the night off from work for this. She's not wearing any of the enormous rhinestone brooches she buys at garage and moving sales. Tonight she's a customer. Then me. I squeeze into the back. Then Roxanne with her white mink stole in the front seat next to Sid Greenbaum. Sid Greenbaum, the funniest man in the world, is driving.

Roxanne has been talking about this dinner at a restaurant for weeks. It's a symbolic moment, an indication. If she can induce Sid Greenbaum to take her family to Christmas dinner, doesn't this automatically portend other things? Of course it does. It opens the door.

In the late afternoons, Roxanne has been discussing the possibilities with Doris, the restaurant expert. You can sense the boulevard winding down a few feet from your face. You can feel how tense the drivers are. They're hungry. They've made mistakes that could put them in the unemployment line if their boss notices. It is hot and they are sticking to their car seats.

I can tell that Doris is taking diet pills again. She's got two cigarettes burning simultaneously. Doris is completely filled with orange and green and white pills that resemble the interior of molecules moving, breathing and decaying. She has swallowed these miniature suns that fall in and out of orbit. There is the matter of gravity and how Doris gets dragged along.

"What do you think?" Roxanne is speculating. "Italian? You think he'll do Italian? Or Chinese? Chinese could be some kind of party with five." Roxanne's eyes have a wild reddish cast to them as if she leaned too close to fire light, perhaps. It was a terrible winter and she got burned or stained. There are avenues of shadows in her eyes and she is sending them out into the almost dusk. It isn't volitional. It's like something with a faulty charge.

Now the moment of revelation is approaching. Sid Greenbaum is parking. He's parking badly. He's scraping the sides of his whitewall tires into the curb but everyone is pretending they don't notice. Now we're unloading Uncle Louie. Aunt Doris is pushing his chair. Then I'm struck with a sense of recognition. It's Fairfax Avenue and everything seems familiar because we are standing in front of Canter's Delicatessen where Doris is the hostess.

We walk in and everyone stares at us. Roxanne has the reddest hair and the shortest white vinyl miniskirt in the room. She is the only person wearing a mink stole and four-and-one-half-inch red spike high heels. The glare of the light makes everything appear coated and plastic. People look like they have been dipped in wax. I think of the fake apples and oranges and bananas everybody has in a bowl on their dining room table. You must display wax fruit and profess an interest in the number fifty. This is obligatory. If you can pull this off, they will think you are coping.

When the waitress takes my order I ask for a Coke. Doris has explained that restaurants make their money on beverages. Only a hillbilly would order a drink. Now I've done it. There. Let the chips fall where they may. It's Christmas and I'm ordering a soda. The cooks are probably pissing in my food. That's what Doris says they do to hayseeds. That's the kind of night it is. Then Sid Greenbaum orders a soda.

"You want a Coke?" Sid Greenbaum asks Roxanne. He seems concerned.

"Of course not," Roxanne tells him. She is sitting up as straight as she can, shoulders back, chin up.

"What about you?" Sid glances at Louie. "Don't you want a soda?"

Uncle Louie shakes his head no. "We never drink in restaurants," Louie says.

Sid Greenbaum appears confused. It's been so long since I used silverware in a conventional manner, I'm afraid I've forgotten how. Then I taste the food. It's the same kaiser rolls only without the thumbprints. Roxanne doesn't say a word until we are back in the car and the car is moving.

"You didn't tip," Roxanne said.

"I tipped big last time," Sid Greenbaum told her.

"You had the same waitress?" Roxanne wants to know.

"Yeah. Her," Sid Greenbaum says, "or maybe her sister." He gives Roxanne a mock punch on her shoulder. He laughs for a while.

I am wedged against the backseat window. We are passing houses with lights strung across the front door, the porch and windows and the border of the roof. The red and green lights delineate the structures. They imply morality and aesthetics. I am thinking about this and Christine Baker and Susan Towne and their mothers and grandmothers and the way their names are connected.

I remember an article I read in science class about a theory that the ancient Egyptians practiced a form of primitive neurosurgery. Skulls had been discovered with tiny triangular holes drilled into the cranium. It was possible they were attempting brain surgery four thousand years ago.

I could use a cranial venting, a small geometric indenture that might let West Los Angeles High School slip out. I could use another one on the other side to allow Louie and Doris and Sid Greenbaum, the funniest man in the world, out. And maybe one designer hole in the middle for Roxanne. Then I realize the whole procedure probably wouldn't work because there is a residue on a cellular level and you need a form of soul bleach to remove it. You need to master the arts of erasure, the names of the ancestors, their villages and gods. You need to learn to cast spells. You must invent avenues of invisibility and bridges where there are none. And even that probably wouldn't be enough.

18

It's afternoon in Mr. Gordon's office. I feel like I'm spending my wretched adolescence here, staring at the surface of the conference table until the grain becomes a kind of primal scene, salty and urgent. Something happens, the random juxtaposition, sudden light and life forming. Smaller units become more complex. They leave the ocean and drag themselves onto the land. If I sit here long enough, I can watch them build cities, high schools, concentration camps and atomic bombs.

At Hiroshima people had the prints of their kimonos etched into their skin. The atomic blast was like the flash of a camera. The arms and back became a wood-block print. The body was a scroll unraveling into willows and maple leaves, the notched petal of the cherry blossom, the peony, the carp and the swallow. The flesh was a stencil of pine bark and floral vines and geometric motifs indicating waves and all of it was burning.

People were blinded and flames came out of the place where they once had hands. Their bodies were a kind of silk hanging tattooed with pomegranates and bamboo, peacocks and dragonflies. It was the end of all subtlety and translucence. There was a river in the city they tried to drink from. There were so many bodies in the water, you could walk across the bloated dead like a bridge.

I imagine what would happen if the bomb was dropped right now. When I hear the air raid sirens, I'm not going to wait around for official instructions. That would be a sucker play, as Louie would say. The roads will become impassable with the carcasses of crashed cars. Motorists would begin shooting and raping each other. It might take hours for the bomb to actually fall. People could have suffered so much by then that impact would seem an act of mercy.

When I hear the sirens, I'm going to run to the bomb shelter under the basement of Palms Memorial Hospital. Jimmy says it isn't just a rumor. He claims he saw it the day Tamiko had her Christmas in July.

In the Courts, when you go out of remission, we call it Christmas in July. If you're a kid, they let you have an entire fake Christmas with a tree and presents. It seems the death sentence always comes in the hottest part of summer, in the most inappropriate season as if to highlight the entire process of aberration.

Jimmy said he went with someone from staff down a flight of stairs under X ray and the basement. He was going to the room where they store the plastic Christmas trees and bags of tinsel and pretend snowflakes for the terminals. That's when he saw the bomb shelter, the one they don't admit exists.

Mr. Gordon is tapping his pen on my file. He's about to ask me why I refused to go to typing class again today. I'm going to tell him that it refused me. After all, there is a sort of lilac drift involved, a dynamic. There is the matter of inland water, how it is isolated and trapped, how it lies under moonlight collecting stories that defile it. There are complexities in these alterations. I am not entirely responsible.

I am thinking about Tamiko's Christmas in July. It was actually August. Usually the terminal kids wished for Disneyland. The hospital had a special van equipped with medical supplies in case they fainted or went into a coma or had convulsions on the way to Anaheim.

Tamiko didn't want to go to Disneyland. She'd already been there. She wanted to go to a Hollywood studio and have herself made up and put into a costume. She wanted someone to fix her hair. Then she wanted someone to take photographs.

Roxanne said she would go to Paramount and get a costume. What did Tamiko want? She wanted to be a dance hall saloon girl. She wanted a satin dress with sequins on the top along the neckline and a bustle in the back. She wanted feathers in her hair. She wanted the dress to have a slit up the front so the sequinned garter on her thigh would show. But she was worried about her hair. It was falling out when she washed or brushed it. Roxanne told her not to be concerned, she'd take care of it.

Roxanne had to take the bus to Paramount in Hollywood. It was a day when Les Downer had pronounced the car impossible and not even a bottle of Southern Comfort could remove the evil spell. It was ninety-nine degrees. Roxanne was gone five hours.

I remembered when Roxanne had fainted in the heat. It was the July when we were searching for the Wonders of the West. It was the day we understood the faces of the women in the windows. It was when we comprehended the nature of rivers. Then night came and we sat on the river bank watching the fireworks.

I waited for Roxanne to return. I was prepared for her to complain. She didn't. Then we went to Jimmy's apartment. Roxanne had the costume in a brown paper bag. She had the high-heeled shoes in a box. I was carrying Roxanne's personal cosmetic case with her makeup, electric rollers, and hair-setting gels.

Tamiko was so pale, she might be coated with a geisha's white paint. Roxanne rubbed rouge onto her cheeks. She filed and polished her nails. She outlined Tamiko's lips with red pencil and filled it in with a purplish gloss. She pasted on false eyelashes with a tube of special glue. She even gave Tamiko a beauty mark above her lip with brown eyebrow pencil.

Roxanne had selected a red dress with yellow and black feathers and red high-heeled shoes. The sequins were purple and silver. Then we stood outside in front of the apartment taking pictures. Jimmy had a camera but the flash attachment was broken. Now it worked only outside in the sunlight. The day was so hot it was devoid of color. It was completely white like exhaustion or smoke. Tamiko leaned against the bleached stucco and smiled.

Later Tamiko folded up the costume and put it back in

the grocery bag. Roxanne told her not to bother, she could keep it. Roxanne made it sound like the costume wasn't important, like she didn't even really care.

"The last of the big spenders," Aunt Doris said. She stared at Roxanne. She seemed astonished. "You can't keep a costume."

"I'm not keeping it," Roxanne said. "I'm giving it away." She moved past Doris into the bedroom, sidestepping her so even their shoulders didn't brush.

"They'll fire you, big shot," Doris said.

Doris was right. They not only fired Roxanne, they put her on the permanent blacklist. She can never step foot on the Paramount lot again, no matter what.

After Tamiko died, Roxanne Scotch-taped one of the photographs onto the bedroom mirror and it is still there. Tamiko doesn't look like a child or a woman or even a human being. Despite the makeup and the sunlight she is insubstantial. She is elegant and sad, as if she knew everything.

She might be one of the women Roxanne and I passed on our journey through America. One of the women pale and partial behind a fold of cotton in a kitchen window facing two twin silos, a few fences, an implication of highway. Perhaps such women spend afternoons considering the abstract tropics, the evolution of music and the graffiti that falls at midnight from a lover's mouth.

In the photograph Tamiko is wearing hundred-year-old clothing. She might be a time traveler. Perhaps people with cancer are caught between times, that is why space is warping inside of them where their modifications are incomplete.

"You don't ask me what I'm thinking anymore," Rox-

anne said one night. "I finally got good answers but you
don't ask."

I am lying on my back, smoking. Louie and Doris are
playing bridge. I can hear their constant arguing. Then I ask
her.

"I'm thinking these are the camps," Roxanne said. She
was staring into the mirror. She tapped Tamiko's photograph with the tip of a nail that was drying. "And these are
the Wonders of the West."

Roxanne was talking about Idaho and Utah and the detour we took to go there, to try to find the West. That was
on our way to California, when we saw the quilts and pelts,
when we heard the gospel and bluegrass under the tents,
when we stood in the replicas of Indian tepees and stage-
coaches. It was the day Roxanne fainted. It was the Fourth
of July and there were fireworks later above the Snake
River.

Now Roxanne is drinking vodka and saying Tamiko was
somehow part of this. I could sense the boulevard outside
our drawn blinds and I was sorry I asked her anything.

"You haven't been participating in gym," Mr. Gordon
says. I thought he was going to ask me about typing. I
feel like I'm in a coma. I couldn't say anything even if I
wanted to.

There is a sort of lavender current that comes in and goes
out. There are harbors where a person can say no. It occurs
to me I can resist. I will refuse to return to gym class. I'm
tired of my awkward one-breasted posture no one seems to
notice. I'm disgusted with everyone's obsession with the
number fifty. It's like Saint Vitus' dance, only nobody has
started twitching yet. That can happen any time. And seeing demons and burning witches.

That's when I know I have to leave. When Mr. Gordon turns to answer the telephone I walk out the door. When I reach the end of the corridor I start running.

I aim myself toward the ocean. I wind down alleys past the fenced yards of intacts. I can determine their status by the extent of their floral borders. They inhabit a world where petals and suggestion are still enough. Sheets are strung on clotheslines, beige towels, yellow and blue shirts. There are agapanthus rising and jacaranda falling and there are purple flowers laying across the pavement and the alley and the grass. I realize I don't have to go to the ocean. If I understand the textures of the city, if I can decode its deceptive intentions, the ocean can come to me.

I change my mind and turn north. Something should speak to me, should march off the flat purple horizon and clarify itself and what it needs. I bend down and try to hear it rising from the earth with its reverse dialect of retrieval. I detect small sounds and feel ridiculous.

I decide to walk to the part of West Los Angeles where Jimmy's family had their house before it was confiscated by the United States Government. They knew the soldiers were coming. Jimmy's grandfather dressed in his best navy blue suit. His grandmother was wearing her hat with the black veil and her pearls. Jimmy's father put on his Boy Scout uniform. His mother ironed the scarf. He had gotten a badge for making various knots in rope. His new badge was for archery. Then the bus took them away. It's a century when the buses are always taking the citizens away. You are always an enemy in the country of your birth.

I walk into a nursery. Jimmy and I used to come here and study bonsai trees. The trees were anomalies, deliberately deformed, compacted and hideous.

I remember Tamiko with her arms tattooed with bruises from the injections. She was wearing a bustle and feathers and red, purple, and silver sequins. She was smiling through the thick white veil of sunlight at the camera. Then the strangeness and ugliness dissolves, I cross a border and recognize that the bonsai trees are magnificent. I understand it is always this way, a thin and shifting line between aberration and beauty.

I realize I could collect such miniature trees. I could have a forest on the side of a terrace, groves and seasonal variations. I could invent hemispheres and planets. I might create arrangements which would imply ocean tides and wind patterns.

It occurs to me that I have touched Jimmy subliminally. We are connected by Tamiko's Christmas in July. I walk to the telephone booth across the street from Les Downer's Flying A Service Station and the phone rings.

"Did you get the package?" Jimmy asks. He seems to be whispering. I push the receiver closer to my ear.

"The record album with the ratty cigarettes?" I glance at the boulevard. A blue bus that is going to the beach at Santa Monica. A lady with baggy black pants pushing a baby carriage. The glare of the sun whitening the pavement and stucco, giving everything facets and a kind of hard polish. "Louie won't let me use the record player. The cigarettes looked defective. I threw them away."

"I'll send you more. You have to smoke them," Jimmy says.

"I don't have time for music appreciation," I reply. "They're trying to put me in reform school."

"The whole world's about to change," Jimmy says. He pauses. Maybe he is evaluating the boulevard where he is, the cars, or beyond. Perhaps the bay. I can hear his cigarette lighter. Then he tells me he is going to quit school and become a candle maker.

That surprises me. I don't know what to say.

Jimmy is telling me about light and candles, their shapes and subtle networks, how the process has integrity, how it is holy. He is going to make sand candles and sell them at traveling art fairs. Sand candles are a kind of wax sculpture. You can dig up manzanita roots and cover them with sand in barrels. Then you pour the colored wax in. There are complex branches like the flowing of rivers.

"I want to make candles, too," I realize.

"You've got good karma," Jimmy says. He sounds confident. "Just hang on."

"Hang on?" I repeat, wondering where the ropes are, if they can detach themselves from the sky and if I might be able to wrap them around my wrists and ankles. Or are they similar to the vines that fall from the mossy sides of certain trees. If I could find these, would it be enough to help me in the drift?

I consider the concept of karma as I walk home. I stop in the library and check out a book about it. Then I remember the ratty cigarettes Jimmy sent me, the ones I threw away. Roxanne has cigarettes that look just like that. I find one under a pair of bronze nylons. I sit on the bedroom floor and smoke it.

There are a sudden series of holes in my head. I have windows and doors, portals, and all of them are opened. They are lanterns and torches. Of course it is all a matter of light. I am at sea, trying to communicate by wind and coded sails. I have seen mica on sand at Santa Monica Bay. Now I know they were millions of shattered mirrors and amulets, indications of how to move through time.

Tiny lilac triangles have been gouged in the side of my skull. They are acid tears, the residue of renegade procedures. I am receiving a cranial venting after all. This must be what the Egyptians were searching for. But this is better, surgery without blood, and images are sliding out from the interior and farther, from their nests within my cells. My thoughts are birds and they are flapping strangely.

Everything is gleaming a kind of antique silver. There are permanent consequences from the moon. Now I comprehend this as the color of transition and hieroglyphics. I have one coherent thought and it is about the desert, something languid and inflamed in the restless magenta sand.

I can sense spring through the glass of the windows. I am a trapped insect. There was a noon of stark collusions. They were unavoidable. No one is to blame. Now it is the dusk that wants to touch my face. I have been lessened, purified and redeemed. Entire sequences of events have been removed from me. Of course the night would find that attractive.

I am crossing the minefield of the living room with its metaphorical metal devices that kill in their own way. Tonight I can actually see them. I am going to step on something and lose my leg. The lower half of my body is going to be ripped off. It will be me and Louie in matching wheelchairs playing hospital basketball on Thursdays with the car crash victims.

"She's heading for the door, Louie," my Aunt Doris yells. "The Poet's loose."

That's what they call me now. The Poet. They've been calling me that since I began carrying my notebooks and journals everywhere. I feel like they are appendages now, almost organic.

Doris lumbers to her feet. She's been on a pastry binge.

She's eaten so much cheesecake, her ankles have swollen. She can't get on a pair of shoes. She has to wear thongs to work. She stands near the front door and puts her arms out like a school crossing guard. Or something worse, a drunken goalie, perhaps.

Doris has insomnia now. The diet pills don't prevent her from eating anymore, just from sleeping. She stays awake compiling lists of places to go and the approximate cost of hotels, transportation, and food. She spends consecutive nights ball-parking herself. She has written on the sides of all the bridge pads in the house, what a week in London would cost, a month in Greece, a summer in Italy. Just before dawn she makes plane reservations in fake names. Perhaps she has developed aliases based on the false initials in her rhinestone pins, whole other manufactured identities, accidental and binding. Last week she reserved two first-class seats one-way to Rome with connections to Calcutta and Nairobi.

I am staring at Doris and it occurs to me that she looks wrinkled and not quite in focus. Somebody should reload her and start over.

Uncle Louie is removing ice cream from the freezer. He says he can't do anything anymore because of the wheelchair and how numb he is. But he is able to stand by himself when involved with ice cream. The refrigerator exerts a kind of magical force field. You touch its cool white metal exterior and you are energized, cured. These are the textures of what is precious. If you open your mouth wide enough, you can live forever.

"What's that smell?" Aunt Doris suddenly asks. "Reefers? You smoke reefers now?" She sounds interested.

Reefers. So that's what they're called. I decide not to say anything. I lunge for the door.

"It's not safe out there," Louie says from the kitchen.

"It's not safe in here, either," I reply. "I'll take my chances."

I prefer my odds on the outside. No subliterate Southerner on a motorcycle is going to spirit me away to a life of forced prostitution, petty thievery, and barbecue cooking. That would be too simple. That would be a fairy tale.

"She doesn't know from white slavery," Aunt Doris says. But she's behind me.

The moon is nearly full above the white jasmine opening along the fences and paths of Palm Courts West, asserting its own junctures of longing and intention. It is the distillation of all possible springs real and imagined. There are no boulevards, only avenues of fragrant green mirrors. I am barefoot. The grass is so many moist stars beneath my feet and I am running toward the old clubhouse.

A senior who just moved into the Courts is lying on a sleeping bag with his girlfriend. He's got a beer can balanced on the lap of the Buddha. It may take him fifty thousand incarnations to work off that act of listless vulgarity.

I can smell reefer in the padlocked laundry room. Last month I had barely heard of it. It was a vague rumor. It barely registered in my periphery. Now it's everywhere. Smoking reefers may be the final mistake they are waiting for. I have become a heretic. I understand the insolent desert, how it engraves itself at your throat, how you can wear it as a kind of brooch.

I sit on a curb in the alley. I can sense the intangible ruins of the city rising into ridges of metallic rust. It makes me think of fire and the patriarchy, why we came here to Los Angeles and what it means. And somewhere there is a river flowing slow behind the insult of obscure smoke.

I realize it must be awful to see God. It would be as monstrous and aberrant as finding the night utterly empty. It would be another form of possession. You would feel as if your skull were polished and you were being held above the tide line. Everything would be gold. It would be impossible to breathe. You would be more expensive than a planet. You would stand at the edge of absolute illumination, which is where the burn and darkness begin, simultaneously, in the same wounded startled breath.

When I get cold enough I walk back to the apartment. Roxanne is standing in the center of the bedroom. She is wearing a black slip and gold stiletto sandals. She seems lost. I notice she is between suntans, somehow pale and stranded. There is something ominous and unnatural in this whitened configuration. Her two large black suitcases are opened on her bed.

"Where are you going?" I ask just to say something, to see if I can order words to come out of my mouth, if they will be human sounds, not birds or howls or drums.

"Location," Roxanne answers. She doesn't look at me.

Location is a magical word. I used to believe it was related to cancer. That's one of the cancer questions. Where is the location? I think of location as being a word that falls somewhere between cancer and real estate.

Of course Roxanne means a movie location. That's what makes it holy and inviolate. A movie location is a glistening word shrine. It's a hanging stupa in the sharp dusk air. You could put branches of ornamental cherry blossoms beneath it, you could offer butterflies and plums. Location is so sacrosanct it creates its own geography.

Roxanne is adorned with supernatural syllables. She collects them. Screening is another divine word. Sometimes at

night Roxanne goes to screenings. That's when they pre-
view the movies to the VIPs before they are shown to the
general public. Roxanne says the word *public* with contempt. The public is farmers and hillbillies. That's who
buys the tickets. Hayseeds. Anybody worth knowing in
this town gets invited free.

At these screenings they pass out a card where you can
rate the movie. Roxanne fills it out but she doesn't return
it. She saves these evaluation cards. On the back she writes
down who she attended the premier with, where she was
taken for dinner, and what she ate. She keeps the cards
wrapped in tissue paper in her stocking drawer. When it's
Academy Award night, we wheel the TV out of the closet.
Roxanne removes her evaluation cards and adds up how
many winners she has. For the past four consecutive years,
she has correctly predicted best costume, lighting, and set
design.

When Roxanne says she's going to a screening I forget
she means a movie. I immediately think of the other kind
of screening, the one they do with your cells and fluids to
see how the cancer is spreading. Sometimes they screen for
other diseases. On Family Day at Palms Memorial Hospital
they screen the blood of all children over twelve years old
for venereal diseases. We wear shabby clothing that doesn't
fit. We eat from charity boxes and don't get our homework
in on time. Our mothers take buses to work. We stay home
and get venereal diseases. The people in our families give
them to us. That's what the staff thinks.

Roxanne has both of her big black suitcases on the bed.
She has also taken down the medium red one and the small
square powder blue bag she calls her cosmetic case. She
looks like she's leaving town permanently. She's already

packed one of the suitcases with dresses layered in tissue paper. That's a trick she learned in Peru when she did the hair on the Tarzan movie. Always use tissue paper layers. They had to do that because there was no hot water at the hotel. They couldn't steam the wrinkles out of anything.

Roxanne is packing her cosmetic case. First the extra-strength hair spray and the three kinds of suntan lotion, then the shampoo and conditioner, the nail polishes and remover. She's already put in the six-month supply of Ortho-Novum and a box of Marlboro hard-pack cigarettes containing what I now recognize as reefers.

''We'd blow reefer in the Catskills,'' Roxanne tells me when I ask. ''Then me and Louie and the jazz guys used to go to Harlem. Ask Louie about it. We'd get the reefer from Pink Eye, the drummer. That was before that drag-ass Ernie.''

I decide to remember that for my book of accounts receivable, my book of reckonings. I like the word *reckonings*, not just for its obvious associations but because one of its meanings is about measuring miles at sea. That's how I feel, completely adrift with lanterns where I once had hands. My book is an anchor. It is going to be filled with my version of forget-me-not rhinestone pins but they will have my own real initials.

Roxanne is removing her shorty nightgowns. Then she takes out her black and red bras. She is smelling them, making sure they have the right blend of floral, of something that is her powder and her skin and some conjunction between them, some sense of cinnamon and almond and a slightly tropical late afternoon crowded with balconies of pink camellias. Nearby the sea is beating itself senseless on the shore. Roxanne is examining her black lace panties with the cluster of miniature red hearts in a circle.

"Do you think I'm still attractive?" she is asking. "For thirty-four?" She sucks in her stomach and turns to the side.

I look at her face. I imagine her behind torn gingham curtains in a kitchen six miles from the interstate. She might be a woman thinking that it breaks her heart to look out such a window. A woman who had already been married and had a child, perhaps. A daughter. A woman who knew there are no light affections. A woman who recognized we are always walking into a brazen windswept dragon of an afternoon the imagination fails to redeem.

When I don't say anything, Roxanne gets angry. "You're such a square," she decides. "You're Ernie's kid, alright. I used to wonder but now I'm sure. You're a drag-ass like your father. You don't get it."

"Tell me," I say with a soft voice.

"We're baboons with hotel reservations. We're baboons with see-through underwear and installment payments." She shuts her medium red suitcase. "Wake up already." She clasps her hands three times. "Come to the party."

I lean in the doorway of our bedroom. The lilac indentures have worn off, the series of tiny windows I had stirring in my skull an hour ago, that choreography of petals and fans. I had an armada of sails, canvas glistening like lightning and pearl, but now they are gone. Everything feels hard again, soldered and impervious. I look down the hallway and watch my mother. She is near the card table. Soon she will wait outside for a cab to take her to the airport. Or perhaps someone has even sent a car.

Louie and Doris are unusually quiet. They're playing with new partners and they're attempting to give them the impression that they are human beings. Johnny J's wife Maureen died. That happens all the time. Everybody is paying attention to the guy with a bypass and the wife turns out to have the cancer. They found a lump in her breast the size of an egg. Eleven days later she was dead.

"Go figure," Louie said. He stared at the tip of his cigar as if the ember was telling him something. He looked depressed.

Now they're playing with someone from Sacramento with multiple sclerosis. Louie must be desperate. I watch Roxanne lean over and whisper in her brother's ear. Then she hands him the money.

There is no light beyond the blinds. Earlier there was a sense of lemon and orange trees, of the sudden and inexplicable and spiced. That was before the sun went down, before the seams were ripped and all the lacerations. The sky looks tentative, broken and malevolent. Maybe they should screen it for something. It is flat and dull. It isn't the reason you crossed an ocean. It isn't the dusk you somehow lost and never stop looking for.

In the morning there will be bird of paradise born from this. Their heads will be translucent, gleaming from within. There will also be a new crop of fuchsias like so many manic suicides leaping into the air, dangling and longing for the pavement.

"Louie. Three spades. It's to you. Three spades," Aunt Doris is saying. She sounds patient. They are playing with new partners and Doris doesn't want to scare them away. She is using her company posture and vocabulary. She has even placed a fork on the card table next to the paper plate of tainted onion rolls.

"Louie?" Doris repeats, her voice starting to rise. "Louie, you coming to the party or what?"

Outside is wild iris, ferns, an accidental eruption of red geraniums. Outside is Sybil Brand and Camarillo. Maybe I could find the party there.

19

I wake up in the darkness thinking about the Wonders of the West and how Roxanne and I got there by accident. We were in New Mexico when Roxanne decided we needed to see the Old West, we had to experience this before Los Angeles, even though we were windburned and hungry and almost out of money. That's when we turned vaguely north and west and lost direction.

We were driving through counties named after metals and rocks. There were occasional fields where the hay was round and smooth as skulls. Some invisible Indian tribe severed the heads and left them there. Or maybe time travelers had done that, had returned to enact a ritual that could save an entire galaxy. We just didn't understand the subtle complications.

We are passing houses with antlers nailed above the front doors. Deer. Moose. Elk. We are learning to decipher bone. There are white horses in pastures with white rocks and white clouds with deteriorating interiors hanging over gray rivers. Palominos. Appaloosas. Arabians. Then the mountains that were red from when the oceans laid on them, burning them for eons.

"Talk about a bad marriage," Rosanne says and smiles.

I don't know what she is talking about. We are driving north and the counties are named for battles and tools and what they take out of rocks, their gutted essences. There is the glory of extraction. In this region, lead and sulphur are evoked. They are conjured. They are rumored to still have power. Then Chuck's Taxidermy in a town where there used to be silver mines.

"It's still the Stone Age," Roxanne says, with a kind of amazement. "I get it now."

On the highways are American tourists. We stare at each other. The roads are filled with people exchanging parts of the country, as if they thought there was something better somewhere else. Families from Florida are driving into Colorado. People from Pennsylvania are going to Texas. I overhear them say this in a gas station. I study license plates, memorizing the color motifs and what the state is proudest of.

America is thin men with Luckies in their pockets and fishing rods in pieces. They carry cartons of beer and Roxanne says they are all alcoholics. You can tell by the way they walk, by the color of their T-shirts, how they hang across their chests. These men look like they just left the electrical or plumbing shop. They do something with their hands that's bad for their health. They look like they got shocked. They lost their lives so long ago, it's impossible to tell what they might have been. Then the women to anchor them, to give them weight, to take the last of the air. Then the backseat with the children, the ice chests, the beach balls, the blue plastic rafts you blow up, the inner tubes, the parts of tents and the dogs.

We are near the Colorado border when we see it. Roxanne notices it, the sign on the road, WONDERS OF THE WEST. 420 MILES. She squints at the sign through the dust and the sun in a valley that resembles the floor of an ocean. Heat rises from the sand like a kind of mist, a blue thing that makes me think of subtraction, violet zeros, and the place before years.

"I've got to see this," Roxanne says. "I've got to see this before California."

Along the roadsides the plants are like stitches. The earth must have been hurt. We are climbing mountains named for their shape, like Eagle Peak and Fish Head. We are crossing lands named for what you find there, like Apple Valley and Bear Meadows, Elk Pass and Sidewinder Ridge. This is a vestige from a world that was once intelligible. There were congruencies everywhere, naturally, you didn't have to contrive them. There were tangible indications. You woke up and knew where you were.

Now we have a destination. We are going to the Wonders of the West. Roxanne has to see this before Los Angeles. There is something absolute about this that I somehow understand. It's similar to the way I want to watch us cross each state border. I beg Roxanne to wake me up so I won't miss it. I keep expecting a ceremony with flags and flowers and men on horseback, perhaps, with trumpets and uniforms and something like red lilies. I still search for the

figures from my puzzle of the United States, the lady with
the tray of glistening round orange cheeses, the farmer
proudly displaying his corn. Maybe here, in this sudden
gorge where the sand might be from ancient oceans or
ground-up shells. I don't know how sand is formed or how
they bring it in.

Always something red is on the hill like a creature died
there. Then the green plants surrounding it. Maybe this is
how Christmas appears in the West. A woman in a country
store tells us iron and magnesium oxide turn the ground
red. I decide to remember this forever. And the mountains
are bouquets of crystal. If you held such a thing, it would
sever your hand.

Colorado is hills with red painted stripes like someone
threw an Indian blanket over them. It is Shoshone Road
and Cheyenne Avenue and mountains with printed sides
below printed clouds. Hills are an absence, as if everything
has been scraped out of them, not just the rocks and metals
with their valuable properties but all the original stories
and reasons, all the skulls and wind.

We are passing fields of cows, a handful here and there.
It's never enough to feed America. I want to know where
the rest of the cows are but I don't ask Roxanne. I want to
know where the roads to the Indian reservations are. What
happens after the sign on the highway and the fence, after
the mountains in the perpetual obligatory distance?

Is there really a town in the aching blue beyond the
gutted ridges, past the rivers named for colors that have
nothing to do with them? Not this White River, this Green
River, this Red River. And the cousins of these rivers,
which are named for animals and qualities, this Virgin
River, this Roaring River. Is this the mouth of the West at

last? If I put my ear next to it, if I trust it with my face, will it say the words to wake me from my sleep? I am under a spell. I am having a terrible enchantment. That's what's happening to my life. I understand that.

Three-hundred-seventy miles to the Wonders of the West. And Colorado is Rabbit Valley, Moose Hills, Fish Lake, but where are these creatures? Bear Mountain and Deer Meadows are uninhabited. The stranded mountains look as if entire refugee families have been carved into them. Faces that argue and watch you, that say you've disappointed them, failed them, ripped out their hearts. I ask Roxanne if she sees this and if this is how cities are born.

"It looks like Ellis Island," she says. She suddenly seems uncertain.

There are railroad cars that have been left in the sand. Who knows why they were abandoned or if they will be reclaimed? There is the sense of contagion. We have arrived in the place without a mouth where the rocks may have taken an oath of silence.

There are the faces of women standing behind hedges where nothing is blooming. Perhaps it is too hot. They seem lethargic, indifferent, glancing up at our car, some-how startled. They are collecting dust with their eyes. They are watching time pass, shine, and blacken. They are computing the passage of hummingbirds with the quality of sunset. Yesterday they counted hawks. At the edge of the field on the silo side the river bends and forms a wide backwater. She could walk there, sit on the bank, watch a crane dive for trout, but why bother? I wonder if Roxanne sees these things. I ask her what the women by the sides of the farms are thinking.

Roxanne lights a cigarette. "I'll be able to tell you that

soon," she assures me. She evaluates the air, seems to be tasting something in the blue afternoon. "I almost know."

There are more towns commemorating what men drag out of the ground. Leadville and Silverdale and Sulphurtown. The one store has a statue of a horse on the roof. The sun feels slow. It's coming from a great distance and it doesn't care if it gets here or not.

We are driving over hills that look so much like clay, I want to stop and touch them, dig my fingers in and make a vase or a mask. I could wrap it with ribbon and give it to my mother. Then the hills with breasts and beards. Hills with trolls. Hills that might be falling apart or wearing talismans and beads. I tell this to Roxanne. I say everything is simultaneously good and evil. There is no way to draw a line and be certain. She says to stop staring at the sun. She says to take a nap.

We pass trucks that are empty, carry only one cable and a few ropes each. I wonder if the vast night proved to be of no use. Perhaps it refused them and what they tried to bring. The rules of the region had been revised. No one recognized their offerings or what to do with them. Maybe they simply gave up and threw their products away, hurled their boxes and sacks and indecipherable bundled items to the side of the road when no one was looking and kept going.

Roxanne turns off the highway. She stops the car. She is showing me a pamphlet about mountain flowers. We have driven to the side of a meadow. We get out. She holds the pamphlet open and bends down to examine and identify what is growing. There are photographs. When she finds something that matches exactly, she lets out a kind of soft moan. She is flushed.

She is walking so fast, I have to run to keep up with her.

She is pointing to alpine daisies and black-eyed Susans. She shows me Queen Anne's lace above a pond with a beaver dam. Then larkspur and magenta fireweed. "I feel like I'm hunting," Roxanne says.

She reads the histories of the flowers she recognizes. She is telling me about the fireweed, how it grew in London after the German bombing. It suddenly appeared in the ruins for the first time since Shakespeare. "The first time since Shakespeare," Roxanne repeats twice.

Then she is discovering wild pink roses, glacier lilies, and pale purple columbine. "It's the state flower," she reveals as if she was telling me a secret. Then she's pointing to bluebells. She shows me monkshood, which contains a property to reduce fever. It occurs to me she could certainly use that. I should pick it and rub it across her forehead. I could put it under her pillow while she slept. I could hide a piece of it in her pocket. We are at the top of Colorado and the Wonders of the West aren't here. They are still hundreds of miles farther, past Idaho.

The sky is the color of wild flowers and rivers. The sky is so blue, it seems to ache. I look at it and think my teeth could fall out. My eyes. There are aspens and blue spruce and I don't think we should go on. The mountains have been a sequence of slow vertigoes. They have been a kind of port. We have finally come to this interior wharf and we should stop here, where the air around the blue spruce turns bruised and dark. I think this is the intimation of a mystery. We should lay our heads on this ground and sleep.

Instead we are moving. Colorado is disappearing. The forests of aspen are behind us. In the towns there are abandoned brick dwellings, just the shells are left without windows or doors. We are passing houses with overgrown gardens and tire swings, rock patios and back doors with the screens ripped. Then houses with horses in the backyards and white picket fences and broken pieces of boats and motorcycles like metal amputations. And lawns with basketballs tossed on them, bicycles, tools, horseshoes and small shovels, children's toys, gardening implements, plastic wading pools. America is this clutter, as if everyone was desperately searching for something to do.

In the towns named for obsolete metals and vanished animals, each house has a porch where no one is talking. There's been nothing to say here for centuries. There are paths with frail roses on the side that look like somebody's grandmother planted them. Then the gutted blocks, the way the wood is dusty, exposed. You can't imagine why anybody ever came here or why they would stay.

We are leaving the town, passing a dead deer by the gravel shoulder of the road. A peacock crosses the street in front of our car, dragging its impossible feathers behind it like a kind of net. Everything is becoming impossible. We are leaving a town where people live wordlessly and then drive off to their farms in the morning.

"They're like amphibians," Roxanne decides. She glances at me. "Don't look so surprised. I know all the words."

We are past the mountains, beyond the flowers Roxanne could identify. We are past the places where the deformed things grew at their sordid elevations. We are approaching the Wonders of the West and I know it is a mistake.

Roxanne stops the car near a brick courthouse. That's what the sign says. Courthouse. We are practicing for the Wonders of the West. There will be forays and scouting expeditions. There will be degrees of preparation and initiation. Now Roxanne pays fifty cents and we climb the steps to take the tour. We are the only people there. I know we can't sign the guest book because we don't have an address.

My mother doesn't pause. She picks up the pen and signs something in the book with its big old-fashioned pages. I look at what she has written. Billie Holiday, NYC.

The courthouse is a narrow room with a staircase leading to an upper floor that is closed behind a thick red rope. I touch it. It is velvet. We find ourselves standing alone in a dark room with glass cabinets with rocks inside. I walk up and down in front of the locked cabinets reading the hand-printed notes next to each rock. These are the rocks you make lead bullets from. This is garnet, tungsten, quartz, agate. This is a geode and this is petrified wood.

A woman appears soundlessly. Her eyes are so incredibly blue, they seem black. There is no pupil, I realize, just a compacted field of absolute blue. Blue beyond larkspur or monkshood, mountain lakes and paintings and dream. These people have different gods, ways of mating and talking to the night. Maybe they get to wear stars in their foreheads. Who knows what visions such people have or what is said to them?

She wants a dollar to let us up the roped-off stairs. Roxanne thinks about it. She lights a cigarette and paces up and down, staring at the dusty carpet. There is nothing left to sell, pawn, or barter. Then Roxanne removes a dollar from her purse and hands it to the lady.

We are permitted to climb the steps. We are edging closer to the Wonders of the West. We must do this in deceptive increments, in sequences of locked cabinets and ruined rugs. Upstairs is a room littered with random junk. The lady with the eyes of isolated midnight explains the objects to us. She shows us a pony express mailbag and antique dentist tools. She points to a portrait of three severe women. You would not want to invite them to dinner. Below the painting is a water keg, a surveyor's chair, and a comb for sheep's wool. Roxanne wants to ask for her money back. I can tell.

"If this is what you learn from the ancestors, no wonder everybody runs from the land," Roxanne says in front of the tour guide, the lady with the icy eyes. Roxanne doesn't care who hears her.

We are walking down the stone steps and we don't look at each other. We continue down the street where everything is closed. We pass a brick post office with statues of soldiers holding rifles, a man made of metal for each of the three major wars. The street is empty. We walk for blocks and don't pass anyone. We have seen something horrible in the courthouse. We avoid mentioning this.

I know what has occurred is somehow irrevocable. It is like a permanent stain. It is like being born wrong. I understand this because Roxanne lets me hold her hand as tightly as I can. I hold it so long I am convinced I have memorized it, the bones and veins that cross her fingers in ridges like rivers. I hold her hand until I am certain I will be able to find her in other lives, when it's dark, when I'm blind and time is completely different.

20

There is snow on top of the mountains in the blue distance but the heat is fierce, relentless, without breeze or variation. The world has deepened and stalled. The sky is crowded with sudden thunderheads but somehow we are driving beyond them. It doesn't rain.

There are towns that look like movies of the Old West. I have seen this in the afternoons I curled up on the green sofa with my mother and watched "Hollywood Playhouse." Now we have actually come here. We have traveled through time and everything is too small.

There are too many people. They are tourists with cameras around their necks. Roxanne says they saved their money all year for such a trip. Her voice rises with contempt.

We watch a crowd gather for a mock shoot-out in the middle of a reconstructed western village. A lady wearing eyeglasses and a blue saloon-girl dress wraps red ropes across the sidewalks. Men appear wearing vests and bandannas around their dirty necks. Their clothing is filthy and I feel it is not volitional. They look like the drunks and bums Roxanne and I saw near the used-car lot. The men who shouted things to Roxanne and made gestures with their fingers and she told me to just ignore them. Now they pretend to be struck by bullets and fall down.

"This is horseshit," Roxanne says. "What do they think they're dealing with? A world of hillbillies?"

We find a museum of guns, and because it starts raining we go in. Roxanne appears serious, studying a navy model Colt from 1852. She points to a feature in the pocket model Colt, Wells Fargo type. She tells me it is from 1848. She acts like she's planning to buy it. She puts it down like she may be back in an hour. She might need it for her collection.

Then we are walking past stores of snake and lizard boots in shops where you can buy saddles. Roxanne examines a Cheyenne saddle with wooden stirrups. There are signs everywhere for Indian jewelry. Roxanne spends the afternoon draping herself in silver and turquoise bracelets, necklaces and rings. The necklaces are called squash blossoms and fetishes. Later she tries on buckskin jackets with fringe hanging down from the sleeves. She looks at herself wearing hats made from the skin of coyotes and beavers.

It is easy to eat in these tourist towns. Roxanne says the waitresses are either inbreds or college girls. In either event, they don't know how to watch. We eat entire dinners with desserts. Then we walk out of the restaurant when no one is looking. We eat steak twice a day. The rebuilt wooden sidewalks are filled with old people and couples carrying packages and holding the hands of children. We walk slowly. No one is behind us.

We read the window displays for rafting trips and floating trips for houseboats and canoes and kayaks. Roxanne stares at a photograph of a raft going through a rapid. She reads the text twice. She shakes her head from side to side as if to clear it. It occurs to me that Roxanne is swaying too much. She is becoming liquid and cloudy, something is leaking in.

There is a stuffed elk in front of a shop. I touch it and it feels like a rug you wouldn't want near your feet. There are pelts hanging in the windows and belt buckles made out of antlers and rocks and shells. We could buy one for Uncle Louie but we don't have any money. Then there are porcupine quill earrings and an iron cowbell that looks like a hundred years of rust and bad luck sat on top of it. There are skulls of steer and cows on the floors of the shops. Roxanne stops to stare at a lamp made out of the feet of an elk. I can still see the fur, the hoofs have been varnished so they are shiny.

"I wish I had a camera," Roxanne says for the first time. She touches the lamp. "Louie wouldn't believe this." She stares at her fingers as if she expected them to fall off.

There are stuffed and mounted heads on the walls of the stores. I can identify them. Deer and elk and moose and pronghorn antelope. There are patchwork quilts made out of hides and pelts and stacks of deerskin billfolds with ornamental stitching around the edges. There are boxes filled with animals carved out of wood, bear and birds and buffalo.

In the Old West Animal Zoo we see a display of stuffed elk with locked antlers on a circular platform that keeps turning. They are perpetually fighting. Behind them is a background of painted trees. I tell Roxanne I want to leave. She says not yet.

It's a zoo of the dead. I understand that. The cells have no glass or bars across the front. I consider the possibility that these dead animals are held in place by invisible force fields. Perhaps the extraterrestrials did this.

The next room contains a stuffed coyote chasing three stuffed pronghorn antelope. There is a stuffed badger and a cow skull on the ground, which is sand. The walls are painted with a river running through the corner. These are the kind of mountains we saw in New Mexico, before Roxanne took this detour. I remember the mountains are called mesas.

In the Real West Art Gallery there are stuffed grizzly bears nailed onto rocks and mountain lions bolted to a wall ten feet high. There are paintings of cowboys on horses riding into Indian camps. There are Indian women standing in front of tepees holding babies. There are sheep in the crags between snow. There are paintings of elk clashing near icy rivers. There are eagles and deer fighting.

"I'm beginning to understand America," Roxanne tells me.

We are driving south now into the heat and Idaho. I can't determine if it is good or bad to understand America. I can't see her eyes through her new sunglasses. She stole them in the Indian jewelry store. She put them in her pocket when no one was looking. And now she won't let me hold her hand.

Then we see the flags. At first Roxanne doesn't know why. We watch a parade where people are marching with red, white, and blue banners. We have come to Idaho Falls on the Fourth of July. America is going to do a slow strip-tease for us. First the clothing, then the skin. Then we are going to look at the heart of the thing. When Roxanne says this, she smiles.

We walk to a park near a river. We have seen this river many times, crossed and recrossed it, glimpsed it to the left, the right. The Snake. Roxanne says they call it the Snake not because of how it curves and slithers. She says they call it the Snake because it is so ugly.

Now we are standing in a city park along the Snake River in Idaho. It is July 4. It is incredibly hot. We are walking through the dusty green expanse and we are having the core revealed.

America is women weaving cloth. It is booths where women display the quilts they have cut and sewed. They hang on clotheslines in the sun as if there were still something left to dry inside of them. In booths women spin yarn. There are woven floor mats and quilted clown dolls on shelves and rising out of cardboard boxes. There are quilted pillows in the shape of hearts with lace running along the edges.

America is a demonstration of beading techniques. It is antique crocheted doilies and antique white aprons with crochet along the cotton hems. There are antique white dresses with crochet around the high necklines hanging on clothespins strung on thin ropes. Then there is a display of old-fashioned kitchen wares laid out on a rough wood table under a pine tree; an iron ice cream scooper, an iron nutmeg grater, a corn dryer, and a colander.

"I feel sick," Roxanne says. She is suddenly very pale. I think she may fall down.

Roxanne lets me take her hand. I close my eyes. When

I touch her skin I feel like I can see perfectly in the dark. I don't need eyes. I find a tent in the center of the park and we sit down. "Bluegrass," Roxanne whispers into my ear.

I look at the grass and it is green. On a stage, a man plays a guitar, a woman plays a violin, and a girl perhaps my age plays a banjo. When they finish, three men come out with instruments I don't recognize. Roxanne tells me it's a mandolin, a dulcimer, and a bass. "It's a standard configuration," Roxanne says. I am still looking for the blue grass.

Roxanne notices a man in the next row with a bottle of whiskey in a brown paper bag. She walks over, bends down, asks him for some, and he gives it to her. Then she says she feels better.

Outside the tent is a sun that doesn't move or bend. It is clearly permanent. Children are standing in line to get into a red canvas booth where they can have their faces painted for two pennies. I watch them having their cheeks made fuchsia, having pastel hearts put on their foreheads, having their eyes made to resemble raccoons.

"Don't even think of asking," Roxanne says. "This stuff is for hayseeds. Don't even let the thought cross your mind."

We are walking through a park under a sun that seems painted, anchored, abusive. Roxanne is permitting me to hold her hand. I am steering her. An old man is explaining how to make log cabins, how you square off the log and cut the notches. Then there are the quilted potholders made from the pattern of the lone star. There are children standing in line for donkey rides. The donkeys are eating hay out of baskets hanging from the end of a lime green trailer. I wonder what else is inside, where the people who own the donkeys go, where they sleep. Then a woman dressed like a cowgirl shows how to outfit a mule for a hunting expedition, how to hang the blankets and rifles and cooking pots, what you do in storms.

I lead Roxanne to a kind of photo gallery of cardboard cutouts where you can put your face and have a picture taken. It is a field of strange decapitations. You can be the face of a woman on an old-fashioned bicycle. You can be dressed like a gunfighter or a saloon girl. You can be Superman. I don't even consider asking Roxanne for ten cents. I wouldn't want to put my face near such things.

At the edge of a park is a banner announcing Early Western Skills. We watch boys lassoing plastic bullheads attached to bales of hay. We sit in a restored stagecoach. We trace the red and yellow paint along the wheels, the gold designs stenciled on the doors, the eagle in the center carrying arrows in his right talon and a branch in his left. Then we watch a man make a rope by braiding leather.

We are walking along the periphery as if there was more air there. We find a cooking booth with free samples. There is a casserole dish with chili. Roxanne fills a paper plate with it. She says it's cold and greasy but she eats it and goes back a second time. She returns with a loaf of bread. She eats three pieces quickly and tells me to put the rest under my shirt. I do.

Everywhere is a sheer blue sky. It looks severed and nailed and it is filled with yellow balloons. The children are carrying and releasing yellow balloons. I don't know why. They are tossing beanbags into barrels and trying to knock over bottles with baseballs. They have butterflies painted on the sides of their faces. Their mothers gave them two pennies for this. I know I am nothing like them.

We have come to the replica of an Indian village. There

are two tepees made out of canvas. The doors are stitched with pieces of pine so white that at first I think it is bone. We go inside. The guide explains that the Indians slept on elk pelts and buffalo hides. There is a pile of furs in the corner. Roxanne lies down on them. Near her are ceremonial Indian shields made from fur and hides with beads and feathers attached to a round wooden frame made from bent wood. The guide points out the features for me. Roxanne has fallen asleep. I pretend to be interested. I ask the man questions. The guide has blond hair and he is dressed like an Indian. Then he notices Roxanne. He shakes her awake. Then we start walking again.

We pass three women wearing identical white layered dresses with black aprons and black fans. They climb a stage where they begin to dance and sing in a foreign language. Their black hair is pinned up and they are wearing red flowers behind their ears. When they finish, there is a sort of play about the evil of drinking whiskey. Men shoot each other with pretend guns. Then men in traditional western buckskin outfits with fringe and Indian beading come on stage. Their caps are made from coyotes. They carry buffalo guns and Jim Bowie knives. It's like a fashion show. A lady holding a microphone explains their garments to the audience.

It is never going to get cooler. Something has happened to the orbit of the Earth. Maybe that's why Roxanne is so pale and why she allows me to hold her hand, to take her by the elbow, to tell her where to go with my arm. We are walking past a booth of dolls made out of rope with gingham blouses and dolls with carved wood faces and gingham dresses. I think Roxanne is going to say something about my dolls, how I could have fit one or two into the car when we packed but she doesn't. And there are cloth pigs with lace bows. There are more quilted hearts and carved wooden hearts and painted wood plaques that say the word *heart* on them in red letters.

Then there are tables with doll clothes and towel sets. It occurs to me that we don't need any of these things. There is a booth with turquoise and silver jewelry hanging from antlers. There are animal pins in thin silver. We walk into a booth that seems cool beneath canvas. It is not. It is steaming inside. There are ornamental wreaths made from native wildflowers hanging on nails. There are bows and crescents constructed from what might be weeds. We pass a table with beer steins and Davy Crockett mugs. You can drink from his scalped open head.

Roxanne leans against a table of carved ceramic Indians. There are entire miniature families, women with babies and men surrounded by wolves. An almost naked warrior offers up a buffalo skull to the sky. Roxanne is unsteady. I am still holding her hand. We are standing near a stack of crocheted hearts and a jar with a sign that says PREHISTORIC POTTERY, THREE SHARDS FOR TEN CENTS.

I am reaching out to pick up what looks like a wedding bouquet. The flowers and ribbon are purple like a certain kind of water.

"Don't," Roxanne cautions. "Touching something like that lowers your intelligence." Then she lets go of my hand and falls slowly down to the grass.

Everything happens in separate increments, the way you build something with blocks, one at a time. People are detaching themselves from the sides of the booth. They are picking Roxanne up from the too-hot grass. They are carrying her down to the river.

Roxanne lays under a willow tree and the water flows below her, the ugly Snake, creased in the heat. A lady puts a cold handkerchief on her forehead and asks me if she is pregnant. I have no idea what to say. Someone gives me a plastic glass of ice. They tell me to keep putting it on her neck. I do this.

I watch the river. I think my secret river thoughts about how water can take you back and forth through time. It isn't spaceships that people need. It is sailing crafts and barges, piers and canals. In such ports, you can trade flowers, spices, verses from songs. You can barter purple bridal bouquets. There are constant ceremonies.

"I haven't fainted since I was thirteen in Atlantic City," Roxanne says later. This is when she leans up on one elbow, when it is cooler. "I'll tell you that story sometime."

People are assembling on the riverbank. When it's dark there will be fireworks. We have come to the heart of America on its birthday. And I don't think Roxanne will ever tell me what happened in Atlantic City.

A woman passes near us in a floral print dress, low cut, with purple and orange flowers and sleeves that can be pushed down and worn across the middle of the shoulders like a kind of high bracelet. Her sandals are fuchsia with four-inch black high heels. She stumbles in the grass and I realize it doesn't matter.

A man has his arm around the woman's shoulder. He's taking her down to the river to watch the fireworks. He spent the afternoon with her in the park. He bought her a quilted potholder and a crown of hearts that glistened. It was only two dollars but it made her face look like rainbows were walking across her forehead. She is wearing the crown now, walking down with him to the river.

It occurs to me that I know what the women in the windows are thinking. They are always remembering that it was summer, the Fourth of July, the evening after the fair in the park. There were thunderheads, but the heat made them insignificant. They drove to the river past fields of barley and potatoes. There were dandelions and milk thistle along the highway. She could have asked him to stop and he would have. She could have gotten out and made thousands of wishes. He would have let her.

She knew the thunderheads wouldn't do anything. Soon she would be beside the river with a man who loved her. People would look up and see her floral print dress with its orange and purple flowers, with its festive assertion of odd power. They would see the way he was holding her hand, see the crown of hearts on her head and know she was loved. It was just a series of plastic shapes but it glittered. It had ribbons that ran halfway down her back.

They drove toward the river past the barley, past the hay that looked like it had been rolled into spools, like some old woman did it in the middle of the night when the moon was full. The woman was wearing high-heeled sandals because she thought they made her startling and elevated, made her turn heads. There were ducks in the water and men whistled from cars. He was holding his arm across her shoulder as they walked past the families setting up their barbecues.

I am watching Roxanne stare at the water, the Snake getting dull green, dented with shadows. Roxanne knows what the women in the windows think. The water is less spectacular than they had planned, less blue, vivid, and intoxicating. Then the women realize it is always this way.

Rivers aren't about color and water, they're about ideas, about the idea of a river.

The woman in the floral print dress and fuchsia sandals hasn't brought a blanket or a towel to sit on. I notice that immediately. That's how new they are as lovers, that woman and man. It simply hasn't occurred to them. They are going to watch the fireworks. The thunderheads are merely decorative, ornamental. They cannot possibly intrude upon the night's events.

The woman in the floral print dress knows she is the most beautiful woman on the riverbank this night. No one else is even trying. She doesn't glance at Roxanne, pale and sick under a willow, in shadow. But she takes in the tableau in general, the women who had been to the fair and were still just wearing shorts. They have so many children, so much had spilled all those hot hours. Now they are spreading out their homemade quilts on the grass.

No one knows where they are going to set off the fireworks. Some said from the island in the river like two years ago. Others said they were going to use the shore in front of the motel. The woman in the floral print dress doesn't care where they release the fireworks. She is certain she will see them perfectly. He will have his left arm across her. She will be embossed, cast like an artifact or something you could sell. The breeze will be rising now in the inverted circle of erupting flowers, the designs that look like flaming fish in the sky, all of this will be indelible. It will be the one Fourth of July she will never forget.

Roxanne and I watch the woman in the floral dress slip off her sandals. We are barefoot, too. Everything about the night is definitive, not just the sky and the sun setting behind the dusty thunderheads but the grass, how it feels between our toes. It is surprising, the mosquitoes, the weeds, the stalks that reach out and scratch.

Then I understand what the women in the windows are thinking, how a riverbank is just the idea of a bank. It is never really the moist soft slope one imagines. Then the breeze comes up behind the willows just as the fireworks begin and the sun sets behind the packing plant.

Roxanne and I have the same thoughts. I am certain. We have decoded the faces in the windows and on the riverbanks. We sit in the darkness until the edge of the river is deserted. The families have taken their children and quilts home. The lovers have left. Then we walk back to the car and start driving.

21

Night into day and there is always the sense of the thick sky where anything is possible, the mountains, the willows and cottonwoods near the irrigation canals. We have seen the fireworks above the Snake River, which was a rubbed-away green like old upholstery, something Roxanne would say not to sit on. It was like vacant lots with broken sofas and refrigerators left there that could kill children. It was something to avoid.

We are aiming south. We have a purpose and we will not deviate again. We are going to see the Wonders of the West in Utah and then we will find Uncle Louie in Los Angeles. We have seen the faces of the women in the windows behind their kitchen curtains and we have deciphered this and the disguised nature of riverbanks, what they really mean. We are draped with subtlety. We know the codes. We can conjure.

I wake up and it's already hot, flat, uncompromising. This is the land of no deal. I can recognize barley now, corn, potatoes, onions, weeds. The silos are like pottery coils made out of strips of tin. This must be what monsters make in art class, rolling the metals between their fingers which aren't fingers and don't bleed.

The hills have painted letters on them, *B, V, N.* Or perhaps the letters are actually carved into the rock. I ask Roxanne why they do this.

"It's part of some colossal stupidity," she says. "Some moronic ritual."

I consider Druids, African chanting, the sacrifice of the harvest and voodoo. Maybe there is a language of stone and color, terra-cotta and rain. One could beseech the spirit of the three islands under the ocean. There are gods of exits and entrances you can ask for protection. There are specific objects these deities desire like gems and perfumes and satins. I saw a program about this on television. People built altars of vermilion cut-glass beads and palm fronds. They listened to the edges of thunder and pounded drums. But I know this isn't what Roxanne means.

Then she stops on the shoulder of the road, the tires scatter gravel. She takes out her map. A woman watches us from her kitchen across a patch of low corn. The woman is holding a yellow dish towel in her hand and I look directly into her eyes.

She is thinking about how it was when he first began to tell her stories. Once he told her about arriving in the Southwest, how surprised he was by the storms. He drove

into one and then out and back again, trying to determine
the precise point where it began. He did this repeatedly.
That was the year he saw everyone was burning sage and
red juniper. She asked him what red juniper smelled like.
He said it was the reason wood had been born and the
answer to why anyone would wish to burn it.

She envisioned him on the edge of some desert running
laps like a sick dog in August and drinking too much. She
imagined him as a kind of delirium, an inflammation.
Things glowed infrared. She could track him in the dark.
She could find his traces where there was no moon, no
lamps. When they kissed she thought of rubbed sand and
fever and lime and afternoons of tequila and glare. She
assumed that he would always tell her what he was thinking, they would reveal themselves in cycles like seasons.

"Maybe three hours," Roxanne decides and refolds the
map.

I follow her back to the car. Later we stop on a ridge. The
sun sets above a river, probably some tributary of the
Snake. The water is metallic orange and fuchsia. Fish jump
out of the surface. There are 141 in two minutes. I count
out loud until Roxanne tells me to be quiet. Then it is dark.

We come to the town with the Wonders of the West and
I know we don't want to see this. We have looked at the
quilts and the boots made from lizards, we have held the
rocks, felt the antlers and watched the mock gun battles.
We have memorized the fireworks like a swarm of inflamed
fish burning to death above our faces. And we were singed.
In Wyoming we saw the heads of animals nailed onto walls
with their eyes in a stasis of sadness and horror and some
final and complete surprise. In Idaho we drove through a
grasshopper storm. We have seen enough.

It is midnight. Roxanne parks near a church and we push back the car seats and try to sleep. That's what we've been doing lately, sleeping near churches with the car doors locked. We have become afraid of dogs and shadows and other people. We have seen something monumental. It feels like the chamber where all things antique and uncharted are. And you cannot clear your head of these interior rivers. They don't disappear in the morning.

We sleep poorly because we are hungry and sunburned. I close my eyes and see the women in the farmhouse windows. They are thinking if he really loved her he would take her away from here, away from that one cottonwood on the mute flat horizon. He would take her away from the field with the dandelions you wouldn't dare to pick, to put near your mouth, to blow on and make a wish. You would be afraid you might get it. It might come true. The women in the windows are thinking if he really loved her, he would take her to a place where she felt like she wanted to breathe, where she wanted to open her mouth and do something besides shout, let me die, let me drown, let me out.

I don't want to open my eyes. We have encountered something intrinsic to the fabric of the night and I know we have changed.

Roxanne shakes my shoulder. It is pre-dawn, the first hot streaked gray. This is the embryo of heat. Somebody should step on it now before it coalesces and ambushes the sky.

We are walking through a downtown I have seen in its sequence of variations. There are always three or four blocks of low faded brick buildings. There is Constitution Hotel and Riverview Inn on Main Street. There is Brady's Bar and the Texas Bar on Broadway. There is a church, a library with boards across the broken windows, three stores selling guns and fishing equipment, a store with pianos, a shop with antiques, two banks, and everything is closed but a café for truck drivers.

The waitress doesn't glance at us. She is thinking if he really loved her, he would tell her stories about Arizona like he used to. In the beginning he would recount the day he saw three rainbows in the arroyo behind his house. He walked down into them, into the end of the rainbow, and he knew the fantastic was possible. Love and rumors, things from dreams and books, vestiges, sacred objects and spells. The next day he bought a silver bracelet from an Indian, for protection, and he never took it off. It occurs to her that if he really loved her, he would give that bracelet to her.

Downtown are the train tracks, the water tower, the grain elevator, the old stockyards, the structures for storing what grows like so many miniature cities. This is a series of repetitions we have memorized.

Then we cross the tracks, the unborn places at the edges. Now there are streets that could be anywhere. They are lined with trees and the sidewalks are torn, uneven. There are two-story houses behind iron and stone fences. There are stacks of wood cut for burning. It is already so hot, the grass looks yellowed. In the backyards behind the wood and stone houses are picnic tables and swings hanging from trees. The streets are named for trees: Walnut, Pine, Elm, Maple, Spruce. The streets are named for elements: Water, Ridge, Valley, Mountain, River.

Near the corner of a street named for something mined from the earth we have come to a derelict structure. Perhaps it was once apartments. The remains of a sign says CABINS. All the doors are opened. You could just walk in.

The paint is peeling. I can see holes in the walls as we pass. There is no more glass in the windows. Outside there are two stoves, pieces of blackened pipe, brown chairs, the remains of a campfire. I don't need to have Roxanne tell me not to touch anything.

Then we see the Wonders of the West. It is a printed sign twice the size of those that offer houses for rent or sale. I don't understand where we are. It seems to be a regular house behind a high wire fence. Roxanne is smoking a cigarette and it begins to rain lightly. There were thunderstorms in the night. I wasn't sure but now I suddenly remember. No one else is on the street but she just keeps standing where she is, like she's afraid if we get out of the rain we might lose our place in the line that isn't there.

Finally an old man unlocks the gate. He is wearing a cowboy necktie with a turquoise disk in it and he has too many keys. It takes him four tries to open the lock. Roxanne pays him five dollars and he lets us walk in.

Behind the house, which looks like any house where a family might live, where a child might go to school and a father come home from work, we find we are standing in a large fenced yard. At the edge there is a tiny log cabin with rusty wagon wheels leaning against it. I walk over, bend down, and run my fingers along the orange ring surrounding the wooden spokes.

"Don't touch that," the old man says to me. He sounds angry.

Roxanne has walked past the miniature log cabin. I can see her red scarf on the far side of the enclosure, past the accidental pyramid of broken tools. There are no spells here. There are no altars. It is a graveyard of empty wagons of various types, all of them inconsequential. Perhaps some carried people and other boxes of farm equipment or crops.

It's a wasteland of rusty metals and machines to sharpen obscure things with and all the edges have turned orange. It smells like heat and contagion, lightning and dust. Somewhere, all the women are quilting.

We are standing in a cemetery of antique tools and barrels and the shells of objects you can't tell what they were for, farming or making war. They could be part of a harvest or a massacre. I identify a seat from an old tractor made out of iron with many holes in it. We have come to a monument of corroded nails and pieces of spikes and fragments that might be partially vaporized. Perhaps creatures from other worlds came here and created this ruin. It had something to do with the nature of their fingers, some chemical reaction, some unavoidable residue.

"You're telling me this is the Wonders of the West?" Roxanne asks with what I am learning to recognize as contempt. She has put her face near the old man. She has lit another cigarette. She may reach out and grab his sleeve with her fingers. The wind is rubbing against the side of her face like it was imparting the precise details of a complex procedure.

"That's what the sign says, lady," the old man answers. He turns and walks away. I listen to his boots on the gravel, how it sounds hollow and final. Before there were words there were stones. I understand this. Now the man bends down and pretends to be interested in a spoke of gray wood.

I am waiting for Roxanne to insist that he give back her money, that he take it from his shirt pocket where we watched him put it and hand it back to her. When we have driven out of the town, when we have gotten back on the highway with its arrow that says Las Vegas, I ask her why she didn't demand a refund.

"You pay to play," Roxanne smiles. There is nothing

happy in it. "And I am learning how to play."

It is downhill from Utah past trees with branches like feathers. Maybe Roxanne could put them in her old hats, the ones in the closet with the coats with torn collars. Then I remember all of this is gone. I am thinking you could blow on these branches and make wishes like you do on dandelions and milk thistle. But Roxanne has said these are the badlands. That must be why the plants look cursed. You could make only terrible wishes in a place like this where the rocks lay on the valley floor in rows that resemble decapitated heads. Maybe some king got angry. Maybe he ordered a slaughter and then he got so mad he just drove away. Isn't that what happened to my father?

We are winding past a kind of ghost town of brush on a hill and everything is calico. It's a world of only three colors and I can name them: dusty moss, brown, and tan. Trains are like snakes with the same fast patterns, the hallucinatory etchings, the way they keep to the edges and night. You don't know their intentions. You can't even be certain you really saw them. The sky is some useless blue. There is no way to determine its mood. Then the sand turns gray or rose. There are places where it looks like it wants to die or give birth to itself. We have arrived in the region where there is no counting. This is the place before rock.

There are ridges of cloud that remind me of white atomic explosions. There are plants that make me think of hair, stubble, something I wouldn't want near my lips. There are Joshua trees with branches like mutilated fingers. My mother could do this to my hands if I made her angry enough. And farther, closer to the highway, trees are growing between gravel and dried riverbeds as if someone had planted and forgotten them. They might be what scarecrows look like after the bomb has fallen and everything is different.

I think we are going to Las Vegas. That is what the highway sign says, the way the arrows keep pointing. I have seen the Las Vegas brochure accompanying the Nevada map in Roxanne's purse. It is a booklet with photographs of swimming pools and hotels and a sense of fantastic shade. I have read the brochure twice.

When I see women in the windows of the houses near the highway now, I think they are imagining Las Vegas. They are thinking, if he really loved her, he would take her to the city that is an oasis. He would give her handfuls of silver money and plates of prime rib and drinks that taste like mangoes. I am surprised when Roxanne doesn't stop in Las Vegas, when the city is behind us.

"I've seen the Wonders of the West alright," she says. "And I'm through being nickel-and-dimed."

We are not going to survive this desert, not when we have to stop every twenty miles and pour water in the radiator. We have water but Roxanne won't let us drink it. We must save it for the car. We are not going to live through this and the way the trucks with their killer faces see Roxanne in their headlights and blast the air around our shoulders with their horns. They are slapping our bodies with their sounds. They are pretending it is their hands.

The sand has become a fact of our life, a lower register we don't bother to question. It's always been there. This is the place before stone. The air has become dangerous and abrasive. It stings my eyes. Once the sky completely vanished. There was no ground or horizon, no color, no outline, no system of measurement, and I thought I was dead.

Then there is a town again. I understand this as an

inevitability. The world remembers to divide itself into Euclid Avenues and Fourth Streets and Vineyard Boulevards. There are the tops of trees I don't know the names of on the side of the highway. Roxanne doesn't know either and she doesn't care anymore. She isn't going to be nickel-and-dimed. And the trees are part of this. There have been cottonwoods along irrigation canals and willows by rivers and blue spruce and aspen in high mountain meadows and Joshuas in the sand and did any of it matter? Did any of it speak, impart the fragment of a dream, provide the shade you never forget?

There are boulevards named for men again and Highland and Sierra and Grove Streets. There are acres of orchards everywhere. Then come roads that crisscross the soft blue of valley floors and look like the sort of streets you would take into some irredeemable internal exile. No one would build you a statue or compose a song about what you did or said. You would wave good-bye once and disappear forever.

A man helps us put water in the overheating radiator. We have come to a gas station in the suburbs of a city. He can't believe we made it across Death Valley. He can't believe we crossed the Mojave Desert in the summer in this vehicle. He says that to Roxanne three separate times. He shakes his head from side to side. He goes to a machine and opens it with a key and gives us each a soda.

Then he tells Roxanne he was born here, in California. She stares at him as if such an event were not quite possible. She whispers to me that he is a native. He looks completely ordinary to me.

But there is a sense of oranges and dusty eucalyptus when he speaks, something slow and spiced and half-asleep. The man keeps talking to Roxanne. I consider the eucalyptus, how the high branches remind me of driftwood. This is how I know the air will be different here and the borders between sky and water will be less assured.

There has been an initiation, but it was ambiguous. We have outwitted the badlands and the places before words or stones. We have survived valleys where it looked like someone had dropped boulders to the ground one by one, as if in a monumental act of severing. We have driven past men in overalls walking by the gravel border of highways in the early mornings as if they had just left the scene of a violent crime. Men with their hands in their pockets and their eyes looking downcast at the earth. Men who look like they might be whistling and hoping no one was following or noticing them. Men who look like they were willing themselves to vanish. Maybe they had just killed their wives.

I fall into a sleep that isn't a sleep. It's a new way of traveling. You send your body on in the car but your eyes keep looking at the trees and the sand and the riverbank. There are always fireworks. It is always the Fourth of July. You aren't really in the car at all. I am the only person in the world who knows how to do this.

When I wake, I ask Roxanne what sick thing is perched above me. I am still thinking of mass murder and the somber vacant edges between towns and the men that walk by highways. I can still see the faces of the women in their kitchens holding yellow dishrags and thinking about Las Vegas, or the Fourth of July, or his stories of storms and rainbows and arroyos. I am thinking it is possible that these are the Wonders of the West.

I want to say this to Roxanne but there has been an inexplicable spillage. There was the pawning, the nights on the blankets beside the car when I looked up and renamed the constellations. I am remembering this when Roxanne turns to me and says, "It's sunset in Los Angeles."

Then she lets the made-up word drift into the tainted red air. The night seems suddenly too cool and I think of contraband and something audacious and flagrant and absolutely lost.

22

I smoke one of Roxanne's reefers as I walk to West Los Angeles High School. I may be arrested and placed in a state facility. There will be some form of incarceration and a drab uniform. There will be doors that lock from the outside and whole new avenues of abuse.

I realize the sidewalk is not simply concrete. These are not merely magnolias with hideous welded-on whitish blossoms, not just derelict shadows from ragged fan palms but the ingredients of an augury.

I have a sense of destiny and revelation. I feel open and raw and it's not entirely unpleasant. I am staring at the neon sign of a doughnut shop and it occurs to me that I can see inside metal, the stark configuration, the interior of the shell like so many yellow heron tracing the swaying horizon.

It's the middle of May and jacaranda is falling brilliant and luminescent, an insistent amethyst no one seems to notice. No one mentions it. It's a small lilac pulsing on the extreme margin. It gets absorbed with the half-lives and X rays. When you look up it's gone.

Nothing from the ground. No contact with soil. No jacaranda. It never happened. If you see it, flagrant and purple, say nothing. There are informers everywhere. There are no trees, not along the boulevards or in your family. There are no names for the ancestors. The only name you remember is Pink Eye, the drummer. He means more than your grandmother anyway.

I walk through the main gate and search for the police they've sent to capture me. Then I remove my best books from my locker, my Baudelaire and Allen Ginsberg, my Camus and Kafka and Rimbaud. And my new book about karma. I sit on the lawn and begin reading. I consider my concept of the continuum and how much like karma it is. When no one confronts me I feel immaculate and reprieved. Then the afternoon bell rings and I carry all my books home.

In the apartment where I somehow live, spring has been outlawed. There are no seasons in this elongated aberration. The rooms are so without features, they might be the unused month from a terminal patient's calendar, the September that never came. The air is the texture of insomnia, obsessions, and soiled bandages. This is where you can actually see suffocation. This is where you can watch the spread. This is the beach where you place a shell to your ear and you do not hear the sea.

"What is this?" Louie asks.

Louie and Doris have wheeled the television out of the closet. They have removed the cloth that covers it. They have switched on the news. Even Roxanne is watching. My first thought is that someone must have dropped a nuclear device on a major urban center. Perhaps the president has been assassinated. Something extraordinary has disrupted ordinary programming and my hands start to shake.

Roxanne has come back early and untanned. No winter. No explanations. No walking. No rituals. Blend in. Don't jeopardize. The fence is electrified. There are guard towers. Don't cry out. No fraternization. They will shave your head. No holidays. Save the wrapping paper. Protect your flank. Everything's coming up roses. And don't even think of asking why. They will put you on a train for the camps. There were infants. Mothers tossed them from the windows hoping some peasant would pick them up. Many skulls were crushed, a slow thud behind you. Boots ground the flesh into the mud.

"What is this?" Louie repeats.

I look where Uncle Louie is pointing. I follow the trajectory of his cigar. I know the answer.

"It's a revolution," I tell him.

Uncle Louie glances at me. "Fat kids don't make revolution," he said. He seems amused.

Roxanne is staring at a point of light lodged at the edge of her left hand. She moves her fingers through the leached air, testing something. Is it permanent? Will it slide off? If it doesn't, will it cost? "It's a lark," she finally decided.

"It's some Boston types slumming," Doris offers.

"They better watch it. Daddy won't put a sports car in their Christmas stocking," Louie said. He makes himself laugh.

I look at the television. I am looking directly at the

continuum, I understand this. I can sense some lilac presence. It's a portal. There's something I'm supposed to do. Then I can get there, across the bridge. And we are everywhere. We are wearing dangling bracelets with smooth silver moon crescents along our wrists. We are wearing amulets. There are so many of us, I can see that now, in the streets, standing along the side of roads. We are giving ourselves the names of hurricanes and ships. The context expands like a highway of violet smoke into the interior.

"They look like hicks," Doris says.

I realize there is no color in this apartment because the horizon has collapsed. It has all been absorbed, bleached. The room has no language, no magnitude or aspiration. Its definitions are obsolete and useless. They are gutted and drift like debris at my feet. I could step over them as I would garbage or kelp. Since there are no boundaries there can be no trespass or absolution. I find that reassuring.

This is what I'm thinking the next morning when I should be sewing. I feel a vague disappointment. I promised myself today would be a new beginning. I'm on time. They haven't put manacles on my ankles yet. They haven't doused me with the glowing maggots that ride on a current into the skull and eat everything back to the rules of addition and subtraction. It's a century where the citizens are the ones who have to worry. The buses come for them.

I am sitting in the sewing room. I have vowed I will not lose control when I hear the word *bobbin*. I am going to fit in.

"You're not sewing," Mrs. Carlsbad says.

She has appeared by my machine without warning like a gingham predator. She wears her own designs. That's why she's so brutally pastel. I understand that now, and the perpetual gathers in the powder blue skirts, the pink and yellow ruffles, the big buttons that match. Mrs. Carlsbad has been hiding in the tall grass stalking me. Now she bends down and removes the plug with a flourish.

"You might as well just go," Mrs. Carlsbad decides. She shakes her finger at me. "There's plenty here want to learn."

There's plenty here want to learn? Jesus.

Everyone else keeps sewing. No one even glances up from a single small seam. Christine Baker and Susan Towne won't even mention my public expulsion when the bell rings and they walk to cheerleader practice. It isn't worth a passing whisper.

"Just get out," Mrs. Carlsbad says. She is handing me an office slip. Her arm is stiff in the air. She doesn't want to be near me. A touch of apathy might rub off, or something vague and shabby, hungry and afraid without the sense to even learn how to clothe itself.

I walk by the front row of sewing machines where Christine Baker and Susan Towne sit. They live directly across the street from each other in tan houses. Christine's wood trim is yellow. Susan's is salmon. They have special signals they make from their bedroom windows with their hands, flashlights, and mirrors. They can practice their cheerleading routines while they wear pajamas and don't even leave their bedrooms. They have private bedrooms with their own bathrooms. They have pink shag carpets. That's what such a material is called. Shag. They have their own pink Princess telephones. They got them for their twelfth birthdays. They carpool in the mornings. Monday and Wednesday is piano. Tuesday is ballet.

I study the fabric they are sewing. They are surrounded

by incomprehensible pieces of cloth and paper patterns with pins stuck in them. It looks like something has been mutilated. Perhaps it's a kind of autopsy. Or are they practicing voodoo? And who knows what they are making by now? Prom dresses? Evening gowns? Baby clothes?

It's the middle of a class period and no one is outside. I imagine nerve gas has fallen and everyone is unconscious but me. I am immune because people who read Baudelaire in French are unaffected. The lyrical sound produces a complex biochemical reaction that provides a resistance. I can save their lives if I get help immediately. They don't have to go into an irreversible coma. I know how to call the paramedics. But I decide to let them die.

If the bomb were to fall at this moment there would be a conflagration of sea gulls and bougainvillea, oranges and lemons, the smoke from the fan palms. A certain form of blue would be removed from the bay at Santa Monica. The sky would be scalped and calm. There would be a seamless quiet. It would be the hour of prediction. There would be survivors.

I am standing alone, feeling my separateness and how clean it is. I throw away my office slip. There are white clouds in the center of the sky like the indication of a highway into some vast interior I always suspected was there.

I glance at the liberal arts building, imprinting the campus of West Los Angeles High School into my personal yearbook. This will be a souvenir item you can't buy at the end of the term or find your photograph in. The sport you played has been obliterated. There was no football or marching band. It was the end of the world and you didn't even know it.

On the other side of the street is a hedge of defiled pink hibiscus. I would not put one of those flowers in my hair. It would stain me. Past the sullen beaten pink an alley slopes parallel to a main boulevard that ends at the ocean. Once I stood in that alley and screamed. I laid down in the border of gravel and trash cans. The sky was an emptiness without shadows or distinction. It was so utterly neutral and indifferent, it was lurid.

I don't do that anymore. If I lose control again, they're going to put bars on my windows and anoint me with electric current to my brain. They may imprison me anyway, even if I suddenly make a prom dress and a meatloaf. It may be too late. They're convinced I'm not going to shape up. They know I'm not coping.

I am sitting very still. The street is a wash of smooth green clarities, tiny mirrors with inexplicable connections to one another. Then I realize I'm not going to Sybil Brand or Camarillo. These are not the syllables I've been searching for. I close my eyes. Somewhere along the lavender continuum something is gathering momentum.

"You won't believe where I've been," Pamela Bruno says.

She has just walked through the main gate as if the waters coughed her up, as if I had demanded a demonstration and here it is. Three-dimensional. I almost don't recognize her. There has been a process of clarification.

Pamela Bruno is wearing a long purple skirt and a scarf in her hair in the manner of a gypsy. Across her shoulders she has draped a shawl with red flowers. There are strands of amber and turquoise beads around her neck and a bracelet of small white and black stones she will later tell me are called snowflake obsidian. She knows how to collect them.

She has big hoops of brass earrings that cast shadows across her cheeks. They are a form of sculpture. Then I realize she isn't limping. I don't say anything. Perhaps she is being held in a spell of renewal and perfection. I am afraid to wake her.

I suddenly remember the photograph of Tamiko with her red satin saloon-girl dress, her sequins and feathers, how she looked like a time traveler. Pamela Bruno is the exact opposite. She is someone who has just landed in precisely the right place. She has indisputably come home.

"I've been to the Haight-Ashbury and Berkeley. I saw Jimmy. We smoked pot and made candles," Pamela tells me. She removes a candle from her bag. She has a kind of pack on her back held by shoulder straps. I've never seen anything like it. "You want to hear about it?"

I say yes. I am examining the candle Pamela and Jimmy made. I touch its cool yellow side as if it were an artifact from another world. Pamela tells me you can see the bridge from the window in Jimmy's apartment. I imagine it looks like an arm across the waters opened in a gesture of forgiveness and resolution. It makes me think of music.

I am staring at Pamela Bruno who isn't limping. Her face seems polished and serene. It could be a kind of glass. You could watch the sand fall inside her forehead and chart your hours.

Pamela is talking about making candles with Jimmy and I am stunned. I didn't realize it was possible to navigate such miles, to move between county lines and cities and cross entire states with their corrosive roads and intricacies, the dogs in packs and the way the wind and sand come to burn. I realize I have never understood the concept of escape before. Perhaps the depots are not all guarded by men with machine guns. Maybe there are broken places in the electrified fences.

Pamela Bruno says a guru is going to give a lecture at the Santa Monica Auditorium. She tells me her name is now Crystal and she doesn't take the medicine they gave her at Palms Memorial Hospital anymore. The pills made her nervous and gave her waterfalls of blue sparks in her hair. They stung and made her crazy.

I can't think of anything to say. It is possible to traverse California from south to north after all. Along the way names can be shed. There are subtle acts of sabotage and insurrection everywhere.

We ride the bus to Santa Monica. The lecture is about karma. I understand everything is about karma and the continuum. Events occur along the edge of subliminal rivers where nothing is solid. These are fault lines like those that cause earthquakes. These are the tremors of ideas. They are the wake from massive passing things you can't identify. They aren't verifiable and they don't come back again. It is night and there are two boys sitting next to us.

"Do you believe that? What he said about karma?" I ask the boy next to me. His name is Alan. I know he has a van and he's driving to Canada. He's going to stop in San Francisco first and burn his draft card. I heard him say that to his friend.

It is a still moment beside the violet continuum, a clearing that elongates near the river with its many strange nuances and unexpected ports. Here is a bend you couldn't have anticipated where everything stops. One hundred thousand white swans are slowly crossing but you can't know this. You can hear the rustle of petals and insects and water only. On all the balconies in dusks the color of wild iris, women are holding their breath. They wear disks with the likenesses of gods around their necks. They brush tin amulets with their fingertips. And I can't believe what I'm doing. I am finally speaking up.

The boy named Alan says yes.

"Me too," I tell him. "And it would be an act of good karma if you took us with you. Good for us in this life and good for you in some other."

I am staring at Alan. The continuum is a network of delicate wooden and iron bridges. We stand at the mouth of invisible rivers where they enter the sea. Sometimes someone appears with a raft, a barge, a limb from a tree. The city burns behind you. Perhaps it has been bombed. But you are on water. They cannot follow because you leave no tracks.

"We're not going until Monday," Alan says. He glances nervously at his friend. He hasn't decided about us yet. He wants to say no.

"Monday is fine," I say quickly. He knows where the main gate of West Los Angeles High School is.

We are walking out to the parking lot. The night is unexpectedly cool and I sense the ocean behind me. There might be stars but I'm not looking up. I'm following his khaki army jacket through the crowd. I have to see his van. I need this evidence.

Then it's there, a blue-purple, not midnight or cobalt but some new combination of the elements. A rainbow is painted on the passenger side. I trace the ridge of yellow with my fingertips, then the blue and red. It's a vehicle from dream. Travel is not as I have known it. There are camouflaged bridges you can cross only by showing your fingerprints. That's how you get through portals. That's how you move through time.

"Taking us will be like money in the bank," Pamela Bruno is saying. She has learned to speak up, too. "Something good will happen to you later. But you have to promise."

It is the season of amethyst. This is where the river curves and whispers your name and the names of your unborn daughters. In such nights everything is revealed in a language of vestal stars above coastal forests. If you stand absolutely still, you can remember every word.

Alan thinks about it. Then he says yes.

On Sunday afternoon, Pamela Bruno comes to my apartment. As she walks into the living room I realize she has never been inside before. No fraternization. No circling. No beverages in restaurants. No prayers. Keep a collection of Seconal. Don't jeopardize. No crying. Smoking cigarettes is okay. Save the wrapping paper. Always demand your money back. Winter doesn't figure. Protect your flank.

Pamela Bruno and I collect my notebooks and journals. We pack my books. There's a free store in the Haight. There are cardboard boxes on the sidewalk. You can just take what you want. You don't even need money.

It's nearly dinner time on Sepulveda Boulevard. They have set the paper plates of kaiser rolls and turkey salad on the side of the card table. Louie and Doris and Roxanne are watching the television news. It's a special report on flower children. I say the words softly to myself, flower children.

The week after the bomb was dropped on Hiroshima flowers appeared in the ruins. It was as if they had been conjured. After the German bombing of London, magenta fireweed grew in the wreckage. Now our bodies are petals and we will cover the spoiled corrupt country with our flesh.

"Look at this," Uncle Louie says. "A convention of ragamuffins." He points his cigar at the television screen.

"It's like a block party for squares," Roxanne says.

"We're going to stop the war," Pamela tells her. Pamela Bruno has lost sixty pounds and she has stopped limping. No one seems to notice.

"Did you hear that? The Poet and the Nutcase are going to stop the war," Aunt Doris says. She glances quickly at Louie.

"How? By throwing flowers?" Uncle Louie likes this. He makes himself laugh. "Maybe you can blow the army down with reefer smoke."

"We're going to build a new world," I say.

"You? And the ragamuffin jerks in Halloween suits?" Louie is still laughing.

"This is the shit of the season," Doris says. "Look at them. They look like farmers."

"You're a square," Uncle Louie decides. He studies me, briefly, then he turns away. I wonder what he sees. "Just like Ruthie always said. You had her pegged."

"Haven't I always called it?" Roxanne replies. "The square wants to go off and build her square world. All the squares sitting in the mud, playing musical instruments and kissing on the cheek. Naming themselves after spices. Christ."

"It's too much," Louie says. "A generation of lemmings. Go figure."

"Hippies, my ass," Roxanne says. She is looking at the television screen. She gives her mean laugh. "You got not a shred of hip."

Later I dust my side of the bedroom and sweep the floor under my bed. I am leaving behind the skirt from the banquet in Bavaria and the sweater with the tennis racket.

I am leaving behind all the garments that don't have my initials. I've already packed my canvas bag. It is filled with books. It's what Roxanne would call carry-on luggage. If you believe the planet is your starship, that's all you need.

I'm holding a blue scarf I've decided to take. I can wear it in my hair if it rains or drape it across my shoulders like a shawl. I could fold it around my waist as a belt or wear it as a veil. It is my world after all.

I understand the continuum now, the blue ports, the way the waters influence the currents that haven't yet been. And I don't want anyone coming at my flank. That's why I've folded my winter blanket at the foot of my bed. I've decided to leave it clean. It doesn't cost.

Suddenly I remember a holiday Jimmy told me about. It was the Festival of Lanterns. Candles were lit in lanterns in tiny boats sent out to the sea. The rivers were arteries of light, golden hatcheries. In preparation for this festival, houses and graveyards were cleaned.

"Don't listen to them. They're dinosaurs," Roxanne says.

She is leaning in the doorway holding a glass of vodka. Her hand sways back and forth like a soft pendulum. For a moment I think we are on a ship. Roxanne is wearing her short aqua blue kimono. If you examine the fabric carefully, you would see a deceptive pattern in charcoal, a series of butterflies with serrated edges and tiny leaves and lanterns. In the center of the lanterns miniature gold letters spell out Honolulu. Roxanne is staring at me like there is something she wants to know.

"Christ. I don't blame you. I've had it," Roxanne suddenly reveals. "Half the time I want to change my name to Rainbow and move to a farm."

I realize my mother is offering me a kind of benediction.

Later I sit in the deserted kiosk and wait for the cab that will take her to the airport.

I am barefoot and the grass is a form of cool caress rising up from the earth. It seems deliberate. I can feel the intensity of the moonlight where it grazes my skin. I consider bronze statues and how the flesh can seem to be a series of thousands of windows, all of them open. The wind can seem lit by candles.

Farther, beyond the city, mountains are like paper cutouts, a disheveled afterthought of ridges assembling themselves from the valley floor. This is what lies beyond the groves of date palms in rows above tumbleweed and orange trees. This is what California taught us.

Then I see her taxi. Somewhere it is a festival of spring grasses. Somewhere people are watching the moon above a river. There are always bridges. When Roxanne passes through the kiosk, I raise my arm and wave.

23

I finally understand the gravity of this world and where to put my feet. The continuum is a blue like the background in dreams and photographs. Or rocks that have been cut open and left for centuries under the moon. In time such stones become precious. It has to do with the starlight that accumulates and the shifting weight of the night with its avenues of complicated demands. This is where you get points for endurance. Eventually, if you survive, you can string such stones to your neck.

It is a Monday in May and I don't have to type or sew or cook anymore. There are no more paper sleeves with pins or mixing bowls, no more sounds of metal. I have kept the bridges to the regions I don't want to enter from my future.

I am simultaneously exposed and protected.

I am sitting in Mr. Gordon's office. It's ten minutes to three and I have been here since early morning. My recent absences have been discovered. Explanations have been required.

Today Mr. Gordon has taken notes. He squints at the pages on the conference table in front of him. This is how he lets me know he finds my thoughts unacceptable. I speak in a kind of hieroglyphics he cannot conceive of translating. Even his eyes resist.

"Have I got this right? You have a vision of the future. Everyone plays guitar and has hair like the Beatles? Women don't cook or sew? They're engineers and lawyers? Supreme Court justices?" Mr. Gordon glances at me.

I don't say anything. Mr. Gordon is poised on the border where irony and sarcasm collide. After this comes contempt. "And ball players? Quarterbacks?" he asks. He decided to cross over the line. It's a small incursion. It's like a little invisible Vietnam. What the hell. No one is watching.

"Maybe," I answer.

In Hiroshima some of the vaporized left an outline of their bodies against concrete walls. Such etchings remain forever. A man pushing a cart. A woman holding plum branches and the hand of a child. A trace on a courtyard wall, a burnt silhouette.

I am thinking about how many of us there are along the continuum. We are dressed in the clothing of gypsies and saloon girls. We are time travelers rising from the margins and alleys. We have woken up. We are what happens after somnambulism and the afternoons with their collection of miserable exhaustions. We have bruises and tattoos on our arms. But we can heal them. We can reach across rivers and oceans if we choose.

The stars are bone white where we look or whiter. It is always a night in the middle of the Festival of Lanterns. There is some pre-arrangement in this. We remember the rudiments. We make candles and offer branches of cherry blossoms and sweet yellow melons to the gods. You cannot count our numbers. We are washing up on shore. We are in the weeds and stones. We are the bank, the sediment and strata. We are the interlude of silence. We are indivisible in a landscape that knows us.

"This force is coming from all over the world? And there won't be families anymore? Or dress codes? Because you happen to know the dress code is illegal?" Mr. Gordon glares at me.

"It's unconstitutional," I correct him. "Yes."

"You're so smart, you'll probably study constitutional law. When you get your law degree you can set us right." Mr. Gordon lights a cigarette and smiles.

I can't think of anything to say. I'm not interested in law school.

"And this thing from the future wears a black leather jacket? It rides a motorcycle?" Mr. Gordon touches one of the pages on the conference table. It's a phantasmagoria. He has to pick it up and put the paper close to his eyes. Even then it doesn't make sense. "And your whole family is wrong? Everyone at Palms Memorial Hospital is wrong? The new governor of the State of California, Ronald Reagan, is he wrong?" Mr. Gordon asks.

I say, "Yes."

"The war in Vietnam is wrong? The Los Angeles Police Department is wrong? The U.S. Army and Joint Chiefs of

Staff are wrong? And President Lyndon B. Johnson is wrong?" Mr. Gordon pauses, presumably for dramatic effect. "But you are right?"

I feel the separate molecules in the air, how they collect into inexorable architectures and densities. They have settled across my shoulders like a form of lace. They have their own weight and direction. All I have to do is listen. It is for this moment all others have existed. This is the door I must walk through. It's where squalor and grace intersect. This is how you move through galaxies. This is where you are found or lost. This is where they keep the antiquities that matter. This is where you receive your real name.

I take a deep breath. I say, "Yes."

They can send nothing to find us. They cannot chart our miles. They cannot even comprehend them. We are what remains after the cool charade. We have mastered camouflage.

Now we are crawling out of derelict apartments padlocked from the outside. We are beneath the fronds of the degenerate palms. We know what malevolence is. We recognize corruption. We are walking slowly back from the beach with the pennies we have gotten from trading in salvaged soda bottles. This time we have saved our coins. We are packing our bags with our scarves and volumes of poetry. And we know exactly what we want.

"You're failing five of your classes and you think you're going to be a writer?" Mr. Gordon lets himself smile. He finds me peculiar. He wants me to know this. "You must be the smartest person in the history of the Courts. Maybe you're the smartest person in the history of West Los Angeles High School."

Jesus Christ. Where do they find these people? Does somebody have a contract to supply them? Do they have agents? Do they hold auditions?

It is essential to remember this section of Los Angeles from this particular second-story window. This is part of my ritual of cleansing and departure. There are half-constructed shells of apartments farther down the street. They are made from a pale wood that might have once meant something but sun has gutted and erased it. There is the suggestion of arches and balconies in this first draft of bleached wood. Perhaps if I look through them at a certain angle, I can see where I haven't yet been. It might be noon above a bay I don't know how to pronounce. No one has taught me. No one has ever taught me anything but the names of the many deaths.

Now I understand each noon has been precisely the same for millennia. The water is a blue that makes me think of absolutes like geometry and the more subtle configurations involved in a lullaby. There is a blue beyond all conventional expectation or longing and I have somehow found it. This is terminal blue. When you walk beside the shore of such a harbor you know it's the end. You don't need the titles, as Roxanne would say. You don't need the musical cues.

It is seven minutes to three. There are palm trees on the sidewalks below the apartments they are somehow constructing, where I cannot imagine anyone will ever voluntarily want to live. The air is too tarnished and malformed. And these are some variety of palm that resemble ferns. They have survived intact from a past so impossible to measure, to assign meaning to, that they are literally unspeakable. We can learn nothing from their history. They come from before bridges and trains and sharpened stones, before intention and regret.

Maybe these palms are doing a plant version of lingering. Perhaps somebody should stuff a suitcase full of Seconal in their mouths and let them go to plant infinity with dignity and class.

Then I see it, driving slowly up the low sloping hill. It is parking across the street from the main gate. The van with the ridges of rainbow. I recognize the configuration. The ridges form a crescent.

Once Roxanne went to Maui. She said there were rainbows every morning. She came back with rainbow paraphernalia, blouses with rainbows stitched over the breast, towels with fields of embroidered rainbows, ash trays where you could put a cigarette out in a rainbow. Roxanne said it was incredible. At precisely eight o'clock each morning a rainbow formed on top of the hotel. The breakfast rainbow.

Roxanne swam and slept for five days. Then she was suddenly overwhelmed by the desire to make things, flower and shell necklaces, wind chimes with stones and driftwood. She never felt anything like that before. They wanted her to see a doctor but she refused.

"I wanted to bleed for Maui," Roxanne said. "I wanted to have a baby or carve a statue. I wanted to choreograph a dance, maybe. I was standing on a balcony watching the palms move. I realized I was really watching the wind. It had nothing to do with the trees. And I suddenly thought, there's a thin line between beauty and suicide. I had to hold onto the railing. I wanted to jump. But it wasn't me really. It had nothing to do with me. It was just my legs."

It was sunset in West Los Angeles. It must have been summer. I could hear plates clattering on Formica surfaces.

I could smell meat. It must have been early in the month. There was the hum of televisions. Everything was etched with the sort of soft blue that made me think it was a memory even as it was happening. It unfolded the way I imagine tattoos do, slow stitches that enter you directly and each is vivid and startling. It's a kind of birth. Then you are different.

Roxanne had been unpacking. She stopped and left a suitcase open on the floor. She was lying down on her bed, smoking and staring at the ceiling. "Was that a crazy thought? I don't even understand that thought."

Roxanne pushed herself up on one elbow. She was trying to tell me something about lines and borders. I thought of the Joshua trees and the California desert after our inconclusive journey when Roxanne and I were simultaneously wounded and purified. I remembered the old barrels and broken wagons, the horseshoes in a haphazard pile oranged with rust, the miniature log cabin where no one could have ever breathed and the padlocked cemetery of useless things, stained pouches, spokes and pieces of tools they called the Wonders of the West.

"I sat on the beach stringing flowers together, making leis," Roxanne said. "I experimented with threads. I bought dental floss in the gift shop. It was perfect. Dino was doing a big benefit and I didn't even want to go. I had bags of plumeria. I pulled them off trees. I climbed fences. The white and pink were easy. The yellow were harder to find. I had to go farther. Security was watching me. They thought I was nuts."

It was night in the Courts. It was summer and I didn't ask her who she was talking about. At this undocumented place between us it wasn't important.

"A huge crowd gathered on the beach around dinner. I thought maybe somebody drowned and washed up. But I didn't understand why it happened every night. Maybe something with the current. Maybe a yacht tipped over."

Roxanne sat up and glanced out the bedroom window. It was an incomplete night, some version of dark where the edges didn't match and something leaked from between the seams.

"So what happened?" I asked. I wanted to hear her voice. I thought about people in depots and harbors. I considered people crossing borders. What they say has nothing to do with words.

"It was right before sunset. The air was purple like a glazed shell somebody spilled silver on. I asked what the color was. They said mother-of-pearl. I kept repeating that, mother-of-pearl. I began to remember my mother," Roxanne took a breath. It was possible she was going to cry. She didn't.

"I was falling in love with flowers. It hurt to look at the beach. The sky was like a coral reef in reverse. It was beautiful and horrible. Everything was tinted rose. The clouds were backlit. The horizon was a hot peach. I was thinking I'd like to see somebody direct this." Roxanne closed her eyes.

I imagined the shore with its streak of rose and the sky falling over the dusk waters like a benediction. I closed my eyes and said, "Then what?"

"The crowd was enormous. I thought somebody famous drowned. I heard Sammy was in town. Someone said they saw Elvis. So I walked down to the sand and you know what?" Roxanne looked at me. "Nobody was there."

"Nobody?" I repeated. "Nobody washed up?"

"Nobody. I decide to wait. I'm thinking maybe they send in a skin diver who does some kind of trick. Something with waterproof cards. Or maybe a frogman with a singing telegram. I've got sand on my black silk and I don't care. My stockings are torn. My high heels are wet. Waves are washing across my legs. I peel my nylons off and the ocean takes them away.

"The world looked like it had just been born. Then the sun dropped into the ocean. There was a flash of green. It was like something a magician did. Then everybody started cheering. They were applauding the sunset. That's what the crowd did every night. Clap for the sunset. Can you imagine?" Roxanne was sitting on the corner of her bed, leaning her back against the wall. She was staring out the window and she was pale.

Mr. Gordon is holding his cigarette lighter. He's studying the side of the plastic like it might contain an absolute answer if only he could turn it to the right angle. Then he looks at me with the same expression.

For no reason I suddenly think of Roxanne and her post-card collection. She keeps her postcard collection wrapped in tissue paper in a shoe box in her underwear drawer next to her reefers and her stack of movie evaluation cards. That's also where she stores her tiny bottles of vodka, gin, and Scotch that she gets on airplanes. She used to keep the parasols from her tropical drinks in there, too. Then she realized only a hick would do a thing like that so she threw them away.

It's another sunset in the apartment and the sky is a hard orange, almost shocking. It could sear you. It's a sunset that makes you think of metal and car crashes and having your face reconstructed on the basis of photographs. It's a hot night and you can feel how wounded it is, how infiltrated. It must be near the end of the month. You can sense the exaggerated density of the quiet. The televisions have been pawned. Some of the apartments have had the electricity shut off.

I have walked into my bedroom and Roxanne is sitting on the floor. It is an era before my mantra of Camarillo and Sybil Brand. I don't seem to be saying anything.

Roxanne is wearing her kimono with the tiny gold etchings that spell Honolulu inside the string of lanterns. She is sitting in the lotus position studying her postcards. She has unwrapped them from their tissue paper. They are spread out all around her. She is completely surrounded.

I can see it is a tropical montage. From a distance it just seems a glaring blue, a stretch of beach with too much sun in it. I bend down. I realize she has arranged the postcards with a sort of geographical coherence. The Hawaiian Islands are to her left, the Caribbean to the right. She has placed Mexico behind her left hip.

"I can name every flower in this picture," Roxanne tells me, picking up a postcard. "Flame ginger, jade vine, spider lily, vanda orchid, plumeria." She points to each blossom with a fingernail like a torch.

I sit near her, in what is now her vast symbolic Pacific. There are piers and harbors with sand that looks blinded and painted, yellow and thick and dreadful. There are wharves and plazas with excessively burgundy flowers. There are illegible plaques for pirates and saints. There are implications of churches and statues. There is a distortion of perspective.

Roxanne is holding the postcard, examining the surface of the blossoms as if she could actually watch them opening into their tainted magenta destinies. In the darkness they enter into their knowledge of red and the intricate constellations with their many strange fires.

"I swam in all the pools," Roxanne said. "I liked pools with islands in them. Islands with pine trees and fountains. Islands with statues of animals with water coming out of their ears and mouths and bellies you could rub for luck. Islands with miniature pyramids and sculptures of dolphins and Greek boys. There were islands with ponds in them that had enormous carp and water lilies. I threw coins in every pool. None of it helped."

Mexico with its hotel pools with islands that have waterfalls and orchids are in a patch behind her, a useless confederation. There were sails in the harbor like huge severed petals. There were fish so startling you wanted to make a dress out of their skin, that's how fantastic and yellow they were. It was as if the sunset had possessed and embossed them. It was a kind of mating. They were a manifestation of fever and delirium. Roxanne has postcards of all of this.

"I learned foreign words," Roxanne is saying. "Mariachis and luaus. The names of flowers and kings. I toured jungles. I looked at ruins from a Jeep. I stared at broken pottery and feathers. I thought I was getting somewhere."

Mr. Gordon is fanning himself with my file. "So you're going to be a writer," he is saying. "Maybe you'll write a story about me someday."

"I plan to do that," I tell him. "I am going to remember every word of this."

I touch my notebook with my personal reckonings and accounts receivable and all my acts of salvage and erasure, sabotage and insurrection. I run my fingertips across their surface. These are my tales of inhumanity and time travel.

It's nearly three o'clock and I am not going to jail.

"I won't be here tomorrow," I say, listening to how these words cut at the air, how sharp and complete they are. I am mastering gravity and precision. I am taking the sullen air and making it clarified and defined.

Mr. Gordon looks interested. "Is that because you're going away in the van with the painting on the side? The one where you don't know anybody's last name?"

"That's right," I reply.

"That's completely implausible. That's a lie. If you can't separate fantasy from reality, you can't stay in a public school. You'll be sent to a structured environment," Mr. Gordon says. "Of course you'll be here tomorrow."

Pamela Bruno is leaning against the rainbow van. She has a mantilla in her hair and a long red rose in her hand. Her name is Crystal now. I can see Alan and a girl with a guitar. She is sitting on the curb with the instrument balanced on her knee. She is bending over and adjusting it. She is curving into it like it was an infant. It occurs to me that you can carry what you love and this is somehow important.

The bell rings and I snap a final shot of Mr. Gordon with my camera eyes. He is gray smoke dissipating behind me. He is lost in a veil of nerve gas and he and his city and his alphabets and his reasons are obliterated now. Then I close the invisible shutter. I am walking down the stairs, through the corridor with its ruined metallic air, with its sunken and broken air. Then I am passing through the fence. I get in the van. Someone turns on the radio. Someone begins to drive.